MARGUERITE
BY THE
LAKE

MARGUERITE
BY THE
LAKE

A Novel

MARY DIXIE CARTER

MINOTAUR
BOOKS
NEW YORK

First published in the United States by Minotaur Books, an imprint of St. Martin's Publishing Group

MARGUERITE BY THE LAKE. Copyright © 2025 by Mary Dixie Carter. All rights reserved. Printed in the United States of America. For information, address St. Martin's Publishing Group, 120 Broadway, New York, NY 10271.

www.minotaurbooks.com

The Library of Congress Cataloging-in-Publication Data
is available upon request.

ISBN 978-1-250-79038-5 (hardcover)
ISBN 978-1-250-79039-2 (ebook)

Our books may be purchased in bulk for promotional, educational, or business use. Please contact your local bookseller or the Macmillan Corporate and Premium Sales Department at 1-800-221-7945, extension 5442, or by email at MacmillanSpecialMarkets@macmillan.com.

First Edition: 2025

10 9 8 7 6 5 4 3 2 1

For Steve

MARGUERITE
BY THE
LAKE

CHAPTER ONE

It would not be an exaggeration to say that Marguerite and I were both in love with Rosecliff. Of all the gardens where I worked, hers was the most remarkable. So I was honored to be included in her party. I didn't expect it.

Marguerite extended her hands, open palmed, to everyone gathered under the tent and spoke into a microphone. "To my brilliant husband, Geoffrey Gray!" The sky darkened and the wind picked up, drowning out her speech. Our view of her silhouette, framed by the sky and the lake, was almost identical to the famous painting of her by Serge Kuhnert, *Marguerite by the Lake*. She had planned it that way, of course.

Geoffrey joined his wife on the stage. Marguerite took his hand and looked up at him. I could hear a hum of delight from the guests. A photographer crouched low, snapping photos. Marguerite was in her mid-fifties, a few years older than Geoffrey, but I wouldn't have known that from looking at them. Her green dress was perfect with her gold hair, which fell in waves around her shoulders. Geoffrey's suit draped loosely over his tall frame. He had delicate features, like a girl, along with the rugged look of someone who spent his time outdoors. The Grays commanded the stage, like shining stars, like a god and goddess. The guests were mesmerized by them. And so was I.

Earlier in the afternoon, Marguerite had posted photos on social media of her flower arrangements, table settings, and stacks of her new book, *Rows of Roses,* as well as the baskets of bright red umbrellas stationed around the edge of the high-ceilinged tent, a precaution her husband said was overkill because the storm was forecast for the evening. But Marguerite loved to play up the drama in anything. In the caption of the post, she'd written: *Welcoming my dearest friends for a joyous celebration. Hoping we make it through the storm unscathed!*

Now, a thin streak of light came down from the sky to meet the horizon. I thought I was imagining it. But I saw a second streak of lightning reflected in the surface of the lake below. The sound of thunder followed.

A wall of rain descended from dark purple clouds. Marguerite looked up and registered the pounding on the tent: "At least we've got the tent!"

"Goodness gracious," Geoffrey said in his British accent.

My eyes zeroed in on the eighty-foot landmark spruce tree,

not ten yards from the tent on the north side. On the south side of the tent was a cliff overlooking Lake Spiro, fifty feet below. Marguerite had insisted she'd chosen the only position for the tent that would take full advantage of the lake view. I didn't agree with her. The Grays' whole property had lake views. It encompassed a peninsula that turned in on itself in the middle of the lake, like a subtle spiral. The tip of the peninsula was not very wide, but it expanded quickly, the angle growing wider until it merged into the mainland.

The wind came from behind Marguerite, so that her hair blew into her face and into her mouth. She laughed and held it back with one hand while speaking into the microphone. "Some of you know that we chose this date for . . ." Every few seconds, her voice was drowned out and I missed some words. ". . . toast my husband of twenty-five years . . . sacrificed so much. . . ." Leaving her microphone in the stand, she spun toward Geoffrey and kissed him on the lips, then slid her hand inside his jacket and around his waist.

His face colored. When he turned to her, I could see his profile—a high forehead and a long, elegant nose.

Marguerite returned to the microphone. "Thirteen years ago . . ." I was still missing a lot of her words. ". . . to leave a boring law practice for all this!" She laughed, but Geoffrey didn't.

The wind was blowing the rain horizontally so that the stacks of books and all of us under the tent were beginning to get wet. A few people had come prepared with rain jackets, but I hadn't. "When Geoffrey . . ." The whistle of the wind grew louder. "... write a book ..." Uniformed staff appeared and began rolling down the transparent plastic panels on the sides of the tent. I focused on the spruce, which was over a hundred years old; its trunk was brittle. Much more likely to snap than a young, healthy tree would be, especially because, a year earlier, Marguerite insisted on installing a granite path that ran under the tree's canopy, too close to its trunk, potentially suffocating its roots. My boss, Frank Brizzi, and I cautioned her against the path. So had the arborist we worked with, but she hadn't listened. She thought she knew best.

Marguerite continued. "'Your friends come to you for design advice. They ...'"

Guests were seated in wrought iron English garden chairs, at tables covered in cream-colored linen. Some held on to their napkins and place cards, to keep them from blowing away. The men were in lightweight pants and linen shirts. The women in sundresses and sandals. My wrap skirt missed the mark.

In the last few months, it became clear that the Grays' spruce was failing, partly because of the granite, partly because of age and disease. I warned Marguerite to take it down. I never waited for a problem to come to me. Because then it would be too late. I learned that lesson early.

Marguerite continued. "... Greenhaven Garden tour ... *Midsummer Night's Dream* ... Titania's woodland bower ... 'I know a bank where the wild thyme blows, where oxlips and the nodding violet grows, quite over-canopied ...'"

More applause. The guests, myself included, stood. Prior to

the party, I'd heard that the group of over two hundred would include Mrs. Gray's publishing team, as well as the producers of her gardening TV series. I saw a few of our clients, like Helen Spielman, a close friend of Marguerite's, who lived directly across the lake. Mrs. Gray liked to host parties, and photos of her gatherings were the main source material for her books. The scale of this event wasn't unusual for Marguerite, but entertaining a crowd was always a big lift, since the Kuhnert painting required security for a large group, like it was a foreign head of state.

One more look at the tree. The wind. And then I stood up, and I yelled as loudly as I could, "Get out. Get away!" I had a strong, low voice, and, under normal circumstances, it carried. But today, there was too much wind, and no one was looking in my direction. Hardly anyone noticed me.

Marguerite clasped her hands in front of her heart. "Every single time . . ." More applause.

I crossed the tent, turning my body to slide between tables and chairs. I called up to Marguerite. "The tree!" She didn't seem to notice me.

I scrambled onto the three-foot platform, grasped her by the shoulders to get her attention, and pointed to the tree.

Marguerite's eyes narrowed. Covering the microphone, she turned her back to the crowd. *"Phoenix,"* she whispered heavily. *"Get down."*

I was interrupting her speech at the high point, but I didn't have a choice. I took the mic from her hands and spoke to the crowd. "Go. Go. Get out. That tree."

Geoffrey understood. He took the microphone from me. "Evacuate the tent," he called out in an authoritative tone. "Move to the other side of the lawn." Then he jumped down from the platform and helped me usher the crowd away from the tree, out from underneath the tent, onto the open lawn.

"Geoffrey . . ." As Marguerite spoke, an enormous branch fell, landing a few feet away from her. Then another branch crashed to the ground. Several guests broke into a run.

In a matter of seconds, everyone was soaked. Thick rain, like heavy tubs of water, hit us from above and water slapped our faces. The baskets of umbrellas were irrelevant.

Geoffrey jogged, head down, across the muddy grass, in the direction of the valet station. Maybe to help them. A few guests were already waiting for their cars.

Geoffrey ran past the granite walkway, underneath the spruce tree.

He didn't realize.

I yelled his name. The wind was so loud.

He wasn't going to make it.

My legs propelled me forward with all my power, the wind pushing me back in the opposite direction, twenty yards, ten yards, five, right into him, and I threw my full weight against him, like a football tackle. I pushed him as hard as I could— away. Away from the path of the tree. I threw my shoulder into his chest. The spruce was on its way down. I could hear it now. Cracking. I could see it. Geoffrey and I were out of the path.

The eighty-foot spruce split down the center and landed, crushing the tent and most of the chairs and tables underneath it. It barely missed us. The uprooted root ball rose high in the air, towering over us like a giant monster, and the ground around us looked like the aftermath of an earthquake.

Geoffrey's suit sank into the soggy grass next to me. He was completely still. I leaned over him. "Are you okay?" The rain was pounding my back and pricking my cheeks.

He blinked a few times and then his blue eyes focused. "My bloody shoulder," he mumbled. He was shaking. He pulled my hand toward his mouth as if he were going to kiss it. His hand was ice cold. My knees were sinking deeper into the mud.

Marguerite appeared over us. Her face was white and unmoving. Her golden hair was matted down against her head. But she still looked like a countess in an old movie.

I moved away from Geoffrey.

Marguerite knelt by his side. "I thought you . . . you're here." She turned inside herself. Her voice was a ghost whisper. She touched Geoffrey's forehead, his jaw, his ribs, his hands. She brushed mud off his necktie and adjusted it, as if his tie was the only problem.

It seemed like I was intruding, so I ran toward the house, the rain like thick needles on my shoulders and back. A few guests followed me onto the verandah.

"I have to give you a hug," one woman said to me. She was probably from New York, because she was holding a pair of mud-covered heels in one hand, shoes that were a bad idea for any garden party.

Under the verandah, several people were already gathered. I recognized Wren Lacquer, who ran the Grays' e-commerce, and Basil Scott and Amar Ansari, two senior executives.

"What the hell . . ."

"I thought we were dead. . . ."

"Geoffrey . . . my God . . ."

A few other guests I didn't recognize circled me.

"How did you know?"

"You saved his life, sweetheart."

"Geoffrey was . . ."

"He owes you one."

"You're welcome," I said to no one in particular. This kind of gratitude made me uncomfortable because I didn't know whether to trust it. I was cold, and my head was hurting.

"I'm very thankful," a pretty woman in a long white dress said. I liked her because her nose turned up, just like my mother's did in the photos.

The turned-up-nose woman, the high-heel woman, and Wren Lacquer were crowding me, and I quickly felt claustrophobic. They were too close and too wet. The pain behind my eyes was constant.

A couple of people helped Geoffrey up and led him to the house, supporting him on either side. I saw him wince when someone touched his shoulder.

Staff members emerged from the house with stacks of towels. I took one and wrapped it around myself. It was heavier and softer than any towel I'd ever used.

Geoffrey stepped onto the verandah. His lips were blue. He had a gash underneath his left eye and on his neck. "Thank you, Phoenix," he said quietly. I didn't remember him ever saying my name before. I didn't even know that he knew my name. When he smiled at me, I had an impulse to reach for him, but checked myself.

Marguerite placed her arm around my shoulder and squeezed. She was vibrating on too high a frequency. I had a feeling she didn't like everyone saying that I saved Geoffrey's life. Maybe it made her uncomfortable. The only reason I was at the party was because of her generosity. She and I both knew that.

Marguerite's sleeves were wet and sticking to my arms, the fabric heavy on me.

When Geoffrey sat on a bench, she left my side to attend to him.

"He needs a hot drink and a hot bath," she said. "We need a doctor. Are there any doctors here?"

A couple of people who might have been doctors moved toward Geoffrey. Now Marguerite was seated next to him, towels wrapped around each of their shoulders. Her hand rested on Geoffrey's thigh.

Meanwhile, several other guests were breaking away, in pairs and singly, bracing themselves against the wind and rain as they crossed the lawn, in the direction of the valet drivers. I saw an opportunity to leave.

"I'll call you tomorrow," I said to Marguerite, but the sound dissolved into the air.

The first time Marguerite and I met, I was a senior in high school. I was going out with Geoffrey's nephew, Peter Gray, and I came as his date to the Grays' house for a wedding. Geoffrey's younger cousin was getting married at their home. The Grays had gone all out, like they'd done for the book launch, but the wedding was even more extravagant, with dancing and a band, and an all-night party that moved indoors in the early hours of the morning. At that time, Marguerite wasn't a household name, but even then, she'd glowed more than the bride. All eyes turned to her when she entered a room. Peter bragged to me that she was from old money—one of the Astors. I didn't know what old money meant or who the Astors were, but I was in awe of her, Geoffrey, and their eight-year-old daughter, Taylor. Their world was unlike anything I'd seen or heard of. Until that day, I didn't know that something as beautiful as the Grays' home existed. Rosecliff took root in my mind.

Then a few years later, I saw Marguerite quoted in *Formal Gardens*. Over time, articles about her became more frequent, and then she was doing interviews on television. She was everywhere. And that painting of her was everywhere. I liked being able to tell people that I knew her.

When I started working for Frank at Brizzi's, I had in the back of my head that the house I really wanted to work on was the Grays'. I knew that Frank had worked on their property on and off for a long time. I'd held on to the image of Rosecliff over the years, almost as if I had a series of photographs to refer to. I remembered the details that well. And then one day, I finally returned to work there.

I reminded the Grays that we had met at the wedding they hosted. Marguerite and Geoffrey both said they remembered me. And maybe they did. I'd like to think so.

Two days after the party, our crew began to clear the Grays' mile-long driveway, which wound all the way down to the road, at the level of the lake.

When Frank arrived, Marguerite greeted him at his car. I joined them, hoping to iron out details of our plan to remove the spruce, which was still hanging over the side of the cliff. "In two hours," I said, "those five river birch will be out of your driveway."

Marguerite angled her shoulders, edging me out of the conversation. "Frank and I discussed that already." And she walked away.

I was used to having easy and friendly conversations with Marguerite. Just a few days before the party, she'd been in a terrific mood because her newly planted Marguerite Gray shrub roses (a famous English rose breeder named a variety after her) were thriving, along with the Lady of Shalott and Manderley varieties we'd planted the prior year. She'd peered at me over the rim of her large dark sunglasses and beamed. "Would you look at these roses?" And then, "Pretty girl, where's your hat? Don't let the sun hit that beautiful skin, 'fair Phoenix bride.'" Marguerite liked to throw phrases of poetry into conversations. Most of the time, I didn't know what she was talking about.

Later, she asked, "Phoenix, how deep do you usually plant tulip bulbs?" She often asked me questions like that and listened attentively to my answers.

But something between us had shifted. Her tone of voice changed. It lost all its breeziness. She avoided eye contact. Maybe it had to do with my saving Geoffrey from the tree. He'd touched my hand, and then my hair. He was in shock though. He probably hadn't even known what he was doing.

My crew and I had been working for months to have everything ready for the book launch. Hours and hours of labor on the roses. Organic fertilizer, compost tea, cow manure, worm castings, Epsom salts. Week after week, we weeded, deadheaded, mulched, watered, and fertilized. In August, we cut back all the roses so that they would shower forth with blooms, just in time for the late-September party. It was a lot of work but gratifying in the end, because the roses were glorious.

But now, the gardens looked like a war zone. By far, the most damage came from the spruce tree. The bulk and weight of the tree falling, more than twenty thousand pounds. The tree's mass had crushed the land underneath it; huge pieces of rock had dropped off the side of the cliff. Fallen branches were scattered over the entire lawn. The root system of the spruce tree was so vast that when the tree fell and the root ball was pulled out of the ground, the earth around it cracked and shifted. The root ball looked like something from a horror movie, looming over us. I felt as though dark forces were released into the atmosphere when that tree came down and the root ball came up.

Our arborist had several men stationed below, near the lake, to warn passersby, just in case the tree trunk fell. We had cordoned off a wide area. We also had to prepare for the possibility that the tree would bounce back up, once some weight was removed. That happens sometimes with a huge root system.

Frank, Geoffrey, Marguerite, and I all watched from the porch as the removal team sawed off branches. They were stripping the tree of its dignity. It couldn't even die in peace. I'd seen trees fall and I'd seen them removed. Some trees' roots travel deep into the ground, and some spread wide near the surface. This spruce's roots did both. The root system was more significant than the tree itself. This tree would not go easily. It would resist. Even after the arborist carried away the trunk and branches from above ground, much of the tree would remain. For most old trees, there isn't one moment when a tree dies. Not like for a person, when the coroner writes down the time of death. It doesn't work like that with trees. I read about a tree that was chopped down five hundred years ago, but the stump was still living.

That day, something between Geoffrey and me felt different. He had barely acknowledged me in the past, but on the occasions when he had, his attitude was strictly paternal. I didn't mind that from male clients. Patronizing was better than flirting. Flirting would guarantee that the wife would eliminate me from the picture.

But sitting on the porch, I felt Geoffrey's eyes on me, and I turned to him. I was pretty certain he looked at me first. Didn't he?

In the late afternoon, when the arborist's team had retired for the day, Geoffrey appeared next to me with a glass of wine, which he offered me. His pale blue eyes were open and generous.

"Where's Marguerite?" I asked.

"Out for the evening."

A voice in my head said, Smile and walk away.

But my hand lifted from my side, like it wasn't even connected to my brain, and my arm extended to take the glass from him. Every impulse in my body was reaching for the glass, reaching for . . . whatever he was offering me.

Go home, the voice in my head said. Go home now.

But I'd stood there for too long thinking about it. Now, it would be rude to refuse the wine. I didn't have a choice. I took the glass, and, in that instant, I felt like the air around me turned warm and balmy. Geoffrey invited me to sit on the verandah, which faced the lake, spanning the width of the house. We could see the orange sky over the rolling hills on the other side of Lake Spiro. The house was perched high, and three sides of the house had a view of the entire spiral-shaped lake, formed by glacial activity during the last Ice Age. Rosecliff stood at the very center of the spiral. The autumn colors gave the water below an orange glow, just like the sky. I was familiar with many of the houses in the area and worked on half of them, but the Grays' property was the most beautiful by far.

Now that I was sitting close to Geoffrey, I could see the cut underneath his left eye beginning to heal. The cut was from the fine, sharp branches that scratched us as the tree came down. He looked like he'd been in a fight.

I reached my hand toward his left eye, almost involuntarily. And then pulled it back.

Instead, I touched my own face, under my left eye. "Is it okay?"

"Does it make me look like a tough guy?" He laughed.

Geoffrey's face would have been too perfect, if it weren't for his crow's feet, his crooked smile, the gray in his hair, and now the cut under his eye, all of which added to his charm. He was about fifteen years older than me, around fifty. His imperfect teeth, no straighter than mine, told me he hadn't grown up in the US or hadn't grown up with money, one or both.

"You're brave, Phoenix."

I found his accent charming, and I liked the way he smelled. A combination of pine needles and mint.

"You saw that tree coming down and you ran toward it. You risked your life for me."

I shifted my body and crossed my legs. "I'm not so brave." I was aware of the wicker digging into the bottom of my thigh and the top of one leg sticking to the bottom of the other leg. I wasn't comfortable, but I stayed still because I was scared any move I made would ruin the moment.

"Those roots are still there," he said. "The tree's in purgatory. I wonder if it's like that for us when we die. Everyone thinks we're dead, but our roots are still here." It was exactly what I'd been thinking, though I wouldn't have been able to say it so clearly.

I felt the weight of Geoffrey's hand on my forearm. For a moment, I thought I was imagining it. Then I looked down and saw his fingers, one by one, wrapping around my wrist. Each finger on my skin sent a current through me. I was self-conscious about the mud and grass stains on my jeans, the dirt underneath my fingernails, but Geoffrey didn't seem to notice.

I couldn't relax. The verandah was out of my normal range, the range in which I worked. The range that I understood. I was trespassing, in a sense. And it was possible that someone was watching us. The Grays had a lot of staff, and there were still a few cars parked in the driveway. Several people in the vicinity. Marguerite might return.

It was reckless to be drinking wine with Geoffrey Gray. Stupid, too. But something kept me rooted to the spot. I couldn't pull myself away. On this evening, there was a disconnect between my thoughts and actions.

The sun was setting, and the air that felt warm and balmy a few minutes earlier was growing cooler.

"This was the worst storm we've had in a long time," I said, trying for a lighthearted tone. I pushed my hair behind my ears.

Geoffrey shifted forward in his chair, like he was memorizing what I looked like. "How did you land at Brizzi's?"

"Frank knew my grandmother."

Geoffrey nodded. He wasn't touching my wrist anymore.

But I could still feel the place where his fingers had rested on my skin.

"At first, I needed cash. And then, it turned out I'm good at this." I laughed and crossed my legs in the other direction. "I never wanted to spend too much time at a desk."

Just then, it started to rain very lightly. I took that as a cue to leave.

"There's a nice bloke at home, wondering where you are?"

"No . . ."

"No?" His lips moved into the beginning of a smile. A light in his eyes.

I stood up and then Geoffrey stood. I could feel his breath, warm on my face. With one finger, he traced the outline of my neck and shoulder.

CHAPTER TWO

After the party and the storm, Marguerite took a walk in the woods on all the days I was there. She was a lot more charged than usual. She walked briskly, coming and going. It was like she was monitoring me, like the walks were a ruse, a chance to keep an eye on me. She might have heard something about me and Geoffrey drinking wine on the verandah. I hadn't kissed him. I'd barely touched him. But it was inexcusable, all the same.

More than once, I saw her watching me from the window of her bedroom. When she came outside, I felt her eyes on me as soon as I turned my back. If Geoffrey happened to be outside also, I did my best to stay far away. I didn't want her to see me looking at Geoffrey or *not* looking at Geoffrey.

When I was pruning the viburnum on the side of the house, I overheard parts of a conversation on the verandah between

Marguerite and Geoffrey, though the lawnmower in the background made it hard to catch all of it.

"It's essentially a gift, an extravagant gift," he said. "We can't afford it."

"We can," she said. "As long as . . ." Her voice faded out.

"What?" His tone was short.

". . . expenses have gone up," she said. ". . . two or three years."

"Yes?"

"I'm just noticing it. That's all."

Was there something strained in her voice?

She continued. "Let's . . ." I was still losing a few of her words. ". . . it's his due."

The lawnmower approached close to where I was standing, so I missed the rest of the conversation. I would have liked to hear more.

Later on, I noticed Marguerite taking photos with her phone, standing near the two rows of pylons we'd placed near the edge of the cliff. She often took photos from that spot. It was her favorite view and almost the exact same place where she'd posed for Serge Kuhnert, only now she had to keep a little more distance from the edge. Since the boxwoods had been wiped out, there wasn't a layer of protection. We wouldn't be able to replace the hedges until the spring. That was one of many things we had to accomplish in the spring, when over a thousand people would descend on Rosecliff as part of the Grays' Greenhaven Garden tour.

I was relieved the day I arrived at Rosecliff and neither

Marguerite nor Geoffrey were there. Teddy and I sat next to each other on the Grays' porch steps. He had been working at Brizzi's for two years. He was getting a Ph.D. in horticulture and took this job to support himself, but also for field experience. He was twenty-five, nine years younger than me, but more responsible than most.

Landscape architects make decent money. I did pretty much the same thing, but I made much less because I didn't have a degree in it. But I didn't care. Frank let me do what I wanted because our clients loved me. I knew how to make every idea seem like it was theirs.

As Frank had pulled back this past year, I spent more time looking over our finances. I told him we had to cut costs. I told him our suppliers were ripping us off. He didn't want to negotiate, because these guys were his friends. So now I was back and forth with our suppliers, trying to save Frank money.

I drank my lukewarm coffee and looked out at the spiral-shaped lake, underneath a bright blue sky. It wasn't a full spiral, but enough of one that, once upon a time, someone had decided to name it Lake Spiro. This view was one of the only things that could clear my head.

"Mrs. Gray wants us to add more Epsom salts to the roses," I said.

"She's a micromanager," Teddy said. "That's for sure."

Marguerite published books about the gardens at Rosecliff—selling herself as the ultimate gardener. I read an article in *Vanity Fair* that described her as an old-school tastemaker, more glamorous than Gwyneth Paltrow or Martha Stewart. I suppose she felt her name was on the line.

Marguerite had five million loyal followers. In a lot of the photos she posted, her hands and face were covered in dirt, like she was immersed in physical labor. But my crew and I handled most of the hands-on gardening, and I liked it that way. Occasionally, she left town and we worked on the property while she was gone. When she came back, she would dig up one of the plants and plant it again so she could get herself on video.

Sometimes I imagined what would happen if I were to post a photo of Rosecliff and claim it as my own work. Which it was, in fact. It was.

But it wouldn't have occurred to me to be resentful or jealous of Marguerite Gray. It would have been like being jealous of a queen or a character in a book.

What's more, my work in these gardens was rewarding, whether or not anyone recognized it as mine.

"It's a weird marriage," Teddy said quietly. "Right?"

"Hmm?"

"Sometimes they walk right past each other like strangers. And other times, Mrs. Gray's like a teenager, hanging on him."

I pushed my hair behind my ears. I'd forgotten to bring a clip. It was too hot to have my hair in my face.

"Whose money is it anyway?" he said quietly.

I'd googled both the Grays many times but preferred not to mention that to Teddy. After Geoffrey graduated from Oxford, he served as a commander in the Royal Navy. Then he studied law in the US and worked at a corporate firm before he quit to run the business with Marguerite. My high school boyfriend Peter was right when he told me that Marguerite was an Astor. According to Wikipedia, they were one of the fanciest families in the country. But *People* magazine said she'd been disinherited the year before when her mother died. I wondered if that was true. I was hoping Geoffrey didn't have to rely on Marguerite's money. I asked myself why I cared about that.

I focused on my coffee and kept my eyes down.

In a few weeks, the temperature would drop, so we needed to wrap up our planting. I had eight guys at the house to plant two dozen PJM rhodies on the south side of the house since the PJMs do well with a lot of sun. And to weed the rhodies' beds.

We were planting the final two rhodies when a black Ford Bronco pulled into the driveway. I didn't recognize the driver or the car. Geoffrey got out of the passenger seat. He closed the door behind him, then turned back and said something to the driver through the open window—something funny because the man laughed, then made a U-turn in the motor court and took off.

Geoffrey waved at me across the lawn. My stomach dipped, like I missed a step coming down the stairs.

"Nice trip?" I spoke loudly over the noise of the Weed eaters.

"A weekend in Boston," he called. "Visiting family. Marguerite's staying on for another day, so I had to find myself a ride home." Geoffrey, wearing his usual khakis and button-down, crossed the lawn and approached me. "Listen, Phoenix, thank you for everything you've done here." I'd forgotten about his pale blue eyes.

"We still have a ways to go." My voice sounded hoarse.

"What a transformation." He was referring to the work we'd done since the storm—removing the spruce tree and filling in the massive cavity in the earth that the root ball had vacated. Then covering everything over with grass and plantings. He placed his hand on my upper arm. I was aware of the pressure of each of his fingers through my shirt and a deep undertow pulling me toward him.

I told myself, Step away, step back.

But I stood still, paralyzed. He slid his hand down in the direction of mine. I thought about wiping my muddy hand on my jeans before his fingers reached it. But I didn't manage to do it in time, so he held my dirty, calloused hand in his. I could feel his wedding ring pressed against my fingers.

Pull your hand away from his.

Why couldn't I move?

He was handsome and charming. But it was more than that. I was dipping my toes into his world, ever so slightly. There was a force stronger than my rational mind, pushing me to jump.

My crew finished leveling out the beds with mulch. They began packing up their trucks.

"I think you and I should celebrate our . . . recovery," Geoffrey said. He managed to make the word "recovery" sound intimate. He spoke to me as if it was acknowledged that we had a shared understanding.

I saw Teddy out of the corner of my eye, walking in our direction.

"I've got to get going," I said to Geoffrey. "Another time."

"Have one drink with me." He mouthed the word "please."

Teddy widened his eyes. "Hey, Phoenix. Remember you wanted to drop your truck off to get serviced."

"Yeah, I'll do that tomorrow," I said to Teddy. "You can take off."

Teddy backed away, his eyes fixed on me. I'd invited him over to my place for a drink after work. I could tell he was disappointed that I was flaking on him, but, in the moment, I didn't care.

On the porch, Geoffrey opened a bottle of champagne for the two of us. When he filled my cup, the champagne frothed over the sides and spilled onto my hand.

It was a cool night, but with no breeze. The lake was a giant piece of glass—so still it mirrored the surrounding hills. The moonlight was bouncing off the water.

Geoffrey sat next to me on the wicker sofa. "To our beautiful gardens." He wanted me to know that he appreciated me.

We clinked our glasses. The champagne felt warm in my throat.

"Phoenix, I'm grateful to you. That's all. I don't want you to think . . ." He paused. "I like talking to you. Listening to you." He looked out at the lake. "You grew up around here?"

I nodded.

"Your parents nearby?"

"They died in a car accident when I was thirteen."

"I'm sorry."

I smiled. "I've managed okay."

The version of my childhood I told Geoffrey wasn't en-tirely accurate; the truth was my mother left when I was two. My brother, Curtis, said my dad and grandma were bullies. My mom didn't know how to stand up for herself.

When my dad had a heart attack, I moved in with my grand-mother, who loved to talk about all the ways that my mom was a loser. That was her favorite subject of conversation. I'd learned to smile and nod when she trashed my mom. My mother couldn't take the abuse. When she left, she told Curtis she wasn't worried about me because I was resilient. I was much tougher than her, she said. Maybe she was right.

"What about you?" I said.

Geoffrey refilled my glass and his. "What about me?"

"I want to know more about you." I was surprised at the words coming out of my mouth. In my conversations with cli-ents, I usually reacted to what they said. I didn't initiate subjects of conversation.

Geoffrey looked down at his glass, studying it closely, from every angle. Then he set it on the side table. The idea that he found my company interesting was hard to believe—especially when someone like Marguerite was his wife.

"I'm relieved that Marguerite's away," he said.

I tried to hold my face still. The champagne bubbles ex-panded into the air around me.

The wind picked up a bit, and so did the current of the lake.

"She's . . ." He didn't finish his sentence, but it seemed like he wanted to. "I love her. Of course, I do. But I always have to prove it to her. When Taylor was living at home, it was easier."

I'd seen their daughter, Taylor, a few times over the years, when she was around, which wasn't that often. She'd been away at boarding school, then college and law school, and had just come home for breaks.

I hadn't ever had a conversation with her. Not since she was a little girl. I remembered her from the wedding. She was the flower girl. She was a little princess. During the reception, I noticed she was upset because she spilled her Shirley Temple on her dress. I got her a refill, and she said thank you. She looked a little like Marguerite back then. But these days, she was practically a clone.

Geoffrey ran his fingers through his hair, starting at his forehead and going straight back. The day I saved him from the spruce tree, I remembered touching his soft hair. I would have liked to do it again.

"I'm sorry," I said.

He looked up at the stars, like there might be an answer in the lavender sky. "Ten years ago, I quit practicing law because we both thought the business needed me. Marguerite asked me to, though she remembers it differently," he said. "Anyway, it was a mistake."

I wrapped my sweatshirt tightly around my body. I brought

my hands up inside my sleeves, like I used to do when I was a teenager.

"Are you cold?" He put his arm around my shoulders.

I backed away from him. I told myself to leave. Go home. *Get the hell out of here.*

"I should go. This isn't . . . a good idea."

But I couldn't stand.

"I apologize." He bowed his head.

"No . . ."

"I'm happy sitting next to you." He twisted his wedding ring on his finger. Maybe he was trying to take it off. "Do you ever see Peter?"

I shook my head. "Not since high school."

"You were too good for him. He was a spoiled kid. Still is."

I wondered why he was telling me this.

"You have grit," he said.

Why was Geoffrey drawn to me? Had I flirted with him unintentionally?

"You don't know me very well," I said.

"I can hear it in your voice. The rest of us, we're like the aristocracy during the French Revolution. Any moment, we're going down." He laughed, but it was a strained laugh.

Maybe he liked me because I was different from him. He existed inside a cushioning system. Blankets of padding, with pockets of air in between each one. I'd seen Marguerite try to shield Geoffrey from pain or disappointment. She gave Geoffrey the soft airy blankets, but she didn't want or need them for her-self. Marguerite wasn't going down. She wasn't going anywhere.

It was several days later that Marguerite approached me, hold-ing her signature pruning shears through goatskin gardening gloves in one hand and a basket filled with freshly cut roses in the other. The velvety crimson Marguerite Gray shrub roses. It looked like she'd cut three dozen of them. When I turned to look at the rose beds behind her, I expected them to appear bare. But they were just as abundant as before. That was a trick about cutting gardens. There were always more flowers on a bush than you could possibly realize were there. Marguerite was especially proud of her cutting garden, which bordered both sides of the path from the front door to the driveway and broke off into a second path that led to the woods.

"Hello, Phoenix." Her lips were pressed into a thin, straight line.

"Hi, Mrs. Gray." Most of my clients would have said, Call me Marguerite. But she had never said that.

"Now would be a good time to cut back the delphiniums"— she pointed to the foundation plantings—"and deadwood the rhodies." There was none of the affection she usually threw my way. She was solid ice.

"We'll get to that as soon as possible." I could feel the heat in my face spreading to my neck and my ears.

"Today," she said quietly. I could see her fingers tightening on the pruning shears.

"Of course."

Marguerite's brown eyes were large and glassy. With no makeup, she appeared vulnerable. The sun shone from directly overhead, and her wrinkles were apparent to me for the first time. She looked her age, which I had never seen before. The corner of her eye twitched. And then it twitched again. She reminded me of a disoriented bird. I felt an unexpected twinge of something like pity.

It seemed like she saw me as a threat, though I was not nearly as beautiful as her.

She'd probably found out I spent some time with Geoffrey.

She rested the basket on the grass, then dropped her shears and gloves into it. She took a pair of dark sunglasses from her pocket and put them on. "And we need to replace the screening around the generator and the HVAC equipment." She looked over the rim of her sunglasses. "The Little Jokers from last year are dreadful."

The Little Jokers were thriving, actually, deep burgundy stems and pale pink flowers; they looked better than I'd thought they would, given the storm. Just a bit of curling, possibly from aphids.

"A reminder," she said in an edgy tone, "I don't want your secondhand plants."

I thought I must have misunderstood her. It's a sleazy move to take one client's rejects and pawn them off on another client. I'd worked with many of my clients for more than a decade. They trusted me. I was very careful about Frank's reputation, and mine.

"Of course not."

"And one more thing." She smiled and placed her hand lightly on my shoulder.

For a moment, I thought Marguerite was going to confide in me, like an older sister or a good friend might. I even thought she might say she was grateful that I saved Geoffrey's life. She lowered her voice and took a half step closer to me, so her face was just inches from mine. "Please check each plant for disease before you bring it onto my property."

I had trouble keeping my voice even. "I've never brought you a diseased plant."

"Are you sure about that?" She paused and held my gaze for several seconds. Then she turned her focus and her body away from me. "Maybe I'm just feeling protective—of my garden, my home." It started to rain lightly. Wren Lacquer's SUV was pulling into the driveway. Marguerite waved to Wren, her hand high in the air making large swooping arcs. Then she turned back to me. "You can understand that. Can't you, pretty girl?"

"Of course, Mrs. Gray." I looked away, unable to hold her gaze.

A little after eight, I arrived back at my grandmother's house on Sunny Valley Road in New Milford, off Route 7. In my mind, it was still her house, even though she'd died ten years earlier. I saw a familiar 2008 Hyundai parked there. It was my older brother's. Curtis liked to show up and start sleeping on my couch. It usually happened to be when he was broke.

He was leaning against my white picket fence smoking a cigarette, his hair slicked back. Curtis had both our parents' coloring: copper hair, blue eyes, and freckles. People used to think I was adopted. My great-grandmother was Native American, and her dark coloring must have skipped the two generations before me.

"Hey, Phoenix." He held up an expensive-looking bottle of tequila.

"I'm exhausted." I stepped out of my truck into humid air. My house was two thousand feet lower altitude than Rosecliff and fifteen degrees warmer. It was unseasonably warm for October.

Curtis lifted a box that contained margarita mix, ice, limes, and tortilla chips and presented it to me.

"Okay," I said. "One margarita." I was on edge from my afternoon at Rosecliff. I thought a drink would help.

Once we'd made a pitcher, Curtis and I sat outside on two Adirondack chairs under my weeping willow tree. The rain had almost stopped. It was just barely a mist and refreshing in the heat.

I'd turned my grandmother's small backyard into a garden that was prettier than some of my clients' properties. My foundation plants looked good this year, especially the bigleaf hydrangea, which Brizzi's used a lot because they're repeat bloomers. The flowers bloom on old and new stem growth. They're cold hardy and can handle acidic or alkaline soil, if you're flexible on the color. My soil was acidic, so my hydrangeas were blue.

Curtis and I ate tortilla chips and laughed about everything and nothing. He was a charmer. Twinkly blue eyes with gold in the center of them. In the end, we each had three margaritas, not one. But I was glad for a distraction. The stories we always rehashed about our childhood were the ridiculous ones from when our dad was still alive. How I spent a week at my friend's house and our dad didn't notice, because Curtis would run the shower in the morning like I was in there. How we ate Sara Lee coffee cake for breakfast, lunch, and dinner, week after week. We both knew, without ever discussing it, to stay away from certain stories.

"Remember the time we snuck into a second movie at Quad Cinemas without paying?" he said. "And then a third one, and then we just stayed for four straight movies."

"Yeah." My eyes landed on the brick pathway that my grandma and I had laid when I was in high school. Though I had actually done most of the work.

"Grandma was pissed when we got back." He whistled, to emphasize his point. "Man, that woman was mean." He smiled and I saw the dimple on one side of his face. I remembered how he looked as a teenager. When our dad died, I was thirteen and I went to live with our grandmother, but Curtis was sixteen. He was a troublemaker. He was a junkie. That's what our grandma had said.

He stayed on a friend's couch until he graduated from high school. I could have fought for him to stay with us. But I didn't want to risk my own position.

Curtis coasted on his charm for a long time. He always had some girlfriend supporting him. He'd had a string of part-time jobs—waiting tables, bartending. Frank even hired him for a couple of summers. For a while, he was in business with his friend Jimmy, who was bad news. I never asked for details, because I had a feeling it was money laundering or drugs or something.

I felt a mosquito bite on my ankle and scratched it hard, making it bleed. All the moisture made the air so heavy.

"I'm sorry I didn't arrange a funeral for her." His eyes filled with tears.

I laughed lightly. "That was a long time ago."

"Yeah. But I regret it."

Moments like this one with Curtis made me feel nauseous. Like I was on a roller coaster that I shouldn't have gotten on. Sometimes I felt like it was my fault the world hadn't been fair to him. But really, the world wasn't fair to anyone. Curtis had a chip on his shoulder, and he was always looking for a shortcut. He thought the rules were for suckers.

We finished off our pitcher and I was ready to call it a night, but Curtis insisted on making one last round. We moved inside when the mosquitoes got worse. I lay back on the living room couch with the fan going full blast, while he fiddled around in the kitchen. I brushed off a couple pieces of plaster that had dropped from the ceiling onto the sofa. I still had my grandmother's fifty-year-old living room set. Every few months, I'd go online and look at buying something to replace it. I hated the furniture in my house, but I couldn't make myself get rid of it.

After my grandmother died, I considered selling the house and moving to another one nearby. Or moving far away. I'd taken the summer off once in my twenties to drive across the country, and I liked New Mexico. A lot of people in my situation would have decided to start fresh. But I chose to stay. It was possible my mom would come back looking for me. If she were alive, she might. I was pretty sure I'd know her if she walked in the door. I had a photo of her pushing me on a swing, when I was a toddler. On the back were the words "Phoenix's 2nd birthday." And another one of her sitting at a picnic table, drawing my grandma's weeping willow. I'd found the drawing and kept it. I also had a book of fairy tales with an inscription: "For Phoenix, Love, Mom." And an envelope with the words "Baby's first haircut" on the outside and a lock of my hair inside. I'd kept all of it hidden, because my grandmother would have tossed it in a fire, if she'd seen it.

I'd tried to track my mother down. But so far, at least, she didn't want to be found.

Curtis returned with more drinks.

"It's time to toast my big news." He sat down and looked me in the eye. "It's finally happening. Jimmy and I are finally doing it."

"Doing what?" I said, though I didn't actually want to know the answer.

"Buying a restaurant." He clinked his glass against mine and some of his margarita spilled over the side of his glass and onto the area rug, which had seen much worse.

"Cool." I widened my eyes and tried to look enthusiastic.

"This is my dream. You know that." He pointed his finger at me. "It's always been my dream."

"That's great," I said. "I'm happy for you."

He took my hand in his. "I need your help, Phoenix. Please. I need to borrow five grand."

I pulled my hand away.

"I'll get it back to you in a few weeks," he said.

I could hear the kitchen faucet from the living room. Drip, drip, drip.

I didn't have that kind of money, and even if I did, I wouldn't hand it over to a shady operator like Jimmy. But it was hard for me to say no to Curtis. "Christ, Curtis. I'll give you five hundred bucks." Maybe I could borrow from Frank.

I stood and went to the kitchen for a glass of ice water. I held the cold glass up to my cheek and tried to block out the image of Marguerite's large brown eyes fluttering, like a butterfly in my face.

After washing out the blender, I walked back in the living room. Curtis was asleep on my sofa, his mouth half-open, snoring lightly.

I didn't have the energy to kick him out of my house. I just left him there.

The house had two bedrooms in the back. Since my grandmother had died, I'd been using her room as my office for design work. Frank didn't know much about computers or AutoCAD, but clients expected drawings these days, so that had turned into my responsibility, along with everything else.

I pictured my brother in the living room, face down, drooling on the sofa. Then I pictured Marguerite's glassy eyes. It was hard for me to fall asleep. I stared at the glow-in-the-dark stars on the ceiling and then at Alanis Morissette on my wall. The room hadn't changed that much in the last twenty-three years. My grandmother painted it pink when I moved in. And it was still pink. I still slept in an antique wooden bed that my grandma had refinished herself. There was a price to pay for the pink room and the antique bed. I'd had to earn my keep or find myself in the system. I knew she wasn't bluffing when she said that because she had no problem shutting the door on Curtis.

The sun woke me up at 6:30 A.M. I showered and dressed for work. My hair always looked the same no matter what I did—dark brown, straight, and silky. It fell in my face, so I generally clipped it back for work. I'd never had much success with makeup. Since my eyelashes and eyebrows were so dark to start out with, it didn't do much for me.

In the kitchen, Curtis had already made a pot of coffee and scrambled eggs. He'd even washed the pan.

CHAPTER THREE

I was back at Rosecliff, scaling back the phlox with my shears. It was a good day for pruning and watering: dry, strong sun and no wind. This last was rare at the Grays' house. The temperature had dropped to the mid-forties and was forecast to dip below freezing soon.

I was purposefully staying away from Geoffrey, but I thought about him every day. I thought about lying on top of him, the pelting rain pushing my body into his, into the soggy ground, with his arms tight around me. Running my fingers through his soft hair.

I lost my focus for just a few seconds, but long enough for my pruners to slip and cut my finger. The blood was an especially bright red, the color of a valentine.

Geoffrey appeared on the walkway. "All right?" he called.

"It's . . ." I was cupping one hand underneath the bleeding hand to catch the blood.

When he got close, his face turned white. "God, Phoenix. Come with me."

I followed him into the large kitchen, preparing myself to see Marguerite. But she wasn't there. I felt a wave of relief. A small arrangement of Marguerite Gray roses in a crystal vase stood in the middle of a round wooden table. These were the last of the roses. Soon we'd be winterizing them, covering their roots with bark mulch. I normally loved the smell of these flowers, but this arrangement had an aggressive scent, like overripe fruit.

I'd been inside this house before, but only briefly. In my mind, there was a very clear line between the exterior of the house and the interior of the house. I'd had no reason to spend time inside, and to do so would have been imposing and intrusive. Not to mention, my boots were usually caked with mud.

Geoffrey held a clean cloth on my wound until the bleeding slowed down. The cut didn't hurt. In my experience, blood didn't necessarily mean pain. Wounds with no bleeding sometimes hurt the most.

"You look pale." He frowned. "Why don't you sit?" For a moment, he looked older to me and less confident. He was wearing shorts and a T-shirt. Why didn't he have on his khakis and button-down? I remembered hearing from someone that Geoffrey used to sail across the ocean with one of his best friends. These days, he went sailing in the lake on a smaller sailboat. I had the impression Marguerite didn't go with him.

He turned one of the brass knobs on an old-fashioned burgundy stove to boil water.

"This is not a big deal," I said.

Geoffrey went looking for some bandages. The blood on my
jeans had morphed into a daisy.

Light from the ceiling lanterns cast a glow over the room.
I'd seen this kitchen in passing, but this was the first time that
I'd ever sat down inside. The interior of the Grays' house looked
like a smaller version of what I imagined European palaces
looked like. Everything was ancient, but it was built so well in the
beginning—with solid stone and bricks, like a fortress—it could
stand for thousands of years, unless barbarians wrecked it.

From where I sat, I had a wide and clear view of my work
through the French doors. I'd designed the plantings between
the house and the cliff to border the two-hundred-year-old stone
walls. The walls and plants were framing devices for the lake. It
was the relationship between the layered gardens and the open
lake that made Rosecliff unique.

I was surprised that Geoffrey knew how to clean my cut and
bandage it. Maybe from his years in the navy.

I heard a floorboard creak from the hallway, and my stomach seized up. I saw a glimpse of someone there. Was it their
housekeeper? I stood, but my knees gave way.

"I'm sorry," I said. "I'll be out of here in just a few minutes."

"No." He raised his eyebrows, like a stern parent. "You're
going to stay."

He poured water over a tea bag and placed a mug of Earl

Grey tea on the table, then sat down in a chair next to me. I was aware of his bare arms and legs, still tan from the summer. He looked into my eyes. "I've missed you."

I wasn't sure how to respond. I wasn't sure who I was in relation to him. Marguerite might be nearby. She might be in the next room.

"Just sitting next to you"—he smiled shyly—"it makes me happy." I could tell it was true. I could see his appearance change when he drew near me. Everything lifted.

He put his hand on top of mine and clasped it tightly. I felt his wedding ring press into my fingers. My hands were fine, until you touched them. And then you'd be surprised by the hard calluses. All the lotion in the world wouldn't soften my hands.

I pulled my hand away from him. "No."

"No?"

"No, because that's not all it is."

I told myself to go. Stand up and walk out the door. What was I doing here?

Sun poured into the kitchen through the French doors and lit up one side of Geoffrey's face. "My marriage is hard." His shoulders moved up toward his ears and then lowered again. "Marguerite doesn't . . . admire me." He laughed. "Admiration is important, isn't it? For self-esteem or something?"

Marguerite didn't admire him? I wanted to believe him. But in my mind, I could see Marguerite's large glassy eyes. I could see one of her eyes twitching.

She would kill me. She would annihilate me.

"We used to laugh." Geoffrey's face went slack. "God, we used to laugh so much. Success changed her, I think."

Geoffrey's eyes filled with tears, and he dropped his head. I could practically hold his heartbreak in my hand, it felt so real to me.

Then he kissed me. Drawing me toward him. His lips were soft and warm.

"I can't," I said.

"Please."

"I'm sorry. I can't."

I stood up then, holding my bandaged hand like a baby bird. I stumbled to my truck and drove away.

I decided to skip Rosecliff for a few days and let Teddy handle it.

I could still feel Geoffrey's lips on mine. I couldn't take a chance on being alone with him again.

In the morning, I visited Helen Spielman. It was my second time visiting her house since the storm. There was a lot of damage on her property, but not as much as at Rosecliff. When I arrived at the Spielman estate, which was fifty acres, even larger than Rosecliff, another of our crews was clearing debris. Helen's house was the oldest in the area. It looked like a Greek temple with Corinthian columns across the front. Since it was a clear day, I could see Rosecliff directly across the lake. The Grays' old stone manor stood on the edge of the cliff. Apparently, years ago,

Helen's house stood on that same cliff, but the owners moved the house to the other side of the lake, because they wanted more shelter from the wind.

Helen came out on her porch to wave at me, her white hair blowing in the light breeze. I walked past the treehouse and play yard, which we'd built for Helen's grandchildren. Helen was eighty-two, but still worked full-time as a psychiatrist.

When I found out that she was orphaned at the age of eight, I felt a connection to her. Sometimes it seemed like she understood more about me than I wanted her to.

She walked me around the side of the house and showed me the honeysuckle vine that was smothering her rhododendrons with a dense tangle. We couldn't get rid of it. Teddy had tried manual extraction, suffocation, cut and spray, torching. Next, we were trying glyphosate solution.

Then she showed me three of her arborvitae, which were damaged from the storm but had only just come down a few days earlier.

It was bad news followed by bad news.

I walked along the border of the property to study the trees, then turned to Helen. "I've been thinking about your gazebo."

She'd been talking about a gazebo for eight years. She had never been able to settle on the location, the material, the size, the purpose. But still, every year, she'd bring the subject up again.

She nodded.

"I saw an incredible fountain last week at an estate sale.

And I thought to myself, this would be perfect for Helen's gazebo." It was funny how words came easily to me if I was talking about gardens.

Helen's face brightened.

I considered it my job to make each client believe that she was the important one—the one I was most invested in. It wasn't a lie. I was invested in all my clients. I needed them—so much more than they needed me. I recognized that I was dispensable. I understood that at the age of five.

I successfully avoided Rosecliff for a week. But I thought about Geoffrey. I missed the way he looked at me—like he and I had a secret that no one else understood.

Eventually, I did return to the Grays' property. A few days away always gave me a renewed appreciation for their gardens, more interesting than any other place I'd seen in person or even in photographs.

Temperatures in the low thirties were forecast for the following day. We always watered heavily before a freeze. Plant cells that are plump with water will be more resilient against the cold. I always told my guys to water deeply and less often. If the water stays near the surface, then the roots of a plant will stay shallow, not strong and deep. The roots go where the water goes.

Near the end of the day, Geoffrey found me. He asked me to have a drink with him. I'd played out this scene in my head a hundred times.

I would say no.

You will lose your job, I told myself. You will lose everything.

"Just one drink," he whispered. "Please."

His light blue eyes were so clear, like how I imagined the ocean in the Bahamas.

"Marguerite?" I said.

He shook his head.

The undertow was stronger than my thoughts were.

It was cold on the porch, but Geoffrey had already poured two glasses of white wine and motioned for me to join him on the wicker sofa. "This is an exceptionally good white." He handed me a glass.

"It's wasted on me," I said. "I don't know the difference."

He laughed and the wrinkles around his eyes grew more prominent. "No one knows the difference. Sometimes you've got to pretend. Tell them the story they want to hear."

I had an impulse to wipe the moisture off his upper lip but checked myself.

"Tell who what story?"

"All the rich people."

I had the same feeling that I'd had before—that the two of us had an understanding.

"Including you?"

"Yes," he said. "Tell me my bottle of wine is better than anything you've ever tasted, so I don't feel like an idiot for spending four grand on it."

I had a sinking sensation. "You spent four thousand dollars?"

"No." He smiled. "But what if I had? Wouldn't you feel sorry for me?"

We both laughed. He was so handsome when he laughed.

The wind picked up. We didn't stay much longer on the porch. He led me in through the back door and we carried our wineglasses with us. I was struck by the strong scent of roses inside the house. I knew Marguerite regularly cut and arranged roses for her home, all of them the fragrant English varieties, but the intensity of the fragrance still surprised me.

"Follow me," Geoffrey said quietly, sliding his hand into mine. We walked through a glass sunroom and down a long, stately hallway with solid walls and high ceilings.

He opened the door to a coral-colored guest room with a king-size bed. Alarm bells went off in my head. In that moment, I recognized the full scope of what I was doing. This was no longer a flirtation—something I could pretend never happened. If Marguerite were to find out . . . But my desire for him outweighed other considerations.

I ran my fingers over his mouth. The outline of his lips was so defined. He kissed my fingers. His hands were underneath my shirt, on my ribs, pulling on my bra straps, then pulling on my shirt. He lay back on the bed. I undressed him and straddled his waist. As we made love, I paid attention to his every breath, to every muscle in his face, in his body. I watched and listened. We could fit inside each other. I could fit into the empty places in him, and he could do the same for me. I could make him whole.

At one in the morning, I lay next to Geoffrey, naked under damp sheets, my head resting on his shoulder, eyelids growing heavy.

He checked his watch, then coughed and sat up.

"Is Marguerite coming back tonight?"

"I'm not sure," he said. "I think you should go."

I felt a rush of adrenaline and panic. How could he have put me in this position?

I found my clothes and dressed as quickly as possible. Geoffrey did, too. He led me down the hall and toward the back door, which was the closest way to my truck parked in the driveway. As we neared the door, I heard footsteps approaching. Was it Marguerite? I'd assumed no one was home. Next to me was the door to a coat closet, which I opened. I stepped inside. I felt childish, but I didn't see that I had a choice.

I heard the footsteps growing louder, then a low, mild woman's voice.

"Good evening, Mr. Gray." It was Gilda, their housekeeper. "Are you feeling okay?"

"Quite fine."

I waited, sweating and suffocating between slippery down coats.

"I heard something and was concerned," Gilda said.

I hadn't hidden in a small closet since I was a little girl. Even then, I'd hated it. I felt like the walls were closing in on me.

"It's your day off, isn't it?" Geoffrey said.

"I'm leaving in the morning."

I was gasping for air—high, shallow inhalations. How long until I ran out of oxygen?

"Okay, then," he said.

I was close to screaming when Geoffrey finally opened the closet. It was three steps until I was out the back door.

The cold air against my damp face shocked me, as did the sound of the lake, almost as loud as an ocean now. Geoffrey followed me out, but I motioned for him to go back.

I'd rarely been on the Grays' property at night. I could barely see my hand in front of my face. I stumbled into a hedge and almost fell on top of it. It wasn't until I was sitting in the driver's seat of my truck that I realized Gilda might hear my engine starting. I didn't know where she slept, but if the noise startled her, she might look out one of the east windows and notice my blue Chevy Silverado. Would she recognize it as mine?

When I returned to Rosecliff the next day, everything looked different to me. The colors were too bright. The air was too clean and cold.

Geoffrey found me after the rest of my staff had left. I could have left earlier, to avoid this moment. Instead, I'd knowingly allowed the opportunity to present itself. Why did I do that?

What could I gain from sleeping with Geoffrey again? Nothing. But the pull came from someplace deep inside me, and I gave in to it.

It was too cold to sit out on the porch. Geoffrey led me to

the coral guest room again. He pulled my clothes off and made love to me. His mouth and hands moved down my body. Then his lean hips were on mine. His arms were golden brown, but his chest, abdomen, and pelvis were ivory. I couldn't keep Marguerite's face out of my head. I imagined her expression if she found out that I slept with Geoffrey. Her lips pressed tightly together, her large brown eyes glazing over. She thought I was beneath her.

This time, I spent the night. Geoffrey assured me Marguerite wouldn't return until late morning. I woke up aware of the coral sheets irritating my skin.

I dressed, then sat on the edge of the bed and kissed Geoffrey goodbye.

His hair was sticking up and he had pillow lines on his face, but he was still beautiful. "I'm going to be away," he said. "But I want to see you when I get back."

Anyone who looked at my situation would say this affair was headed for disaster.

Frank and I were wrapping up our weekly meeting at his office, which was situated over his garage. "The Grays are in Italy on vacation," he said.

I'd assumed Geoffrey was going to New York or to Boston.

Did Marguerite know about us? Had she taken him away on purpose? To prove to me that he belonged to her? To prove to *him* that he belonged to her? A marriage like the Grays', it would take a lot to end it. No matter how much Geoffrey liked me, or even loved me. Marguerite had a stranglehold on every aspect of the Grays' life. She would never release her grip.

"Listen, kid." Frank cleared his throat. "Send Teddy to the Grays' place. I want you to focus on nailing down new business."

"Hmm?"

"Send Teddy or Finn to Rosecliff." He looked down and adjusted the band of his watch.

"I still have a lot to do."

"It's just winterizing," he said. "You stay away from there. Maybe you'll go back in the spring."

I caught Frank's eye. *Marguerite told Frank.* She knew about me and Geoffrey.

"I don't—"

"It's what the Grays want." His voice was barely above a whisper, but his intention was sharp.

"They said that?"

He met my gaze. "They said that."

Geoffrey wouldn't have said that. I didn't believe he would have said that.

In the days that followed, energy slowly drained from my body. As hard as I tried to focus, I couldn't concentrate on my work. I visited Rosecliff every day, in spite of Frank's instructions. I couldn't help myself. I was hoping I'd get some information on Geoffrey. When he was returning.

And then finally, I heard an exchange between Gilda and

Raoul, the chef, a discussion of the airport pickup that after-noon.

I longed to see Geoffrey, even if it was only for ten seconds. I wanted just to catch his eye. Just to assure myself that I still had his . . . affection, or attention, or something. At five, the Grays still hadn't arrived. I usually packed up by 4:30, but I was find-ing work to do, anything to keep me there.

Finally, at around six, an SUV pulled into the driveway. I stood behind the gardening shed. A chauffeur helped the Grays out of the backseat. Geoffrey was holding a large, heavy sculp-ture of a bird. Geoffrey and Marguerite carefully made their way to the house. It seemed like they were discussing where they were going to place the sculpture. The driver managed the five suitcases. No one noticed me.

Gilda came out and greeted them. Geoffrey handed her the sculpture, issuing some kind of directions. He was so hand-some, even from a distance.

Once Gilda went back inside, Marguerite kissed Geoffrey. She leaned her weight on him; she kissed his face and his mouth and his neck. Her arms around his waist. Most of the time, Marguerite reminded me of a predatory animal, like a lion. But sometimes, when she wasn't performing, something shifted, a veil dropped from her face, and I could see desperation under-neath.

Geoffrey responded to her kisses. Marguerite whispered something in Geoffrey's ear. He laughed. I found myself wishing I had made him laugh.

I looked away, suddenly aware it was a scene I didn't want to witness. I felt a heaviness in my gut and realized I didn't want Geoffrey to love her.

It was two days later when I was back at Rosecliff, against Frank's wishes. I stayed all day, hoping to find a few minutes alone with Geoffrey. As the hours passed, I planted more asters than I'd intended to, just to have an activity.

I was planting the last of the pansies, along one of the stone walls, when I saw the bright red sky. It was the most startling sunset I'd ever seen. It was otherworldly. I crossed the grass to take a picture. That was when I noticed Marguerite. She was walking past the two rows of pylons we'd placed near the edge of the cliff.

I approached close enough to call to her. "Mrs. Gray, you shouldn't be standing there."

She didn't appear to be listening to me, or maybe she couldn't hear me. It was below freezing, but she was wearing only a bulky gray sweater and a long floral skirt, which billowed in the wind. I moved farther, now standing ten yards away from her.

"It's icy," I yelled over the wind. The black ice was almost invisible, but a practiced eye could recognize it.

She continued to ignore me. She took several photos in the direction of the sunset, and then in the other direction. She'd probably done so a hundred times before, but now the cliff was precarious. The pylons weren't for show. I didn't allow any of the

Brizzi's staff to walk out past those pylons, unless they wore a harness and followed our safety protocol.

But I didn't enjoy giving Marguerite instructions. If only Teddy were here.

When she stepped closer to the edge, I raised my voice and yelled louder. "Mrs. Gray, turn around please. And walk back. Without the boxwoods, it's extremely dangerous."

She finally turned to me, and her eyes were pools of rage. She knew. She knew about me and Geoffrey. "Have you forgotten whose house this is?"

"I can't allow you to—"

She laughed, but the sound came out choked. "You can't *allow* me?" Her voice rose in pitch and in volume.

I remained standing where I was. I didn't know what to do.

It was getting colder, and rain was expected. I would gladly have left, if only she wasn't standing near the edge of the cliff.

I approached closer, so I stood just twelve feet away from her. "It's hard to see, and you can't tell, but there's a slope."

Her eyes narrowed. "Please leave." She pointed to the driveway.

She turned her back to me and walked three feet farther, then stopped to take photos. The sky was turning from red to orange.

I followed her. When I was two feet away, I took her elbow in my hand in an effort to lead her away from the edge. I didn't have a choice. Wasn't there liability if I stood here and watched her walk to the edge?

She pushed me off her, and I stumbled back.

I felt heat spreading from my face to my neck and down my body. She was putting my life in danger as well as hers. I was trying to be responsible.

I told myself to turn around and go home.

But I didn't because I was scared she'd fall off the cliff and die and I'd be to blame. Or maybe because I was angry. She was dismissing my warning. Dismissing *me*. Over and over and over.

I took her elbow in my hand again. But she slapped me hard across the face. Then, she raised her fist. Instinctively, I blocked her with my forearm. Her fist made contact with my arm. I guess that she didn't expect to meet resistance. So that resistance caused her to stumble back slightly. Just two steps, but enough to lose her purchase, to lose her footing, just enough to slide backward over the ice, the imperceptibly sloping ice. Her eyes wide with the recognition of what was happening. Over the edge of the cliff.

She disappeared.

She was gone.

It took a moment for me to understand what had happened.

She fell. Back. She . . .

She wasn't standing in front of me anymore.

It was a fifty- or sixty-foot drop.

Was she dead? What happened? Was she dead?

She . . .

Help. Help.

I could feel my fingernails cutting into my palms. I could feel the cold air in my eyes.

I didn't know, what should I do? Should I call someone?

But . . . it was no . . . it was too late. I couldn't. She fell, and there was no way . . . She was dead. She was already dead. It would . . .

There was nothing to do. There was nothing.

She was already dead.

I stepped backward. One foot and then the next.

She was already dead.

I kept backing away from the cliff, away from the pylons, backing up toward the driveway, toward my truck. Marguerite might rise up from the lake and come after me. I didn't believe . . . I didn't know what to believe. I opened the door to my truck. I got in. My house was twenty minutes away from the Grays'. I kept driving and the only thing I could think was, No. The only thing I could say was "No."

People came from miles around for the garden tour. To see that particular view from that particular spot. Some called it the most dramatic view in New England. The place from which she fell.

Thick, dense rain slammed against my windshield. I could hardly see the road. My truck skidded into the oncoming traffic. I lost control of the wheel. I thought, Maybe it's for the best that I die right now. Maybe it would be a good thing. But I didn't die.

In my driveway was Curtis's car. I felt such relief when I saw him, knowing I wouldn't be alone. Curtis was standing under the portico. I stumbled out of my car and toward him, my face dripping with tears and rain.

He walked with me into my living room and led me to the sofa. He put his arm around me. I was so very grateful for him. Someone who would not judge me.

"Phoenix, tell me what happened."

"Mrs. Gray . . . Mrs. Gray . . ." I cried for a long time. I didn't know if I'd ever be able to speak again.

"Okay," Curtis said. "It's okay."

Finally, my breathing slowed down. "Mrs. Gray . . . *fell.*"

"Mm-hm."

"I told her not to get so close. She wasn't listening to me. She was walking so I tried to . . . I was trying to stop her from going toward the cliff. And she wouldn't . . . so I took her arm and I was pulling on her. And I think she knew about me and Geoffrey. . . . And she was mad and pulling away and she hit me and then she fell back. . . . And I was so scared. . . ."

I was hyperventilating again. Curtis didn't rush me at all. He just rubbed my back like I was a child with a stomachache.

"I was so scared. I left. She's dead. And I was there alone with her. When she fell she was trying to hit me and I was just . . . all I did . . . I just held out my arm to defend myself."

"It's okay, Phoenix," he said. "You didn't do anything bad. You were trying to help her. If someone asks, just say you left the house like normal. You did your job and you came home."

Eventually, I must have gone to sleep, drained and exhausted. I felt him drape a blanket over my body before he left.

I forgave Curtis for everything. All the money he'd borrowed. All the nights drunk on my sofa. I forgave him.

The death of Marguerite would follow me for the rest of my life. I could go to the police now. But they'd think . . . I didn't harm her. She was already dead when I left the house.

The days and nights after her death ran into one another. I lay in my bed and played versions of the scene in my head, on repeat.

"Mrs. Gray, turn around please. And walk back. Without the boxwoods, it's extremely dangerous."

"Have you forgotten whose house this is?" she said.

I said: *"Of course. I won't bother you anymore."*

I turn around and I leave.

If I played that scene over in my head enough times, maybe it would become real. Maybe I would believe it.

My mind circled. Over and over. On the same images. The same concepts. Where she was standing. The force of her hand. The force of my resistance. The slope of the hill. The ice on the hill. The lack of friction. I had been good at physics.

I could have left. I didn't need to warn her. Why did I stay?

I washed the blue sweatshirt and jeans I'd been wearing that day. In hot water, twice. I shoved both to the back of a closet shelf.

Occasionally, I went to the kitchen for a glass of water. Occasionally, I looked outside. Through my bedroom window I could see my weeping willow tree covered in frost.

A team of underwater CSIs found Marguerite's body. I read it on my iPhone. I dropped the phone on my kitchen floor. It burned my hand. I backed away from it.

Her body had settled on the bottom of the lake. It appeared she fell from the cliff above. She would have died upon impact.

Probably. She probably would have died upon impact. There was nothing I could have done to prevent her death. Even if I'd called 911. She was already dead. She was probably already dead.

Marguerite Gray died at the age of fifty-six in a tragic accident at her home on October 25. The cause of death has not been confirmed. Mrs. Gray was well-known as a cultural and lifestyle doyenne. She was also known as the muse of artist Serge Kuhnert. He painted Mrs. Gray at least ten times. One of Kuhnert's lesser works sold last year for $3.6 million at Christie's. The most famous of his paintings, Marguerite by the Lake, *which now resides at the Grays' Connecticut home, is considered one of the most important paintings of the last century. It has been loaned out to The Metropolitan Museum of Art several times, and to the Getty Museum. In it, Marguerite is standing on a cliff with a lake in the background. The New York Times described the painting as "raw and unfiltered and confrontational."*

Mrs. Gray leaves behind a husband, Geoffrey Gray, and a daughter, Taylor Gray.

CHAPTER FOUR

The rain started again the day that Marguerite's body was found, and it wouldn't let up. The local police asked everyone on the Grays' staff, as well as the Brizzi's crew, to report to the police station in the morning for interviews as part of standard protocol. They asked us all the same questions. What time did you leave the Gray residence? Did you see Marguerite Gray? Did you speak to Marguerite Gray? My answers were two or three words long.

In the afternoon, I knocked on the door of Frank's office. When he didn't answer, I let myself in and sat down across from him while he finished a call. Through the window, I could see his house and the long field beyond it. Photographs of his late wife covered the office walls. He had never remarried after she died, twenty years earlier.

Frank hung up the phone. He had dark circles under his

eyes and looked older than he had one week before. "I told you not to go there." He rocked forward and backward in his big leather chair.

"I know, but—"

"What time did you leave?"

This was what I was dreading. These questions. I didn't want him to hear a crack in my voice. "Could have been four."

"Did you say goodbye?"

"No." My throat was swollen. I didn't have a place to rest my tongue.

"Was she outside when you left?"

"I don't know." My words echoed. *I don't know.*

"What does that mean? You know if you saw her. So you didn't see her." Frank's tone was sharp.

"No."

"Listen to me, kid," he said. "The Grays are not your friends. You work for them."

"I know that."

"This is bad business. It looks like negligence. Someone could sue us. And Brizzi's could go under like *that*." He snapped his finger.

I tried to keep my expression sad, but not distraught. I needed to show him I was deeply distressed about the situation. But not taking it personally.

"Who else was there that day?" he said.

"Teddy, Finn. Geoffrey was out of town. I'm sure some of the house staff were there, too."

Frank closed his eyes and took his glasses off. He opened his eyes wide and squeezed them shut again. Then opened them again. Maybe he was hoping that something would change each time.

"When I had a couple of bad years, Mrs. Gray loaned me ten thousand dollars, no interest. She didn't even tell her husband," he said. "There's erosion there on the cliff. We talked about it. But we didn't even need to. That's a smart lady. *Quella dannata* stone path. Why did she walk to the edge?"

Because she wanted a picture of the sunset. Because I told her not to. Because I slept with Geoffrey. "I don't know why."

A funeral service was held at the church in Litchfield, open to the public, and a reception at Rosecliff afterward. Frank told me we had to go to the funeral. It was the last thing that I wanted to do.

I drank two shots of vodka, followed by a piece of bread, followed by mouthwash, and forced myself out of the house. I met Frank at his place. I couldn't remember ever seeing him in a suit and tie. He drove us there in his ten-year-old Maserati. Frank's pupils were dilated. His eyes looked like Curtis's did the day he came home with a concussion in seventh grade.

I was glad that Frank and I were seated in the car next to each other, so I didn't have to look at his eyes. He was more agitated than he was when we met in his office.

"I don't believe these stories." He pounded his fist on the steering wheel.

I looked down and saw a stain on my black dress, and one of the buttons in the front was coming off.

Another car tried to pass us, and Frank accelerated, causing the car to lurch.

"These things don't happen," he said. "Not to a lady like this."

A car cut in front of him. He slammed on the brake. My seat belt tightened around my waist and torso.

"I drove over to Rosecliff to pay my respects, but no one's there," Frank said. "The whole place is a crime scene. They've got half of Lake Spiro roped off. I hear the cops were waiting on some harnesses to go out to the edge of that cliff in the rain. So, while they're waiting, Rosecliff gets nine inches of rain in one hour, nine inches, and that big mass of rock that was splintering when the spruce fell? The whole thing breaks off and boom, falls straight down into the lake. So, the poor cops are left sucking their thumbs up there. Because all their evidence is in the god-damn lake."

All the evidence was in the lake? Could that be true?

Frank said Marguerite's cell phone wasn't recovered, but they found photos of the sunset in her backup that she had taken right before she died—similar to ones she had taken many times before.

It looked like four hundred people attending. We were early, but even so, almost every seat in the church was full. We entered to the music of an organ, strings, and a choir performing hymns.

My father's funeral service had been nothing like this. He was cremated, and we had a small service at our Catholic church. Fewer than a dozen people showed up. My biology teacher came. I asked Curtis: "Why is Mrs. Fowler here? She doesn't know anyone."

"She knows you," he said.

That was what I remembered best about that day. Mrs. Fowler drove forty-five minutes to go to my dad's funeral.

There was no service when my grandmother died. I was in the hospital with eighteen broken bones.

Frank and I found seats in the back of the church, in the far corner. The congregation grew silent when the pallbearers walked down the aisle with a casket covered in white roses. I recognized Peter Gray, my high school boyfriend. He looked in my direction, but I couldn't tell if he saw me. I also recognized Basil Scott, Amar Ansari, and Wren Lacquer, all seated together. Serge Kuhnert, the artist who painted Marguerite, was seated in the second row, behind Geoffrey and Taylor. Several people were whispering and pointing in his direction. It was the first time I'd seen him in person, though I recognized him from photos. He was possibly more famous than Marguerite. He was wearing a silk tie the color of purple delphiniums. My grandmother would have called him "posh."

A priest presided over the ceremony. The liturgy seemed familiar to me. Curtis had told me that my mother used to take us to Mass when we were little. Maybe I remembered some of it.

Halfway through the service, Serge Kuhnert stood and

made his way to the podium. I noticed Geoffrey's head was tilted down, like he was praying. There was a murmur from the crowd. They quieted when he spoke, reciting a poem: "*She walks in beauty, like the night of cloudless climes and starry skies; And all that's best of dark and bright meet in her aspect and her eyes . . .*"

When he finished, he stepped away from the microphone. Then he stopped and turned back. "Thirty years ago, Marguerite Gray saw something in me that no one else saw." His voice broke. He adjusted his horn-rimmed glasses, then continued. "She believed in me." The crowd's murmurs grew louder as he made his way back to his seat. Geoffrey's head was still down.

Wren Lacquer, in a black minidress, stood and walked to the front of the church to delivery her eulogy. "Marguerite Gray inspired everyone around her. She demanded a lot, but she gave so much more." She continued talking about Marguerite's brilliance and her generosity. When she finished, Taylor spoke. She was a young Marguerite. The tilt of her head, the outline of her chin, the way her gazelle arms swung by her sides. It was Marguerite twenty-five years earlier. Taylor referred to her mother's "tragic and unaccountable death." She started crying in the middle of her speech and couldn't finish. She stumbled back to the pew. Geoffrey stood to embrace her.

After the funeral service, I stood in line and waited to speak to Geoffrey. Serge was in front of me. "We have to talk," Serge said to Geoffrey. At that moment, a woman I didn't recognize cut in line to hand Geoffrey a glass of water. Serge departed.

I was sweating through my dress when I finally spoke to Geoffrey. "I'm sorry for your loss," I said. "If there's anything I can do."

"Thank you for coming," he said quietly. I looked up and we made eye contact for one brief moment. His face was very pale against his dark gray suit. I tried to read him but couldn't.

"What a tragic . . . so tragic," I stammered, turning my eyes down. And then ducked out of the way.

A group of reporters and photographers crowded around the base of Rosecliff's driveway, probably hoping for a glimpse of Geoffrey or Taylor. They were disappointed when they saw me. The Grays had a security guard at the gated entrance, checking off names.

Geoffrey had hired valet drivers, but the motor court was still packed with cars. I parked on the grass.

A week had passed since Marguerite's body was discovered. Rosecliff was released back to the Grays in time for the funeral and the days of mourning.

Marguerite's parents were both dead and she was an only child. But it seemed like there was extended family—maybe two dozen cousins, aunts, and uncles—milling around.

I noticed one woman who was probably twenty years older than Marguerite but resembled her. She was old-school, with blond coiffed hair under a black straw hat and a heavy string of pearls, along with large pearl-and-diamond earrings. Another woman, who looked like a young Kate Middleton, was wearing low heels and a black velvet cloak with a gold clasp at the neck. Did one of these people cheat Marguerite out of her inheritance?

I thought I could tell the difference between Marguerite's relatives and her friends. The friends were a less conservative group with a lot of Botox. One fortysomething man was wearing sunglasses, a fitted suit with pants that hit him above the ankle, a thin tie, an AirPod in his ear, and lots of hair gel. The crowd parted when he came through.

I also saw some of the guests from the garden party, like Helen Spielman and a few other Brizzi's clients. Wren Lacquer was talking to Amar, Basil, and a small group of unfamiliar faces who might have worked out of the New York office. From a distance, I could see her clocking the guests. She eventually left Amar and Basil to talk to an older heavyset man and a younger emaciated woman who wore a clunky emerald necklace. I had the sense that Wren knew who was important and was making the most of this opportunity.

I needed to be seen like I had nothing to avoid. But I didn't want to be there. I kept my eyes away from the cliff. Someone might be able to read my mind if they saw me looking at it.

I circled around the outside of the house, just to get my bearings. Through the living room windows, I could see Taylor, her blond hair twisted up on her head, revealing her swan neck. A security guard was standing near the fireplace, guarding the Kuhnert painting.

I brought brownies. When my father died, a few people

showed up with unappealing casseroles, but one person brought a basket of brownies. Curtis and I went through two dozen of them in one day. It was the only thing we ate.

I rang the Grays' doorbell and a wispy young woman who worked for the Grays opened the door. Geoffrey, in his dark gray suit and sapphire tie, was standing in the gallery talking to a small group. He had bloodshot eyes and a dazed look, like he hadn't slept in days. He saw me and approached the door. "Hi, Phoenix."

I handed him the brownies. "If there's anything I can do . . ."

He nodded. "Thanks." He gave me an awkward salute.

I considered what would seem most natural. Should I hug him, pat his shoulder, rest my hand on his arm?

In the end, I didn't touch him at all. I heard Taylor in the next room, and I ran away. I was coming to believe it was over. Everything with Geoffrey. He would probably feel loyal to Marguerite's memory. It was probably for the best. Distance. Space. Maybe it was for the best.

In the days after the funeral, Helen's house was a tight ball in my stomach. Thinking about the view from Helen's house. Of Rosecliff. Helen's house stood at the same elevation as the lake, and you had to look up to see Rosecliff on the cliff across the lake. I didn't know how much of the property was blocked because of the angle. I couldn't remember, because it wasn't necessary before.

My crew and I were scheduled to visit Helen's house to cover trees for the winter frost.

I arrived earlier than everyone else. I needed to see.

I sat on Helen's porch. My worst fears were confirmed. Since the Rosecliff property sloped slightly down in the direction of the lake, I had a clear and open view of it. I recognized Geoffrey. I could tell by the way he walked, the way he moved. His body was long and lean, and he had grace. It was difficult to identify others, until Wren arrived and walked across the lawn. I knew it was her. I also recognized Taylor. It was easy to recognize Taylor's movements. So similar to Marguerite's.

I proceeded slowly across the waterfront of Helen's property. There were no cliffs here. The lawn gave way to the sand and shallow water. I stopped every few feet to analyze the view from each angle. If someone had seen me—could someone have recognized me? Helen's housekeeper, her relatives, her children or grandchildren? It was unlikely that someone was staring at Rosecliff in that five-minute period before Marguerite fell. And it was even less likely that the person had good enough eyesight to identify who was on the lawn. A very small chance. If I knew how often people visited Helen, what days and what times they visited, what they did while they were visiting, maybe I would have known how likely it was that I was in danger.

Later, at home, I took a long hot shower, changed into sweats, and turned on the TV. I didn't have friends over to my house often. Most of my friends had graduated from college, but I'd quit after two years. And then they'd all gotten married and had kids. When I saw them, I could tell they were thinking, *Phoenix has still got that same job working as a gardener?* Like they felt sorry for me. They probably thought their desk jobs were better. But they didn't realize I would never have wanted that life.

When it was almost dark, through the light rain out my window, I could see the headlights of a stripped-down black Dodge Charger pulling into my driveway. And then a short woman with a long braid got out of the car and walked to my front door. She rang the doorbell.

I opened the door. I recognized her.

"Hello, Phoenix." She stood underneath the portico protected from the rain.

"Hi, Rachel," I said. "What can I do for you?"

She showed me her badge. "I'm investigating the death of Marguerite Gray."

Acid from my stomach rose up to my throat. Rachel Hanna. She had the same sharp face and long braid that she'd had in high school. Except now there were two deep vertical lines between her eyebrows and her hair was lighter.

"Just wondering if I can ask you a few questions?" she said.

"Of course," I said. Because what else could I say?

She made a show of carefully wiping her boots on the doormat.

I motioned for her to sit across from me on the mustard-colored living room sofa. As she sat down, her eyes landed on a piece of plaster next to her hand on the sofa cushion. She looked up at the peeling paint on the ceiling.

She took a small black spiral notepad and a retractable green pen from her jacket pocket. She wasn't wearing a police uniform. She was wearing corduroy pants, a sweater, and a damp rain jacket. I could picture her sitting next to me in French class.

"I heard that you saved Geoffrey Gray's life?" She smiled.

"I . . . what?"

"He was going to be crushed by a tree and you risked your life to get him out of the way."

I hadn't expected this subject. "That's an exaggeration."

"It was brave of you." Was she being sarcastic?

"Thanks." I looked down and noticed my worn-out socks with no shoes.

She pulled her braid around in front of her shoulder, like she used to do in French class. "Helen Spielman said the tree could have killed a lot of people, if you hadn't warned everyone."

What else did Helen Spielman say?

I smiled. "I notice these things."

"Why were you at the Grays' party?"

I cleared my throat. "I was a guest."

I remembered when our French teacher, Madame Sophie, told the class that my father died. She suggested I go sit outside and read a book. To take my mind off everything. I could picture how Rachel looked at me. It was a mixture of pity and curiosity.

"How did you happen to notice Geoffrey Gray's location when you came to his rescue?"

"I was paying attention to the spruce," I said. "I kept telling Mrs. Gray we should take the spruce down."

Every few seconds, I could hear the kitchen faucet dripping.

"Have the Grays invited you to a lot of parties?"

"No."

She blinked a few too many times. Her mascara was flaking off. "Why this one?"

"I don't know."

Rachel clicked her pen. Her nails were cut to the quick. "And . . . just one more thing." She held her notepad vertically as she wrote. "Looking at the timeline of October twenty-fifth. Do you have someone who can confirm where you were at five that evening?"

I smiled. Casual. "My brother Curtis can. He was here."

She wrote several words.

"Thanks for your time, Phoenix. Nice to see you again."

She left. I closed the door behind her.

What did she know that she wasn't telling me? What was she keeping from me?

I had to talk to Curtis before she did. I had to talk to him now. Right this minute.

He was living with his girlfriend, Maya. I'd never been inside their place, but I'd dropped him off there once. I drove to their one-bedroom apartment in the center of Waterbury. Curtis buzzed me in.

There was a small white laminate table with two steel chairs against one wall and a sofa that smelled like weed across the room. I could hear the television playing behind the closed door of the bedroom. Maybe it was Maya in there?

Curtis looked like he was high. "What are you doing here?"

"I need to talk to you."

"Yeah?" He motioned to the table and chairs.

I didn't sit down. "Remember Rachel Hanna?"

"Sounds familiar."

"She's investigating Marguerite's death."

"Yeah?"

"I told her you would confirm I was home at five that day."

He exhaled through his mouth, like he was blowing bubbles. "You want me to lie to the police?"

I put my finger to my mouth. "Shhh." I didn't like how Curtis was framing this. I thought he'd be more flexible. "I was home at five."

"Really?"

"I've helped you out of some scrapes," I whispered.

"You've helped *me*?" He laughed, a little too hard and too loud.

I had a strong metallic taste in my mouth. "Please, Curtis."

He shook his head. "I don't know."

"Please," I said. "And for the restaurant, whatever you need."

I visited Helen's house three days in a row. Sometimes the light was too low to see details. Sometimes the glare of too much light made it harder to see them. On the fourth day, Helen called to me: "Phoenix, I usually don't see much of you this time of year."

"I've been thinking about your gazebo," I said quickly.

Helen and I sat at her kitchen counter since it was bitter outside. She brought me a cup of coffee. I needed a shot of whiskey
in my coffee, but I didn't ask her for it.

"We've got three sets of plans," I said.

"Oh, Phoenix. Plans stifle my imagination. Let's think out
of the box."

Helen stood and pointed toward the back of the house. "I want
the gazebo up on the hill. That's where I always wish our house
was situated." Each property has its own built-in constraints. And
sometimes the owner doesn't recognize those constraints.

I sipped my coffee. "Interesting idea." But I didn't think it
was a good idea at all.

"Two hundred years ago my house stood on that cliff." She
pointed to the Grays' home across the lake. "Before Rosecliff was
even built."

Helen had told me this story, but I didn't mind hearing it
again.

"The Eden family thought it was too windy up there, so
they moved the house to this side of the lake." Helen smiled.
"They lowered it to the ice, which was three feet thick that winter, wheeled it straight across the lake, then used a pulley to get it
up here. If only they'd pulled it a little farther." She turned again
and pointed behind her. "To the highest point." Helen returned
to looking out the window at Rosecliff on the other side of the
lake. "I used to sit on my porch and just stare at Marguerite's
place," she said. "It's so dramatic, the cliff there. I used to wish
my house was still there. I feel like there's an invisible connec-

tion between the two houses. Marguerite and I were so close, and I often thought that was the reason."

I felt as though someone had turned up the lights in Helen's house. It was blindingly bright. It was important to keep my face composed. Was she taunting me with this information? I'd been working on her property for eight years. She'd never mentioned sitting on the porch and staring at Rosecliff. She'd never mentioned an invisible connection. Why was she telling me this?

"But now, it's painful. It's hard for me to look at the cliff without thinking about Marguerite's fall," she said. "We were friends for thirty-five years. I was friends with her parents, too. What a mind she had. A brilliant mind." She sat back down on the kitchen stool. "You know, her mother never liked Geoffrey. She always thought he was after Marguerite's money, but she was dead wrong. Geoffrey adored Marguerite. Not that they didn't have problems in their relationship. She thought he was cheating on her." She sighed. "I've had a lot of patients who cheat on their spouses. It's usually because they want to be noticed. They're not getting enough attention.

"That detective's been over here. I told her everything I know. I want to help," she said. "Of course, some of it is speculation."

Helen had probably told Rachel Hanna that Geoffrey was cheating on Marguerite. My potential paths forward were fewer and narrowing all the time. I didn't have a lot of room for error.

As I pulled out of Helen's driveway, I saw in my rearview mirror a Corolla sedan turning in. The car was similar to one

I'd seen before at the Grays' house. I didn't get a good look at the driver. I had an impulse to turn my truck around and go back to find out who was in that car. But I kept driving.

My conversation with Helen had unnerved me. What she said about the invisible connection. What she said about Geoffrey sleeping with me to get Marguerite's attention. Was it possible he cared so little for me?

The next morning, I went to CVS and purchased three pairs of eyeglasses, to approximate three different people with a range of distance vision. I visited Helen's house again to examine the views of Rosecliff from every angle. The person with the worst vision would probably not be able to identify anyone. The person with the best vision would possibly be able to identify certain people, depending on the weather and the light.

Frank had told me not to go to the Grays' place, but he didn't realize I had to. Rosecliff fed me in a way that Frank couldn't understand. And Geoffrey was there, even if I didn't see him or talk to him. Knowing that he was close was somehow consoling.

When I arrived, I noticed Rachel Hanna's car in the driveway. Geoffrey was on the porch talking to her, along with a man in a jacket and tie. Maybe it was her partner.

I went to work on the foundation plantings. If I was gardening around the corner from the verandah, behind one of the viburnums, I had a good chance of hearing a conversation, without being seen. And if no one else was nearby, I could look through

the sliver of space between the copper gutter and the siding of
the house. There was the added advantage that the foundation
plantings around the Grays' house legitimately required a lot of
tedious work.

"Anything I can do to help you." The sound of Geoffrey's
voice was comforting, even though he wasn't talking to me.

"I appreciate that," Rachel said.

"Only, if possible, we'd like to avoid an autopsy. Marguerite
was a strong Catholic."

"We'll try to respect your wishes," she said. "Russ Marks
confirmed that you were sailing together on October twenty-
fifth."

"Right."

"And . . . just checking on a few facts." She raised her voice
over the wind. "Mr. Marks is employed by Greenhaven Gardens? That's the charity that you and Mrs. Gray founded?"

"Right."

Why did she care where this guy worked?

After the detectives left, I shifted my focus to planting tulips.
I rarely planted tulips earlier than November because they were
vulnerable to tulip fire, a disease that made them look burnt. I
preferred species tulips, like the dark Queen of the Night, because their performance improved every year, unlike bedding
tulips, which faded after a couple of seasons.

Lake Spiro wasn't very big, about one mile across at the
widest point. When I was a kid, Lake Spiro would freeze solid
every year. I'd heard stories about ghosts walking across the ice.

Most years, I would see ice-skating and ice fishing on the lake. But over the last few winters, that had changed. Gradually less and less ice. So far this year, it was scant, just a thin layer in certain sections.

I wondered what would have happened to Marguerite if she had fallen in the summer with no ice at all? How quickly would she have died? How quickly *did* she die?

I was surprised to see Frank's car pulling into the motor court.

He crossed the lawn to where I was standing near the cliff. "Why don't you let Teddy take over here, like we talked about?" He pulled his hat down over his ears, to protect them from the biting wind.

"There's a lot that needs my attention." Before he could stop me, I jumped in with ideas for drainage and stormwater management strategies. We needed to replace the protective layers of vegetation that had stabilized the site. "What do you think about golden bell?" Where the branch touched the earth, it would form new roots. Could new roots be as strong as old roots?

He shook his head in frustration. "I'm telling you, kid, back off."

I didn't listen to Frank. I was compelled to go to Rosecliff. Occasionally, I'd catch a glimpse of Geoffrey and we'd make eye contact. He'd smile at me, like we had a secret between us. But that small acknowledgment was enough to sustain me.

A few days before Thanksgiving, I saw Taylor Gray from a

distance. She was returning from law school. A young Marguerite. The way she glided across the frosted lawn in her long white woolen coat. I tried to swallow, but my throat tightened.

Taylor saw me looking at her. She nodded. How would it feel to return home to a grand house like hers?

She was a few yards from her Honda CR-V. I looked down, and then when I turned back, she was on the driveway in a heap. Teddy was by her side in an instant to ask if she was okay. He helped her to her feet. I was relieved because I wanted to avoid her. I was sure she would sense my unease.

Teddy came to my house that night and brought hamburgers and fries. We split a bottle of Heineken, and then a second bottle, and sat at the kitchen table. He knew more about my relationship with Geoffrey than anyone else did, except for Curtis. He'd seen me and Geoffrey together more than once, before Marguerite died. He didn't know the specifics, but probably guessed.

He hadn't seemed to care before. But now, I sensed something different. Was he more guarded?

"I feel sorry for her." Teddy opened a packet of ketchup and put some on his cheeseburger.

"Who?"

"Marguerite's daughter." He took a bite of his burger.

"Why?"

"She hurt herself when she fell. I think it was her wrist," he said. "She seems like a nice kid."

His interest in Taylor struck me as a betrayal.

"You like her?" I said.

Teddy's face had a pink glow to it, but I didn't know if it was just from too much sun. He rolled his eyes. "No. I mean she's cute, yeah. But I just feel sorry for her."

"Right."

"Her eyes were red and swollen," he said. "Like she'd been crying. Probably about her mom. Man, that Marguerite was a stone-cold biatch. But, you know, if it's your mother, it's your mother."

I added salt to my fries. I didn't usually add salt. But today, the fries were bland. The burger was bland. Nothing appealed to me.

"And it's gotta be confusing, too." He was finishing his fries. He didn't seem to notice how tasteless they were. "Marguerite was sharp and alert, you know. I'd seen her take pics from that spot. Some of our crew were like, the spruce tree changed the grade, blah, blah, blah, and she didn't realize it. Bullshit. We talked about it with her. Of course she knew it. It's sort of like, what was going on that day?"

"Hard to know." The back of my neck felt hot.

Teddy looked out the kitchen window. "There's something else," he said. "If that's what I'm thinking, it's gotta be what Taylor's thinking."

I drank a glass of water in one go. I felt like jumping out of my skin. I couldn't allow this rumination.

"Detective Lee showed up at my place," he said.

I remembered the man in jacket and tie who was with Rachel the other day. Was that Detective Lee?

"He asked me what I was wearing that day. What the rest of the crew were wearing."

I frowned like I was curious. I could feel my heart pounding in my chest.

"I don't remember what I wore *yesterday*," he said. "I mean, come on."

He was trying to sound off-the-cuff, but I thought there was something tense in his posture. Maybe Teddy left out part of his conversation. Was there something he was choosing not to tell me?

When Taylor arrived at Rosecliff, my interactions with Geoffrey changed. He seemed self-conscious, so I stopped smiling when I saw him. I stopped making eye contact.

Stay away from him, I told myself.

I tried to, but I couldn't help myself. In spite of Frank's instructions, in spite of everything, I kept going back.

I was spraying the foundation plantings around the corner from the verandah. Geoffrey and Taylor came out on the porch.

"Detective Hanna's on her way over," Taylor said to her father, then lowered her voice. "She's talking to Gilda again."

"Don't worry," Geoffrey said, "your mum went to bat. All charges were dropped."

Charges? What kind of charges?

Rachel Hanna's Dodge Charger pulled into the driveway.

She left a teenage girl sitting in the passenger seat, listening to music. Was it her daughter? Why did she bring her daughter?

Rachel walked from one side of the property to the other, her long braid swinging, taking notes the whole time.

She walked back and forth across the portion of the cliff where Marguerite had fallen. Where the mass of rock had broken off. She traced the same line with her steps, at least five times. Then she stopped and looked across the lake. Was she looking at Helen's house? Did she consider Helen's house important? Had a witness come forward?

She stepped too close to the edge. I wouldn't have stepped as close as she did. When I was a kid, I used to be scared of heights. If I was near a cliff, a balcony, or an open window, I'd think to myself, one split second of losing my sanity was all it would take. And I'd be dead. Watching her near the edge, I thought the same thing. One split second was all it would take.

Rachel joined Geoffrey and Taylor on the porch.

I had a partial view of Taylor's profile, sitting ramrod straight, with her perfect little nose in the air. The wind had picked up, so I couldn't hear what she was saying.

Rachel shook hands with Taylor.

Taylor turned to her father. She seemed agitated.

While Taylor and Geoffrey were talking to each other, Rachel walked to the edge of the verandah and looked out.

I had a fear of being spotted, so I circled the house and ended up behind the shrubs on the other side. I could still see them, and I would be more protected from the sound of the wind there.

"Ms. Gray, if you have other information," Rachel said.

"My mother wasn't reckless. I don't believe she fell," Taylor said. "I want to know, what happened to my mom?"

Taylor had a subtle tone of superiority when she talked to Rachel. If I were Rachel, I wouldn't like Taylor's attitude.

"An autopsy would make a big difference," Rachel said.

Taylor turned to Geoffrey, then looked back to Rachel. "We'd like an autopsy."

"Are you sure?" Geoffrey said.

"I'm sure."

"You two need to discuss the autopsy." Rachel wrote something in her notepad. "My team is still canvassing the neighborhood." She pointed to Helen's house. "We spoke to the lady in that house. Spielman. She said she's a friend of the family?"

"Helen and Marguerite were close," Geoffrey said.

"Mrs. Spielman was confused about a couple of things when we spoke," Rachel said. "But I'm going to try again. Of all the houses across the lake, that one has the most open view of your property."

Rachel was going back to Helen's house. She thought Helen had more to say. This was what I'd been scared of.

I'd been crouching in an awkward position for several minutes, in the guise of adding bark mulch to the flower beds, and my feet and calves had fallen asleep. But I still didn't move. I needed to hear the rest of the conversation.

"Thank you both." Rachel looked at her watch. "I have an interview with Gilda Reynolds."

Taylor escorted Rachel inside, then returned and sat next to Geoffrey.

"Please consider the possibility that more information will hurt you," he said.

Taylor squeezed both hands into fists and held them on top of her head, her elbows forward. "I could find out that someone chopped Mom's head off with an axe," she said. "It won't be worse than what I already know, which is that she's dead."

"I'm sorry. That's not what I meant. I just . . ." Geoffrey put his arms around her and kissed the top of her head. She cried. Her body shook in wracking sobs.

"We'll figure this out," he said.

When I saw Geoffrey embracing Taylor, I was strangely jealous. I wanted him back. I wanted to feel his arms around me. It was like there were several miles between us that I couldn't bridge. Only five weeks earlier, his naked body was next to mine. Only five weeks earlier, his body needed mine. I could feel it when I was in bed with him. I had power over him.

And now, I was no one. The gap between us grew larger each day. And I'd allowed that to happen, because I thought it was necessary. It *was* necessary. Wasn't it?

Rachel Hanna showed up at my house again that evening. The sight of her Dodge Charger turned my stomach. I knew she'd be back but didn't expect her so soon.

It was only when someone besides Curtis or Teddy visited my house that I noticed how bare the living room walls were.

How dark the room was. Every few months, I'd look at buying a lamp, but I never did.

Rachel pulled out the same spiral notepad and green pen.

"So . . . um . . . let's see," she said. "Just following up on our last conversation. Trying to track exactly what Mrs. Gray was doing on October twenty-fifth."

"Of course."

She pulled her braid around in front of her shoulders. Her honey-blond hair contrasted with her dark roots. I wondered if she dyed her hair at home or walked into a hair salon carrying a concealed weapon.

A memory came back to me. High school graduation wasn't the last time I'd seen Rachel. I could picture her in the corridor of the rehabilitation unit where I was recovering after my accident. I was walking down the hallway with a cane and she stepped to the side.

"You didn't talk to Marguerite Gray that day?"

"No, I didn't."

She clicked her pen a few times. "She wasn't gardening?"

"No."

"We found traces of plant material and fertilizer on one arm of her cashmere sweater."

My brain went into overdrive, like the dial on all my senses was turned up to eleven.

Keep your mouth shut.

"So, we're trying to figure out how the fertilizer could have gotten on her sweater."

"Maybe it was from a different day?"

Don't offer theories.

"Could be."

I focused on maintaining eye contact.

She tapped her boot on the ground. "Is it possible that you touched Mrs. Gray's arm? Maybe you just casually bumped into her?"

I frowned like I was bewildered by the question. "No."

Could she be bluffing? My mind was moving quickly, trying to assess what information Rachel might have. Or what she might pretend to have.

"Did Mrs. Gray know how dangerous that cliff was after the tree fell on it?"

"Yes," I said. "We told her. We all told her."

When Rachel left the house, I felt my body collapse. I was exhausted from the energy I'd exerted. I had two vodka tonics and then went to bed. After several hours, I got out of bed and had one more.

I had a splitting headache the next morning. When I walked into the kitchen, Curtis was sitting at my table with a Starbucks coffee. "Hi, scrawny," he said. "Are you eating?"

At the sight of him, I had a wave of anxiety. "I'm fine."

"So, Rachel Hanna called yesterday," he said. "I had the conversation you asked me to have."

"Thank you."

"I said exactly what you asked me to say."

"Thank you." I was trying to put it together. Why did she come back over here after she talked to Curtis?

"My friend José works with her," he said. "I asked him what he knew." With his two index fingers, he spun his Starbucks cup in a circle on the table.

I poured myself a cup of coffee. "Hmm?"

"The CSIs found blue fibers on Marguerite's cashmere sweater."

Blue fibers. My blue sweatshirt. I felt a searing pain in my skull. Rachel didn't say anything about blue fibers. Why didn't she say blue fibers? I focused on how to hold my face still, how to position my body, so that Curtis wouldn't notice the raging storm inside me.

"And they're analyzing DNA traces on the sweater, too."

DNA? How could they get DNA?

"The sweater was in the water for two days," I said.

"Yeah, but they've got techniques," he said. "And his daughter asked for an autopsy."

Was Rachel telling people this was a homicide?

"I don't want anyone finding out about that night," he said.

"I didn't do anything wrong." I was trying for a smile and an unemotional tone, but Curtis knew my real smile, and he probably knew this wasn't it.

This was my treading water smile.

"Yeah. No. But . . ." Curtis shifted in his chair and spun his cup on the table. "It's just a bad look. If . . . you were there and . . . you know."

I turned my back to Curtis to open the refrigerator. I took my time adding milk to my coffee so he couldn't see my face. I wanted to scream, "Get out of my house!"

But I needed Curtis to vouch for me. I needed him. And on top of that, I would have lost my mind if I hadn't told someone. When the world is shattering, you just need to talk to someone.

Curtis had too much information. About the night that Marguerite died. About other accidents from the past. And sometimes, he had bad judgment. As long as Curtis was in the world, I needed layers of protection, cushioning. I needed alliances. Was Geoffrey my ally? Could he still be my ally?

When my grandmother died, I ended up in the hospital, and I was on painkillers. I had five surgeries in a row. I was stoned out of my mind half the time. So, it was weeks later that I even knew she was dead. And by the time I realized, what was there to discuss? What could I have said about it? It was just a deep dark ball of emptiness and confusion. I had no past. No history. Because the one that was there, it was all wrong. The only person connecting me to anything larger than myself, she was gone. And if I was glad she was gone, it was balanced by the massive pit of loss.

I needed to find my way back to Geoffrey. My body told me I was too far from the center of gravity. I needed to be right up next to him, under him, to surround him, envelop him, in his bed. His confidante. His other half. I needed to find my way back.

I needed reassurance. Assurance or reassurance. Geoffrey's warm arms around me.

I could talk to him about his driveway, his roses, his trees. Helen's house. Helen's house. Helen's house. Sometimes when I closed my eyes, the only thing I could see was that house. I would drive other images into my head, just hoping to cover up the picture of Helen's house. But any image I came up with, it rolled over and mutated and grew and transformed, like a beast, into Helen's house.

Or I could talk to him about "us." Our relationship.

Did Geoffrey still care about me?

Sometimes my rational mind told me to back away from him. To back away from the light and the attention and the role of mistress. To return to a familiar state of invisibility, where I knew how to exist. But now I wondered if hiding would look weak. My mother had thought everything would be okay if she was quiet and invisible. But sometimes hiding doesn't work. Sometimes it makes you sick. Maybe it was making me sick.

I texted him. I called him.

Finally, I knocked on the door and asked him to sit with me on the porch.

The sky and lake were gray. The cold of winter had sucked the color out of everything. I was sweating under my down coat, in spite of the biting wind.

I couldn't feel my toes. They were numb. I didn't wear the right socks this morning. I didn't usually make mistakes like that. Dressing for the weather was part of my job. But my mind was off.

"If there's any way for me to support you." I needed to keep talking. Keep the conversation going. I rested my hand on top of his.

"I remember the day you saved me from that spruce tree." Geoffrey looked at the spot where the spruce used to stand.

"Seems like that was years ago."

"You saved me from the spruce, but you couldn't save her."

Why did he say that?

I found my hands shaking again. I clasped them tightly together and held them against my body. "No one could have saved her."

Blue fibers. Fertilizer. Plant material. Words were bouncing around in my head like Ping-Pong balls.

I was looking for answers. I needed to be close to Geoffrey. Didn't I? His starting place for anything was so much stronger than mine was. Powerful people, like Geoffrey and Marguerite, they claimed their space. They showed their faces and their bodies. None of them hid.

He zipped his high-end down jacket all the way up to his neck.

I'd brought two large file folders with me: three drawings of the driveway in one and a stack of photos in the other. I removed the drawings from one folder and handed them to Geoffrey. He tried to look at them, but he couldn't keep them flat. They kept flipping up in the wind. I put them back in the folder and took out the photos. "These are just to take your mind off everything. If you're interested? A plan for your driveway." I looked to him for a reaction. "Would you like to see?"

"Sure."

I had to keep talking. "Your driveway should be a story," I said, "with a beginning, a middle, and an end."

He handed the photos back. "I'm sorry. I don't have the mind for this now." He touched his forehead with the palm of his hand. "To pay attention."

My hands were trembling. I laced them together to hold them still. "I know. The truth is, I just wanted to see you."

"You did?" His eyes glistened. "I didn't know. . . . These last few weeks, there were so many times when I would have given anything to be near you."

His words were like a balm.

"Even if I couldn't touch you," he said. "Just to be in the same room as you."

I allowed my lips to brush against his rough chin.

"I miss you," he whispered in my ear. "I miss the rich, low tone of your voice." His hand came up behind my head. "I miss the way you push your hair behind your ears, when it's already behind your ears. I miss the line of your beautiful shoulders."

"Just my shoulders are beautiful?" The question sounded pathetic. I was begging for his affection.

"Not just your shoulders." His hand slid up my thigh.

I needed to know that he wanted me, that he was thinking about me, that I mattered.

I brought his knuckles to my mouth.

The wind was subsiding.

I wanted to fold myself into Geoffrey's arms. I couldn't bear all these forces. Rachel Hanna. Helen. Taylor. Teddy.

"You make me happy, Phoenix," he said. "Looking at you makes me happy."

The sun was beginning to set. Helen's outdoor lights were on. She was standing on the lawn. Could she see us together? Geoffrey was looking in the same direction. Was he wondering the same thing? I felt him shift away from me. Just barely.

"How's work?" he said.

It seemed like a trick question. "You want to talk about my work?"

He nodded.

What was he looking for?

"Okay. Let's discuss your driveway," I said. "Your driveway. It will be long and curving. The Japanese maples on either side. It's all about the rhythm of the trees building anticipation. The grading and the trees will hide the view for as long as possible. When you arrive at the entry and the drive penetrates the gardens, the view is revealed. It's better than what you remembered. The colors are deeper and stronger. It shakes you to your core. It changes everything."

"Phoenix . . . ," he whispered.

I was drawing him in. "I want you."

I put my hand on his face. His skin was cold. The smell of pine needles and mint was combined with something like laundry detergent. He turned to look at me. I kissed the tip of his nose.

"Let's go inside," he said.

An exhilarating rush of adrenaline coursed through my body.

He led me to the living room. The heady smell of roses confronted me. Then I looked up and saw, hanging over the fireplace, *Marguerite by the Lake.* The sight of the painting was a sharp blow. I heard myself gasp.

I'd seen the painting before, but not since Marguerite died.

It was as if she was in the room with us. The painting captured her eyes, her intention coming out of the canvas. I could see inside her brain. She was standing with the lake in the backdrop, *exactly* where she'd been standing the last time I'd seen her. Her voice, her face, her eyes, filling the room. She was saying, *Have you forgotten whose house this is?*

Geoffrey sat next to me on the sofa. I put my fingers on his perfect lips. His mouth was still ice cold. His face was, too. I lay back and pulled his body down on top of mine.

CHAPTER FIVE

Taylor was staying for a week at Rosecliff over the winter holidays and then returning to school. I knew I wouldn't see Geoffrey while she was there.

I went to Frank's house for Christmas Eve, like I always did. Frank would invite me and Teddy and the rest of our team. He always bought a huge Christmas tree and some of us came early to help him decorate.

He made traditional Italian Catholic dishes like salt cod and fried fish. There were ten of us in the end. I usually had a nice time at Frank's house, but my ability to enjoy myself was severely compromised these days.

It was clear that Rachel knew things. And I was sitting here doing nothing. At night, I lay in bed going through options—ways I might protect myself. I'd come up with nothing.

Frank pulled me aside after dinner, before I left. "The detective asked me if I knew about anything between you and Geoffrey Gray." He looked concerned. "I told her no."

"Of course not."

I could tell he wanted to believe me.

On my drive home that night, I could see Frank's worried face in my head. Maybe a relationship with Geoffrey was dangerous. But maybe the alternatives were no better. My whole existence was fragile. Should I sit around my house and wait for Rachel to arrest me? And when she did, I wouldn't have a dime for a lawyer or anyone to vouch for me. She probably knew about me and Geoffrey. She already had her sights on me. How much worse could it get?

I didn't hear from Geoffrey for a week, and then, on the morning of New Year's Eve, he texted me. I want to kiss you at midnight.

An uplifting sensation expanded through my body. A feeling of hopefulness.

At home, I heated up leftover pizza and turned on the TV. I watched a movie called *Flawless,* starring Demi Moore as a jewel thief.

I needed devotion. Unconditional love. I needed an ally. I was a woman with good intentions in the wrong place at the wrong time.

I kept an eye on my phone. I was looking for reassurance that he was thinking about me. Reassurance that we had a connection, a deep connection.

Later that night, Geoffrey texted me again: I just want to talk.

I could feel some of my strength returning. Maybe I had some hold on Geoffrey. But I wanted to explain to him that I had no use for casual sex. He needed to know, that wasn't good enough.

I needed loyalty. But I wasn't certain how to communicate that.

The following morning he wrote: Will you come for dinner?

I reread his text and the tight feeling in my chest loosened a little. Will you come for dinner?

I didn't know how to respond.

Two days later he wrote: I want to hear more about my driveway.

I might have laughed if I'd had any sense of humor left.

I spent a long time deciding what to wear for our dinner. I tried on a striped sweater dress that I hadn't worn in five years and a paisley skirt that I hadn't worn in ten. I couldn't remember why and when I'd purchased such hideous clothes. I ended up wearing the same pants, sweater, and boots that I'd worn to Frank's house for Christmas. I drank two shots of vodka before I left the house.

At Geoffrey's kitchen table, I sipped a glass of red wine slowly. Geoffrey was cutting pancetta into strips, prepping for his pasta carbonara. A pot of water heated on the stove. He seemed comfortable in the kitchen, which surprised me because I had the impression that the staff cooked for him most of the time. I wasn't sure where the staff was. Maybe they were off tonight.

He told me about a British mystery series he was watching on PBS called *Sent from the Grave*.

"Is your family in England?" I said.

"Most of them," he said. "We're not a close bunch. They packed me off to military school at the age of eight."

I smiled but wasn't sure if he was joking.

I sensed the presence of the painting at the other end of the house. I was purposeful about avoiding the living room. Oddly, the rose smell in the house had not faded with Marguerite's absence, in spite of the fact that she was no longer cutting and arranging roses from her garden. Today, the scent had a hint of cloves and bad wine.

During dinner, Geoffrey talked about his years at boarding school. "I begged my mum and dad to come home, but they wouldn't hear of it." I could see a trace of sorrow in his eyes.

"Marguerite's parents were cold, too," he said. "But she didn't let it get to her. She was remarkable. Her will to overcome. She was determined to give Taylor a happy childhood. We both were. When Taylor was in eighth grade, she was dead set on boarding school. I said no way. But her best mate was going and Marguerite thought we should let her." He finished his glass of wine and then poured us each more. I paid attention to how much Geoffrey was drinking and tried to stay at the same rate. "I thought it was wrong to send her away, when I'd been so miserable at boarding school. But it was a different school. And she was a different person, with loads of confidence. Whereas I was small, skinny, awkward. Teased mercilessly. I was terribly lonely."

It was hard for me to picture Geoffrey being teased mercilessly. It was the opposite of what I would have thought.

He smiled at me. "I bet you were part of the popular crowd, weren't you?"

"No." The truth was high school had been a blur. I hadn't been part of any crowd. I'd just moved along, putting one foot in front of the other. I kept to myself, and most people left me alone.

He wiped his mouth with the corner of his napkin. "I saw you at that wedding. You must have been the prettiest girl at your school."

"I was miserable in high school." As I said it, I realized it was true.

"We were both miserable." He smiled. "Is that what we see in each other?"

His eyes clouded over. What was he thinking about?

He kissed me and pulled me close to him. His hand rested low on my back.

I wanted to be near him. I wanted to possess him.

"Stay." His voice was warm and soft. He was beautiful and gentle.

I held my hands out in front of me. "I need more than this."

"What do you mean?"

Geoffrey didn't understand that I was grasping.

"I need to know that this, between us, that this is special to you." A scrambling sensation inside me. Blue fibers. Fertilizer. Plant material. Words and images batted around in my head. "I need to know that."

I went home, but I couldn't sleep that night. I lay awake thinking about Geoffrey. How to hold him. I replayed his words in my head on repeat.

Marguerite was remarkable.

I'll always love her.

And then Rachel Hanna's words.

Is it possible that you touched Mrs. Gray's arm?

When I finally fell asleep, I dreamt about making love to Geoffrey in an attempt to drive Marguerite from his mind.

The next time Geoffrey and I had dinner together, I learned more about his relationship with Marguerite. Or maybe I just learned what he wanted me to believe about his relationship with Marguerite.

"I could never be successful enough to impress her," he said. "I tried to make her happy, but I wasn't perfect. I made mistakes."

I didn't know what his mistakes were. Maybe I was one of his mistakes.

I asked about the Grays' friendship with Serge Kuhnert. "I was a law student," Geoffrey said. "But I wanted to be an art student. I spent all my time in galleries and befriended the owners. And one day, one of my friends introduced me to Marguerite and Serge."

I had the sense that there was more to tell, but that it wasn't a subject Geoffrey enjoyed.

When I kissed him good night, I could feel his fingers barely touching my shoulder blade.

"Stay," he whispered.

Every sensation in my body was heightened. I longed to stay, but again I resisted.

Each time I went to Rosecliff, I was careful to avoid the living room. I stayed at the other end of the house and didn't even look in the direction of the painting.

Every time I pulled into Geoffrey's driveway, I braced myself, fearing I'd see Rachel Hanna's car. And every time I pulled into my own driveway, I had the same fear. Eventually, she would be back to question me.

One evening, I arrived at Geoffrey's house and heard him finishing a call. "That was about the autopsy," he said when he hung up. "The results should be in next week."

I tried to swallow, but my throat was closing.

The results should be in next week.

Valentine's Day was a mild, sunny Saturday. Geoffrey invited me to go on a two-mile hike. My job was like one long hike every day, but he didn't realize that. On the ascent, a couple of people waved at Geoffrey—people I didn't recognize. When we arrived at the top, we had an aerial view of the entire lake and a 360-degree view of all the mountains beyond. It was more extraordinary than the view from Rosecliff.

But then, as we started back down, a white-haired woman

was coming up the trail. She was bundled in a down coat and hat, but as she drew closer, I recognized her. It was Helen Spielman. I was so startled that I stumbled and twisted my ankle.

It was the first time Geoffrey and I had been out together in public. Of course, we had to bump into Helen Spielman.

Her mouth opened like she was going to say something, then it closed. She finally spoke. "What a surprise."

"Helen," Geoffrey said. "Good to see you."

"Geoffrey, Phoenix." She nodded at each of us. "Happy Valentine's Day."

Would she consider this a betrayal of Marguerite? She would. Wouldn't she?

I felt sick for the rest of the hike down, and was limping, too.

After a candlelit dinner that night, Geoffrey poured us each a glass of champagne.

My ankle was still throbbing, but the champagne helped to take the edge off.

"I'm happy when I'm with you." He traced the line of my shoulder with his finger, like he did the first time we sat together on the verandah. His light blue eyes glistened in the candlelight.

"Stay with me tonight, Phoenix."

I shook my head. "People will—"

"I don't care what people say." He raised his eyebrows and smiled, a hopeful look on his face.

What if I said yes to Geoffrey? What would happen if I said yes?

I didn't make a conscious decision either way, but somehow, I found myself walking into Marguerite's bedroom. I told myself, *It's Geoffrey's bedroom now.* But in my heart, I knew it was Marguerite's. Floral chintz curtains were hanging over the windows. A canopy bed was covered with lace and silk pillows and a puffy duvet.

Geoffrey took off his shirt. His torso was muscular and lean. He looked like some kind of Italian marble statue.

I stepped closer to him. He smelled like pine needles and mint. I unbuttoned my shirt and placed his hand on top of my bra, with one hand. I felt a pull of desire. I kissed his chest, and then his abdomen.

"Phoenix."

The idea of making love to Geoffrey on Marguerite's bed made me uneasy. But maybe I needed to send a signal, making it clear to Marguerite that I wasn't scared of her. I wouldn't give in to her. Maybe the time had come to assert myself. To look forward, not back.

I didn't think I could keep it a secret that I was seeing Geoffrey. I would have to tell Frank before he found out from someone else. In our weekly meeting, I gathered my courage: "Listen, I have news."

"Yeah?"

"You may not like the news."

Frank frowned. "What?"

"I'm seeing Geoffrey Gray." I tried to hold eye contact, to communicate that I wasn't defensive.

He rubbed his forehead with his hand. His face darkened.

"That detective is out there talking to people." Frank searched my eyes. "It's only been three months since she died. It looks suspicious."

He used the word "suspicious." I felt slightly short of breath.

"I don't want people saying things about you," he said.

What might they say? That I was fucking Geoffrey for his money? Or something much worse?

"Mrs. Gray could have told people things," he whispered, though no one was in earshot. "You don't know what she told people."

He closed his eyes. "She was *famous*. And there's this *interest*. From all these types all over the place. The cops are gonna be investigating this thing for months. Maybe years. And you're stepping right into the center of *la merda*. People will start to look at you."

Everything he said was true. Did I want people to look at me? Why was I doing this?

I wanted to slide in and out of Geoffrey's house without making a scene. Ideally, the staff would never notice a big shift. I would just happen to be there . . . sometimes.

I worked late the following night. Partly because the last house I visited was over an hour's drive from Rosecliff. But also because I dreaded the painting.

The night before, I'd overcome my fear of Marguerite's bed. I'd even fallen asleep with my arms around Geoffrey. But in the middle of the night, I woke up and I could sense the painting of Marguerite downstairs in the living room. I didn't say anything about it to Geoffrey because I knew he'd think I was absurd.

"I tried calling you," Geoffrey said in a tight voice when I arrived back at Rosecliff and walked in the kitchen.

"I'm sorry to keep you waiting."

Either Gilda or Raoul, the Grays' chef, used to serve dinner for Geoffrey and Marguerite every night. But I was relieved to see that everyone except for Geoffrey was gone. Raoul had left a tenderloin on the stove.

"The dinner's cold," Geoffrey said.

"I'll heat it in the microwave."

"Do you always work twelve-hour days?"

"It takes as long as it takes."

"But Brizzi's is not yours," he said. "You don't own it."

He didn't realize what Brizzi's meant to me. Brizzi's was my independence—the only good thing that had ever happened to me. I tried to explain this to him, but he didn't appreciate what I was saying. There was no way to cut back on hours unless I gave my job to someone else.

But also . . . I was avoiding the house. It was absurd. How could I live in the house if I didn't want to be there? The problem was the painting.

And in addition to the painting, the staff made me anxious. What were they thinking? What were they saying? Some of them might guess that Geoffrey and I were sleeping together before Marguerite died. Even if they didn't guess that, they probably thought our relationship happened too quickly. They might question what I was after.

It was hard to explain that, even to myself, and I didn't think Geoffrey or anyone else would understand. He gave me a buffer zone, like a moat around a medieval castle that keeps your enemies away.

Geoffrey poured us each a glass of red wine and we ate dinner at the kitchen table.

I wanted to ask him about the investigation but couldn't come up with a way of leading the conversation in that direction. Instead, I asked him about his day.

He sighed. "Marguerite's book is pretty much written, but she didn't choose the photos. She had her own process and she didn't always share it with me," he said. "Wren and I are going to New York tomorrow to sort this out with her publisher."

It was hard for me to focus on what Geoffrey was saying. My ankle was still hurting, and he was drinking his wine way too slowly. I was waiting to see if he would pour us each another glass and was relieved when he did. After my third glass, I could block out the rest of the world and stay in the room with him. I could lose myself in his pale blue eyes and his perfect lips. For a little while anyway.

Geoffrey barely slept, and he kept me awake most of the night. I heard him walking around the house for hours.

I dreamt that thick, hot red liquid was erupting from the ground where the spruce tree used to stand and spreading everywhere. It looked like my blood. My body jerked awake. It was 3 A.M.

An hour later, Geoffrey returned to bed.

"What is it?" I rested my head on his shoulder. The physical contact with him was comforting to me. I felt grounded when I was touching him.

Did he feel the same way? I couldn't always tell if I steadied him.

"The book deal, the series. I can't afford to lose these things." His words folded into each other, like an accordion. He'd lost the ability to separate his words. "I've got to convince them the brand is strong without her." His usual scent of pine needles and mint was muddied by something acidic and sharp.

"It'll all be okay." What did I mean by that? How could I possibly know if it would be okay?

"I need to know that you're going to stand by me." His voice was breaking, cracking, so that he sounded like a thirteen-year-old boy.

"Always."

He wrapped his arms around me. "You support me," he murmured. "And I support you."

His fragility gave me a tad of confidence. As long as he needed me, I could stay here.

I was even more uneasy being in the house when Geoffrey left for New York. I stayed away until after eight—visiting clients' properties that weren't even on my schedule, just to avoid

Rosecliff. When I finally returned, I parked my car and walked down the long driveway, and then on the road, which continued alongside the lake.

There were no streetlamps, but the moon and stars were so bright it was like daylight, like how I pictured summer nights in Norway.

The road was quite narrow, so drivers avoided it if they could. Even in the middle of the most crowded day in July, there were few cars on this road. And at night in the winter, it was absolutely empty.

I'd never walked around the lake at night. I wasn't worried about getting mugged in rural Connecticut. But there might be bears. I was wearing black, so if a car were to approach, I would have had to step off the road, and since there was no sidewalk, that meant stepping close to the edge of a steep slope, below which were multiple sharp granite ledges.

But I saw no cars and no one. There was nothing. Just the sound of the lake, the leaves, the wind. For a few minutes, I had quiet.

I turned around and walked back to Rosecliff when I was certain the staff would be gone. I knew that my behavior was cowardly. If I was scared of the staff, how was I going to handle Taylor when she came to visit?

In the kitchen, when I opened one of the cabinets, I saw the image of *Marguerite by the Lake* printed on all the coffee mugs. It was also printed on the umbrellas that were kept by the back door, as well as the duffel bags on the shelf in the coat closet, not to mention the T-shirts stored in the garage. This wasn't just at Rosecliff. *Marguerite by the Lake* was like the *Mona Lisa*. Sometimes you can't see something, and then it's everywhere.

Marguerite took up all the space in the house.

I had to find a way to live with the painting.

In the living room, I built a fire, the way I'd seen Geoffrey do it. I placed three logs on the cast-iron grate in the fireplace. I struck a match and lit a piece of newspaper, then stuck the newspaper up the flue to warm it. Then I stuffed the same burning newspaper underneath the logs that were resting on the grate, and they went up in flames. The temperature of the room shot up in an instant.

I'd been through the entire house looking for roses, in case Gilda had been buying them someplace and bringing them inside, but there were none. Still, the pungent smell of roses persisted, and it was particularly strong in the living room.

I sat on the sofa and told myself to appreciate this work of art in front of me. Maybe I could try to enjoy it. Maybe I could try to understand it.

There was a disconnect between the intense anger in Marguerite's face and the romantic windswept cliff. I could see anguish in her, too, even in the muscles of her left hand. She was holding a dead flower; the veins in her left arm were noticeable. Her gloved right hand hung by her side holding pruning shears. The blade of the shears reflected sunlight. (In her Instagram posts, she was always holding her signature pruning shears, whether or not she was using them.) This image of Marguerite captured the mature woman, as well as the young adult. Her hair was pulled up away from her face, but several strands had come loose, one falling in front of one of her eyes. Her face was ever so slightly damp and flushed. The painting wasn't Marguerite at her most beautiful. It was Marguerite filled with rage.

I could recognize rage. Rage was baked into my identity.

I approached the fireplace and placed my hand on the painting.

I wasn't supposed to do that. The moisture and bacteria in my hand could cause serious damage. Like a child who'd been caught, I jumped away and looked behind me to see if anyone saw what I did.

When I looked back at the painting, Marguerite's eyes appeared to grow wider. Up close, her large brown eyes, framed by thick lashes, were so intense, so alive. So present in the room. A raging energy pulsing from the painting.

Her mouth was slightly open, lips rounded, as if she wanted to say something.

I didn't know how Kuhnert had painted her brain, her thoughts—her state of mind right before she died. The painting was almost thirty years old.

How could he have known?

How could he have known what would happen?

CHAPTER SIX

"Gilda, don't worry about dinner tonight." I practiced that sentence ten times in the mirror, hoping to sound friendly and easygoing. When it came time to actually say it, Gilda's back was facing me and I was trying to get her attention, so I spoke louder than I needed to.

She started and turned away from the spice rack, which she was in the middle of organizing, and looked at me. "Very well, miss." Gilda's gray hair was pulled back in a bun. She was wearing slim black pants and a white blouse, which was what she always wore. I didn't know if that was a uniform, or just what she liked to wear. Gilda had perfectly maintained pale pink polish on her nails, one clue that she didn't do much cleaning herself. She managed the rest of the staff. I was beginning to recognize the distinctions between the different jobs and the hierarchy.

I made risotto for Geoffrey that night. It was one of three dishes Frank had taught me to cook. Either Raoul or Gilda would usually make dinner in the evenings and leave it on the stove. Geoffrey had requested that they leave the house by six, along with the cleaning ladies, Nina and Bess. At first, I was grateful to him for sparing me interactions with them. But over the course of the week, I grew uneasy. Maybe he wanted to keep me separated from his real life, so it would be a cleaner job to remove me when the time came.

We ate in the kitchen. Geoffrey and I had not eaten dinner in the formal dining room yet. I found the kitchen table more intimate and relaxing. I wasn't drawn to the dining room because it was north facing and one of the darkest rooms in the house.

"Simply delicious," Geoffrey said when he tasted the risotto. He was in a better mood because he'd bought himself a little time on the next book. The new deadline was April. He said the new publication date next year was timed to coincide with The Met's *Female Gaze* exhibit, for which *Marguerite by the Lake* was the signature image. "But it'll be a job to pull together the photos."

I nodded but my mind was elsewhere. There was a question that had been on my mind since I moved in. I couldn't avoid the subject forever. "How's Taylor?"

He sighed. "This is a tough time for her."

I frowned, trying to demonstrate concern. "I'm just wondering if . . . Have you told her about me?"

He paused. "I had to tell her. She'll be visiting in a couple of weeks."

"Right," I said. "So . . . um . . . what did she say?"

"I don't know." He rolled his eyes.

"You don't know what she said?" I took a bite of the tasteless risotto.

"Phoenix . . ."

"Tell me."

"She's not happy that you're here."

"She's not?"

"Of course she's not."

"Right." I tried to appear neutral. I knew she wouldn't be happy. Even so, hearing him say it out loud was a blow. I took a bite of the risotto and almost gagged.

"Her mother died," he said. "She's in pain. She's angry at everyone."

"I guess that's a coping mechanism." I didn't really know what I was talking about. When my grandmother died, I was driving her to a doctor's appointment, and I made a left turn into oncoming traffic. The sun was in my eyes. The right side of my car was totaled. I spent nine months in the hospital, on painkillers the whole time. Drugs were my coping mechanism.

I swallowed my wine.

"And there's the investigation," he said, "and . . . everything."

"Right." It was a natural lead-in to the investigation. I might not get a better one. I needed to know the autopsy results. "Any developments?"

He paused. "Developments?" He studied me in a way I found disconcerting.

"On the investigation?" I tried to sound casual, but my voice went up too high on the question.

"The autopsy results suggest Marguerite fell backward. So, they ruled out suicide." He cleared his throat. "And they saw some bruises on her arm."

Bruises? What? How could there be bruises?

"As if someone was gripping her arm tightly," he said.

I could barely keep my face composed. "You must be glad to have the information," I said. "Just to have any information."

He didn't say anything, but suddenly he seemed more re-laxed than he had been, as if some of his burden was lifted.

"Yes, I'm relieved," he said.

Bruises on her arm.

"But listen, Phoenix," he said. "Tell me about your day."

It was hard for me to move on after I heard him say, Bruises on her arm. I tried to shut that information out. It could para-lyze me, and I couldn't afford to be paralyzed.

"How's the house treating you?"

"It's intimidating." I smiled. "Right?"

"Intimidating?" He looked around the kitchen.

"It's hard for me to feel like I belong here."

"Rubbish. Of course, you do." He closed his fingers over my hand.

I took a bite of risotto. It turned my stomach.

Bruises on her arm. Rachel Hanna would be fitting puzzle pieces together, connecting dots.

He wiped his mouth. "Maybe you should bring something from your New Milford house, like . . . a piece of art."

A piece of art? He had no idea what my real life was like. I drank my wine, trying to delay my response.

"So that Rosecliff feels more like home to you," he said.

"You want me to feel like it's my home?"

"Of course, I do."

That was what I was hoping to hear. "I don't have anything nice enough for this house."

"Ohh, you must have something. Childhood photos?" He pushed his chair back from the table and crossed his legs.

I'd already brought the two photos of my mother. The envelope with the lock of my hair. The book of fairy tales. The other things were better left behind.

"Not really," I said.

"We'll figure out how to make Rosecliff feel like your home. We'll pick out a new . . . set of knives." He laughed. "Or a new dishwasher? Or get a . . . golden retriever?"

Rosecliff is my home. He said it. *Rosecliff is my home.*

That night, when we made love, he was calm and gentle. He kissed me and I could feel the roughness of his beard against my face. I inhaled pine needles and mint. The way he looked at me, it was soft, rounded, blurry edges. No sharp points or hard borders.

Later, I lay awake in bed. I couldn't get the image of Marguerite's bruised arm out of my head.

The following morning, Geoffrey noticed that I was moving Marguerite's belongings out of a small drawer in her closet to make room for a few of my T-shirts. He frowned and, for a moment, I thought he was upset. I should have asked him first.

"Phoenix, darling, I'm sorry." He shifted his body weight from one side to the other. "I should have sorted this already." He pulled me close to him and rested his mouth on the top of my hair—a kind of half kiss. I was relieved he wasn't angry.

He took a step back from me. "We need to start fresh," he said. "Don't we?" I thought I heard real affection in his voice.

He was anxious, tired. But the bags under his eyes didn't detract from his looks. Nothing ever detracted from his looks. "Please give me a little time to look through all of this." He motioned to the dresser and the closet. "I don't look forward to it. It's overwhelming." He squeezed his eyes shut.

"I know. If you want me to do it for you?" I wanted him to believe the offer was a generous one. And it was. But it was also true that I wouldn't mind having a reason to sift through Marguerite's belongings.

"I can't put that on you. No. But . . . in the meantime"—he gestured around the room vaguely—"rearrange things how you see fit."

Maybe we'd been making it too easy for Marguerite's

spirit to stay. In most ways, it was still her house. So little had changed.

He gently placed his fingertips on the side of my face. "Shall we plan a night out, darling?" He had soft, warm eyes and a soothing tone of voice.

"Yes."

"The house has a mind of its own," he said. "Sometimes we need to get away."

What did he mean by that? "A mind of its own?" Was he acknowledging Marguerite's presence?

He fastened his Blancpain watch around his wrist. It was his favorite. There was no engraving on the back—I'd checked— but I felt certain Marguerite gave him that watch. How could I complain about what Marguerite had given him? Where would it begin and where would it end?

"A strong personality," he said.

"Marguerite's?" It was obviously Marguerite's personality. Why wouldn't he just say that?

His tone hardened. "No."

Geoffrey didn't always confide in me. There was a part of him I didn't have access to. Thoughts, feelings, and ideas that he didn't choose to share. About Marguerite. About the investigation. I couldn't look inside his mind.

"But Rosecliff *does* have Marguerite's personality," I said. "Doesn't it?"

"It has Marguerite by the Lake's personality," he said. "Rosecliff helps us sell the books, the garden supplies, the merch. It's our Buckingham Palace."

Was he joking?

"So, we're stuck in this gilded cage." He smiled. "Even if . . . if we wanted to live somewhere else one day, we can't." He paused. "If we care about the business. And we do." He raised his eyebrows. "Don't we?"

Geoffrey had said *we're* stuck in this gilded cage, not *I'm* stuck in this gilded cage. He was talking to me like we were partners. It was what I wanted. What I'd hoped for. We could get through anything if we were partners.

Maybe Geoffrey would be secretly relieved if I handled Marguerite's belongings. He'd said, Rearrange how you see fit. Maybe he'd be relieved if they were just gone, without too much of an explanation.

Late that afternoon, I returned from work early, glad to see that Rachel Hanna's car wasn't in the driveway. I shut myself in our bedroom with my tools and a carton of cleaning supplies. I started by taking down the floral chintz curtains and all the hardware from our four bedroom windows, leaving the white shutters exposed and unsightly holes in the walls where the screws had been drilled in. I'd have to ask Gilda if someone on the staff could fill in those holes with plaster and paint, though I could do it myself if need be. I felt a little sorry for the windows. They were so naked now. I had a moment of hesitation, wondering if Geoffrey would think I was being too aggressive. Or Taylor? As much as I hated to think about it, Taylor would eventually return to this house. She would eventually walk into this room.

In the end, I didn't feel I had a choice. I needed to breathe.

I opened all the shutters. I could see a glorious view of the lake and the hills beyond it. I held my thumb up to block Helen's house, so I could enjoy the view without that eyesore. Through the windows on the opposite side of the room, I could see the gardens I'd been working on for the last ten years, much of them covered in frost and a thin layer of snow. Many plants had been destroyed in the storm, but the structure, the architecture, conceptually it was all still there. And quite beautiful.

I started in Marguerite's marble bathroom, assessing what was there. I'd been using this bathroom for several days, but I'd only had a quick look inside the drawers.

Spanning the width of the room was a stone vanity, with two large windows above it overlooking the lake. At least a dozen framed photographs of Marguerite with friends and family hung on the walls of her bathroom. Several of her and Geoffrey. Several of Taylor and Marguerite. A few with Marguerite, Geoffrey, and Serge. In a large group photo, I recognized the man in the Ford Bronco who drove Geoffrey home from Boston. It had never occurred to me to hang photographs in my New Milford bathroom. But I recognized it as a good idea. To hang my own pictures and make this bathroom feel like mine.

There were some pictures of Geoffrey and his extended family, pictures I considered keeping. But the problem was that

Marguerite had breathed on all these photos. I could smell her on them. I could feel her. Taking the photos, selecting them, framing them, hanging them. Her sweat, her bacteria, her skin cells—all that she was—would have coalesced on those framed photos. It was true of so many items in the house. But in her bathroom, it was hard to ignore. She'd wandered around in the bathroom naked. I needed to start with a blank slate.

One by one, I placed the photos together in a box.

If Geoffrey objected, well . . . I would have to tell him. I couldn't exist in the midst of Marguerite.

Heading to the top of the stairs, I could hear a conversation between Gilda and Nina downstairs in the gallery. Nina spoke in broken English, with a Russian accent.

"It expires," Nina said.

"Expired?" Gilda asked.

"Before three months," Nina said.

"She doesn't care about your visa," Gilda said.

Who was Gilda talking about?

I used the pause in conversation to descend the stairs. I didn't want to talk to either one of them, but I couldn't hide from them either. When Nina heard me, she vanished into the kitchen.

Gilda remained at the foot of the steps. As I neared the bottom, she reached to take the box from my arms. "Can I help you, Miss Sullivan?"

I held tightly to the box. "Geoffrey asked me to rearrange a few things."

She pulled the box. I pulled. She pulled, and then I yanked the box away from her and walked quickly to the basement door. Did I imagine that? Did she really try to take the box from me?

I deposited that box in the basement, then gathered extra cleaning supplies. I ascended slowly, listening for Gilda, hoping she was gone. But when I opened the basement door into the butler's pantry, she stood in front of me.

"Can I help you with anything else?" A pinched look had come over her face, so that all her features were closer together than before.

"Not at all." My heart was racing, but I tried to keep my tone calm and composed. I tried to hold on to a soft smile.

"All right, then."

I walked past her toward the front staircase.

"Miss Sullivan."

I turned back.

"I neglected to mention," she said, "Detective Hanna stopped by yesterday when you were out. She's scheduling follow-up interviews with the staff. With all individuals who work on the property in any capacity."

I pressed my lips together so that I didn't say anything I'd regret.

"I've already spoken to her." Gilda smiled. "So did Nina."

I had an impulse to tell Gilda that I knew about her criminal record. I held my hands close to my body so they wouldn't tremble.

"She'll probably be reaching out to you soon," she said.

I nodded.

Upstairs, I closed the door to my bedroom. I locked the door to my bathroom, but I was still scared Gilda might find her way in.

There were hours during the day when I was able to shut out thoughts of the investigation. Now, Gilda had successfully pushed Rachel Hanna to the front of my mind.

I made myself return to the task at hand.

In Marguerite's bathroom, what remained was the depressing sight of a dozen nails and the surrounding blank walls. I would frame my own photos and replace the ones I'd taken down. Personal photos of my landscaping perhaps. Flowers, trees, stone walls—at Rosecliff and other clients' homes and my grandmother's house.

I quickly cleared out three cabinets, looking over my shoulder for Gilda every few minutes. All the fancy cleansers and moisturizers in glass pots, as well as deodorant, bandages, sleeping pills, mouthwash, toothpaste, all of it went into a large cardboard box. I needed to breathe. I couldn't bear to have all of Marguerite's belongings around me.

I emptied each drawer in her bathroom: the makeup, makeup brushes, hairbrushes, combs, nail polish, blow-dryers, hot brushes, hot rollers, curling irons, hand creams, perfume, every kind of antiaging potion and cream I could imagine, with brand names I'd never heard of.

When finished, I wiped down the entire place with Windex until it sparkled.

I emptied the shower of all the shampoos, conditioners, soaps, sponges, and razors and put everything in another large box, along with all the towels. I scrubbed the shower down with bleach and wiped the brass faucet and plumbing fixtures.

I looked over the bathroom when I was finished. A coat of paint would help. That was for another time. I stacked five boxes in a corner of the room, deciding I would deposit all the boxes in the basement at once, but I would wait until Gilda had left for the day.

Geoffrey had given me a credit card to purchase new sheets. I wasn't sure whether it was for my sake or out of respect for Marguerite's memory that he wanted new sheets.

He also said to use the card for any "necessities" for the house. I wasn't sure—what qualified as necessities?

The towels that Marguerite had in her bathroom, the ones I'd been using, were thick and lush. But from the beginning, it felt wrong for me to use them. Unseemly. Similar to how I felt about the sheets. I looked up Marguerite's towels online and learned that they were nine hundred grams per square meter (the most luxurious towels that exist) and each one was two hundred dollars.

I could have bought towels that cost thirty dollars each, and I wouldn't have known the difference. They would be so much better than what I had in my New Milford home. But purchasing thirty-dollar towels, being content with them, would that reveal me to be a commoner, not a real princess, like the one in "The Princess and the Pea"? The real princess can feel a pea underneath twenty thick mattresses and twenty eiderdown comforters. I remembered the conversation with Geoffrey when he'd said, "Sometimes you've got to pretend."

So, I purchased Marguerite's brand. The two-hundred-dollar towels were better. I would have to learn to tell the difference.

The towels, the sheets, the shower faucet, the wine, the antiques, the art, these things would bleed into me. I needed to inhabit the role of the princess, the queen, the lady of the manor. I needed my movements, my words, my facial expressions, all of it needed to speak in one unified voice and all of it needed to say: "I belong here."

Looking around the bedroom, I noticed four shallow drawers in Marguerite's nightstand. I opened them and found that each one was lined with black velvet and divided into small compartments. They were meant for jewelry, but all were empty, except for a few buttons and safety pins. Maybe Taylor already had the jewelry?

I moved on to Marguerite's walk-in closet. It was almost the size of my New Milford living room. Taylor had already taken many of the clothes, but I packed up every remaining item: dresses, pants, blouses, sweaters, suits, underwear, bras, shoes, hats, all of it into boxes. I tried to work quickly, though I paused a few times to look at the brand names she wore, or look up articles of clothing online for the price. Marguerite spent more money on one blouse than I'd spent on my wardrobe for the last three years.

When I heard a car in the driveway, I looked out the window and was relieved to see Gilda's sedan pulling out.

I made a trip to the basement with one of the boxes and bumped into Nina. She was wearing a black blouse and black pants that emphasized her washed-out appearance and were too big for her. She looked like a child in her mother's clothing.

She had usually left by now. I had a strong suspicion that Gilda told her to spy on me. I was still trying to get a handle on the staff's schedules. Nina's hours and days were always changing. But Gilda wouldn't share that kind of information with me, if she could avoid it.

"Hello, miss," Nina said. "I came for to help you."

"I'm fine. Thank you."

I made several more trips to the basement and the whole time, she was hovering nearby, asking if she could help. She wasn't as oppressive as Gilda, but she had a nervous energy that I couldn't tolerate. My grandmother would have said she was "frightened of her own shadow." Maybe there was a problem with her work visa.

I carried the last box down to the basement. Then I went back up to the bedroom to see what else needed to be done. The surfaces were all clear. The bathroom was completely empty. The closet was completely empty, but for the first time, I noticed a panel on the wall behind one of the hanging rods. It was hidden when Marguerite's clothes were there. The panel looked like it was meant for access to HVAC controls. I pushed and the door sprung open to reveal a shelf covered with a stack of papers and photos and a drawer underneath. Inside the drawer, I found two jewelry boxes.

The larger box was black leather. It contained a delicate diamond bracelet. The smaller jewelry box was blue velvet with a gold latch. I opened it. Inside was . . . an extraordinary ring. I'd never seen anything like it. Not up close. It was a five-sided pink diamond. It looked bigger than J.Lo's rings. Ten or twenty carats maybe. The larger diamond was surrounded by small pink diamonds, the most sparkling ring I'd ever seen. Like a bright light.

I had a confusing desire to take the ring. To steal it from . . . whom?

I tried it on. The enormous diamond extended beyond the width of my finger. The pink cast of the diamond looked beautiful against my skin. The ring gave me strength. It made me feel seen. It made me feel like I was untouchable.

But I couldn't wear it in front of . . . anyone.

Put the ring back, you idiot. Put it back.

I returned the ring to its box.

Did Taylor know about the secret panel in her mother's closet?

On the shelf was a photo of Marguerite and Serge. She was wearing a silver sequined dress. They were drinking champagne. It looked to be taken more than thirty years earlier.

I flipped through the papers and read a letter from Marguerite to Taylor.

Darling Taylor,

I'm worried about your father.

You and I need to figure this out together. And the other thing we discussed as well.

The letter was unfinished.

What did they need to figure out? What was the other thing?

I found a Mother's Day card from Taylor to Marguerite. Inside the card, Taylor had written: *Wish I was with you, Mom. Love, T.* On the left side, she'd written: *The loan came through. BTW I'm not surprised about how this went. They were always out to screw you.*

I had so many burning questions. And nothing was becoming clearer.

Another letter was from Serge, dated last October, a few days before Marguerite died. It read:

Dear Marguerite, I'm distressed by our conversation, though it's nothing new. I'm glad you spoke to Frank. Will wait to discuss in person next week.

> *All my love,*
> *Serge*

I reread a few of the lines. *I'm glad you spoke to Frank.* About me?

She must have told Serge. Serge knew that Geoffrey and I were together.

What else did he know? How long would he stay away?

It occurred to me that Geoffrey might have a secret access panel, too. Geoffrey's closet was smaller than Marguerite's, but much bigger than a normal closet. He had three whole columns of shelves with sweaters and T-shirts in perfectly folded piles. I looked behind his hanging clothing, but there was just a regular flat wall. No panel. In addition to the shelves, he had a built-in dresser with two shallow drawers on top. Inside one of them were his watches, all lined up, in a velvety tray.

The second shallow drawer was full of odds and ends: paper clips, coins, scraps of paper, business cards, and a large envelope filled with photographs and held together with a rubber band.

I flipped through the stack of photographs. A lot of pictures of Taylor as a little girl, pictures of Geoffrey and Marguerite together, including some from their wedding and presumably their honeymoon in a tropical location. Then a few more wedding photos, some that included Serge, who was maybe a groomsman. There was one from a later period, with Geoffrey and the man in the Ford Bronco. Both men were in tuxedos at some event. I turned the photo over and saw the word "Greenhaven." Was that Russ Marks?

After I rummaged through the papers, mostly phone numbers and names I didn't recognize, I returned to the watch drawer, pulling it all the way out. A scrap of paper was underneath the tray in the back. I lifted the tray out. Underneath were a few photos. One was of a twentysomething brunette woman. She was sitting in Geoffrey's lap. Her limbs were wrapped around him. Who was this woman?

There was another photo of Geoffrey and a large-breasted redhead in front of a theater.

Who were these people? Why was Geoffrey keeping their

photos? Were these his girlfriends? I had a horrible feeling that I'd missed a lot of important information staring me in the face. Could I have misinterpreted . . . so much? I thought he'd been faithful to Marguerite until me. I was still standing in Geoffrey's closet, staring at the photos, when I heard Nina's voice. "Good night, miss."

I started and looked up. She stood there in front of me.

I didn't want her to think I had anything to hide. I smiled like nothing was wrong. "Drive safely."

"Soon my husband comes, miss. I don't drive by night." She bobbed her head and left the room.

How dare she walk into my bedroom without knocking? Did Gilda tell her to?

Would she tell Geoffrey I was looking through his closet?

I went to the window and saw, parked in the driveway, the same Toyota I'd seen turning into Helen's driveway.

I ran downstairs to stop her before she got to the door. "Nina." I was out of breath.

"Yes, miss."

"Do you ever go to Helen Spielman's house?"

Her face looked blank, like she didn't understand what I was saying.

"Helen Spielman. Do you know her?"

She nodded mechanically.

"Do you go there?"

Her eyes were wide. "When Miss Helen broke her arm, Mrs. Gray asked for to help her."

"Okay."

"Good night, miss."

That was the car I'd seen at Helen's house. Why had Nina been there? How often had she gone there?

In the morning, Rachel Hanna left me a voicemail asking for a follow-up interview. Was her tone of voice different? I heard something different. She knew I was dating Geoffrey. Would she suspect me more?

I was distracted all day. Thinking about the photos from Geoffrey's closet, Nina's car, the voicemail from Rachel. Occasionally, I had the disconcerting feeling that Marguerite was controlling Rachel's every move. Rachel was just a pawn.

After work, I sat down in the living room to view the painting again. My memory of it was slightly off. I remembered Marguerite's lips being just barely parted, but I was wrong, because her mouth was actually more open than I'd thought.

"Can I get you something to drink, Miss Sullivan?"

I turned to see Gilda standing there with a bright aggressive smile. For the first time, I noticed a thin gold chain and locket around her neck. It was partially hidden by her blouse. Whose picture was in that locket? Her son's? Her lover's? Maybe Marguerite's? Had Gilda done something illegal for Marguerite's sake? Or was it the other way around, Marguerite covering for Gilda out of the kindness of her heart?

"I'm fine," I said.

"Very well," she said before turning and leaving.

The wind was loud. It was whistling through the trees, rustling the branches.

I could hear a light whisper. It was almost muffled by the sound of the wind.

Leave. Go.

I returned to studying the painting. To studying Marguerite: her blood, her brains, muscles, sinews, tendons, bones, skull, skin, organs. It was her. Or something greater than her, concentrated and infused into that canvas. I was frightened of this version of Marguerite.

I was trying to eat a bowl of strawberries for breakfast, but every few minutes, I imagined I heard a car approaching and that it was Rachel Hanna, who would be wondering why I hadn't returned her call.

The strong wind had blown the snow from the previous night into a checkerboard pattern on the frozen lake. It looked otherworldly. I'd never seen a pattern like this on a lake.

"Look at that," I said to Geoffrey. "Did you see that?" I pointed to the lake.

He was having bacon and eggs while answering emails on his laptop.

It seemed like he didn't even hear me.

"Geoffrey." I shook his shoulder, and in doing so, I bumped his hand and made him spill his coffee on the side of his laptop and on his pants. He had ten pairs of identical khaki pants. They were almost disposable.

"Damn." He pushed me away from him.

I jumped up and grabbed a dishcloth to mop up the coffee on the laptop. "I think it's fine," I said. "It just got here . . . on the side."

When I looked closer, I could see that a little coffee was crawling between the keys, finding the lowest point and sinking deeper. "I'm sorry."

He was silent and I felt my stomach drop. I was trying to read him. To get a handle on his state of mind. I wasn't going to confront Geoffrey about the photos. Not now. Not ever. But I had to accept the possibility that Nina might tell him she saw me looking through his closet. He would be so angry. It was an invasion of his privacy.

But did he have an obligation to share his past with me? And what if it wasn't just his past? What if it was his present, too?

We sat in silence for several minutes while he finished his breakfast.

Finally, he spoke. "Did you see the bow rake we added to the website?" he asked, moving his laptop closer to me. It was open to the shopping section of the Marguerite by the Lake app, which included various garden supplies, tools, plants, and seeds.

I zoomed in on the rake and recognized the brand.

"Is it good?"

"It's high-end," I said.

Geoffrey didn't appear satisfied by that answer. "And?"

"That was the rake everyone wanted five years ago." I

was relieved to have something Geoffrey needed. Some knowledge.

His face clouded over. "What bow rake do you use?"

"My rakes aren't glamorous. They're for professionals."

Geoffrey raised his voice. "Then, bloody hell, tell me what
rake to put on the website!"

I didn't appreciate his tone of voice. "Who manages the
website?"

"Wren," he said. "She's sharp. But she came up in market-
ing. She doesn't know plants. She used to run everything by
Marguerite. Everything."

"Okay."

"We tripled revenue four years running," he said. "But now
we're down, and we don't have a cushion anymore."

I thought about Marguerite's lost inheritance. "Okay."

"And Serge is . . ." He stopped mid-sentence.

"Serge is what?"

He rolled his eyes. ". . . asking for a cut."

"A cut?"

"A percent of revenue. The day after the funeral he starts
on this." Geoffrey pursed his lips, like he'd sucked on a lemon,
like the taste of Serge's name on his tongue was sour. "We were
counting on PR from this *Female Gaze* exhibit. But . . ." He
raised his eyebrows. "Please tell me which rake."

I could see desperation in Geoffrey's eyes. "I can help you,"
I said. "If you need me, I can help you."

"I didn't mean to snap at you." His shoulders dropped and

his whole body seemed to sag. "I'm just worried." He looked vulnerable.

Maybe the photos of the women in his closet were ancient history. I could choose to believe they meant nothing.

I browsed through the rest of the merchandise. "Nothing here is current enough. It's all last year's. . . ." Marguerite was strong on aesthetics, but there was a whole market she hadn't captured. "You should be selling plant sensors. And an infrared heat blast for weeding. Also, the plant selection is narrow." Marguerite was too traditional. "You're not including popular new varieties—like New Dimension Blue salvia."

"Please. Talk to Wren," he said. "The website is just a small part of . . . We have these social media platforms. We should be keeping our followers abreast of our plans: the trees, the driveway, the patio." He frowned and squeezed his eyes shut. "Marguerite always posted specific advice and photos."

"You should keep posting photos," I said. "That's important."

"We need real content, too." He ran his fingers through his hair starting at his forehead and going straight back.

"That's not too hard," I said. "Is it?"

His face lifted into a smile. "Could you . . . ?" He seemed to have forgotten the spilled coffee. "Wren and I could use your help."

Marguerite's brand—the entire Rosecliff business had relied on me and my skill and images of the property I created. Marguerite had been presenting my work as hers for years. But Marguerite wasn't here and . . . now . . . to the degree my schedule permitted, it made perfect sense for me to step into this aspect of Marguerite's role. And, of course, I wanted to help Geoffrey. He needed me.

Nina walked into the kitchen, just as we both stood. Her light hair and pale features faded into her white face. "Good morning, Mr. Gray," she said. "Good morning, miss." Her eyes darted around the room like a frightened animal. Maybe she was scared of being deported.

"Nina, you're just the girl I was looking for," Geoffrey said. "My favorite glasses have gone missing. Would you keep an eye out?"

She nodded. "It is hard missing your glasses." She tapped her own glasses, maybe to assure him that she understood his request.

Wren came to the house that evening, after I finished work. I prepared myself for the fact that she might hate me. She might be loyal to Marguerite.

"So obviously," Geoffrey said to Wren, "Phoenix is ace when it comes to gardens."

"No shit." Wren's auburn hair was pulled up in a ponytail, revealing a bird tattoo on the back of her neck.

"If I can help in any way," I said.

"Are you kidding?"

"I don't want to step on anyone's toes."

"You're a fucking lifesaver," she said. "We've gotta start posting shit. I mean, this has been brutal. Margie didn't delegate social media."

It took me a moment to realize that Margie was Marguerite.

"We need gardening content from a gardener," Wren continued. "That's what Margie was doing. She was like, here's what you do with the two pots you've got on a stoop in the middle of nowhere. Aspirational. But super practical. You have three square feet? It'll be the most brilliant square feet anyone's ever seen. That's why I was, like, *Hey dude, we could use your help.* When she died, we were screwed," she said. "So now, I think we have to be, like, *This was Margie's vision. And we're carrying out her vision. Bottom line, it's all about her name.*"

When our conversation was over, Wren started to leave, then turned back. "The detective called me. She said she needs to talk to me again." She shifted her weight. "I was like, *Damn, lady, I already said everything I have to say.*" Wren was trying to sound like the call from the detective was no big deal.

"Sorry about that," Geoffrey said. "Hanna says she's capturing a three-dimensional history. She's going back to New York to interview Serge for a second time."

If Serge knew Geoffrey and I were together before Marguerite died, he would probably tell Rachel. If he hadn't already.

Geoffrey continued. ". . . and Marguerite's cousins, aunts, uncles, everyone." He sighed. "I wish . . . I don't know. I just want closure. But Taylor disagrees."

"Poor kid," Wren said.

"Maybe you should talk to Taylor," Geoffrey said. "She'll be here next weekend."

"Nah. When she has her mind set on something, she's

gonna drill down on that motherfucker," she said. "Just like her mom."

I had an image of Taylor walking toward me holding a hammer drill high in the air.

A three-dimensional history. Rachel Hanna wants a three-dimensional history.

In the morning, I greeted the Brizzi's crew in the driveway. Eight guys had come to work on my property. But was it really my property? I felt like a child pretending to be someone fancy.

The weather had turned mild. So some of the team were direct sowing early blooming annuals, while some were checking for frost heaving and adding mulch where needed.

I trusted myself when I was working in a garden, more than I trusted myself at any other time. I had the intuition and the years in the field. But for the first time, I was self-conscious talking to my staff. If I started being too polite, the guys would notice the difference, and it would seem like I was talking down to them. Like I wasn't one of them.

After an hour of sowing sweet peas, I heard a car and then saw the same stripped-down black Dodge Charger. Rachel circled the side of the house, walking in my direction. Bile rose up in my throat.

"Hello, Phoenix," she said as she approached.

I looked up at her. I was kneeling on the grass, with a shovel in my hand, and I was covered in dirt.

She smiled at me like we were close friends.

These days, I didn't do as much manual labor, because managing the teams was a better use of my time. But today, it was lucky that I'd decided to pitch in. I was less available to her.

"I didn't realize that you live here now." She turned and pointed to the house. Her long braid swung with the movement of her body.

I nodded.

"We just have to confirm some information." And then, like it had just occurred to her, "Would you want to sit down *now*?" She motioned to the house.

I could feel and hear my heart pounding in my chest. "I'm in the middle of"—I held up my dirty hands—"all this."

"Of course. Well, then . . ." She pulled out her spiral notepad and green pen. "Let's see. . . . Just filling in a three-dimensional history. Do you know Russ Marks?"

"He's a friend of Geoffrey's. I don't know him."

"Do you know anything about Greenhaven Gardens?"

"Not really." I was trying to remember what I knew about Greenhaven Gardens. What, if anything, I knew about Russ Marks. Other than a couple of photos. Other than the time I saw that man who drove Geoffrey from Boston. That man might have been Russ Marks. I had the same feeling I'd had when I saw the photos in Geoffrey's closet. There was information I'd missed. Information I was still missing.

"And Serge Kuhnert?" she said. "Do you know him?"

"No."

"Were you aware of tension between Mr. Gray and Mr. Kuhnert?"

"No." I was aware of plenty of tension, but the last thing I would do was share that with Rachel.

"Okay. Thank you. And, um . . . let's see."

I tried to focus on the sweet peas, hoping my voice wouldn't carry any strain. "Yes?"

"As I mentioned, we found fertilizer and trace plant material on Mrs. Gray's sweater. And we're trying to figure out how it got there."

I nodded.

"Did you have any physical contact with Mrs. Gray on October twenty-fifth?"

I wiped the sweat from my forehead on the sleeve of my shirt.

The sun was in my eyes. "No."

"Even just something like, I don't know, showing her a . . . flower," she said, "when you might have accidentally brushed up against her sweater?"

I held my hand up over my eyes to shield them from the sun. The gesture prevented eye contact with her, while creating the illusion that I was doing my best to look at her.

"The placement of the fertilizer on Mrs. Gray's sweater matches up with bruises on her arm," she said. "So, it seems possible that someone was grasping her arm that day. And that same person was gardening that day."

Where were my layers of defense? There were none. "I wish I could help."

She nodded. "Right, okay. And . . . um . . . one more thing. Your relationship with Mr. Gray?"

Why was Rachel Hanna in a position to question me, to judge me? Why couldn't I control her information, limit her information?

"Yes?"

"When did that begin?"

"Last month."

"And you moved into the house . . . ?"

"Last month."

"So, it was right away?"

"We were already friends." Why did I say that? I pressed my lips together.

Stop talking.

"Close friends?"

"We were very good friends."

She blinked her eyelashes too many times. "Did Mrs. Gray know that you were very good friends with Mr. Gray?"

Again, I had the horrible feeling that Rachel Hanna was Marguerite's emissary.

In my peripheral vision, I could see Teddy looking in my direction.

Finn was standing closer than Teddy, but he had AirPods in his ears.

I turned my focus to the sweet peas again. "I was friends with her also," I said. "Equally with both of them." I pressed my lips together again.

"You worked for them."

"Yes. But Mrs. Gray invited me to her book party, so obviously . . . we were friends."

Rachel smiled at me. "Thank you for your time, Phoenix."

I was up half the night vomiting. I woke up on the bathroom floor at 5 A.M.

I was trying to ignore the conversation I'd had with Rachel. Pretend it never happened. I was trying to ignore the photos from Geoffrey's closet. I was trying to shut it all out. Everything bad. Shut it all out.

On Saturday, I reserved the whole day to work on Instagram. Wren and Geoffrey wanted a post about the driveway, because it was our largest upcoming project, scheduled for late March. The design of the driveway was mine, but they wanted me to give Marguerite credit. It pained me to give her credit, but I didn't see that I had a choice.

For my first video post, I wrote down my script ahead of time. I put together a list of phrases Marguerite had used in her posts, so I could sprinkle her language throughout.

I quickly learned that Wren had only given me partial access to Marguerite's Instagram account. I was not allowed to delete content or engage with followers. Wren retained full control. She was trying to keep me on the periphery, as someone who belonged to the world partially, not fully. I would look weak if I argued with her about it.

Starting at the bottom of the hill, I walked up the snow-covered path that was designated for the new driveway, which was going to have much more curve and grandeur than the original one. *Marguerite designed a winding driveway with Japanese maple trees that will repeat on either side, creating rhythm and offering sharp contrast with the glorious moment of surprise when the lake comes into view. Soon, you'll see pea gravel bordered by reclaimed granite cobblestones. The stonework will serve as a nod to Rosecliff's past.*

After I posted that video, I continued taking videos that I could use in the future. It was an opportunity for me to explore the whole property, which I hadn't done in recent years. The wooded areas of Rosecliff were beautiful and vast, twenty acres. They didn't need landscaping. But I thought it would add dimension and texture for me to video the wooded property and juxtapose that with shots of the open lake. In the wooded areas, there were thousands of white oaks and white pines, most still covered in snow, so that the number of downed trees was barely noticeable.

I walked through a sparsely wooded area, downhill at a slight grade on a lightly traveled path, and gradually the path became more and more densely forested. It was quiet, except for the sound of snow crunching under my feet. No one walked here. I was glad to be on my own, surrounded by trees.

The tree canopies blocked more and more of the sky and the sun, until it was no longer possible to tell what time of day it was. It was almost dark when I turned around. I wasn't sure if I was still on our property. I was embarrassed to realize that I didn't know exactly where the property ended. I'd been walking for a long time. I made my way back up the slight hill. Following the same path. But I came to a fork in the road, and I didn't remember it. I didn't know if I'd wandered away from my initial path or if I just hadn't noticed the two paths crossing the first time.

The light had changed, and my surroundings looked so different than they did before. I stood still, but everything around me was shifting. I'd assumed that this property would be easy to navigate. I'd assumed because I was on my own land—was it mine?—that I would know my way around. But that wasn't the case. I looked at my phone, but it wasn't getting any cell reception.

If I was exploring an unfamiliar area, I always made a point of marking my path and noticing the details. But this time, I'd allowed myself a misplaced feeling of ownership walking through these woods. And now, it was dark, and I had no idea which way to turn. I couldn't see the sun at all. The shadows of the trees were warping and changing, taking on various distorted shapes: hooded figures, beasts, wolves, lions.

I told myself that this was a temporary disorientation. There are always handholds. Though you might not see them at first. If I could relax and let the information come to me. So, I lay down in the snow, sinking into it, my whole back wet and cold, my hair filled with ice. But I stayed there, growing numb all the while.

Then I closed my eyes, and I said to myself, When I open my eyes, I'm going to stand up, and I'm going to follow my instincts. That's what I did. I opened my eyes and started walking. I didn't think about it. I just walked. And walked. And finally, the forest thinned out, and the house came into view in the distance.

I entered the house, so relieved to be back, but immediately felt a familiar magnetic pull in the direction of the living room. I couldn't bear to face her. I felt like I'd been revealed as a fraud. Like the walk in the woods was a test of some kind, one that I'd failed. Maybe no one else knew about my humiliation. But Marguerite did. Marguerite was relishing my distress.

I didn't allow myself to look in the living room. In the kitchen, I poured some vodka into a coffee mug and ran upstairs. I went straight to my shower. The intensity of the hot water on my back was helpful in returning me to my own body. After the shower, I climbed into bed. When Geoffrey came looking for me, I told him I wasn't feeling well.

That night I dreamt of Helen's Greek-columned house suspended over the lake. Marguerite stood on the cliff. And then she slid backward off the edge. When I turned around, the red eyes of two hundred deer were burning hot into me.

CHAPTER SEVEN

In the morning when I checked Instagram, I felt a warm surge of pride. My post had twelve hundred likes. That wasn't unusual for Marguerite's account. In fact, much of the time, her posts had more than ten thousand likes. But it was different now, because her followers knew that she was dead. They knew that someone else was posting for her.

So, it was a victory of sorts. A small victory.

If only the investigation wasn't a constant pressure on my temples. A searing pain in my skull. The conversation with Rachel Hanna had shaken me.

That evening, I joined Geoffrey on the sofa in front of the living room fire for a glass of wine. The sun was low in the sky. A pink glow was cast over the light blue living room walls, turning them lavender. I sensed a calm in his manner.

"Darling Phoenix," he said. "I think that you and I should take a trip this summer."

A trip?

"Where would you like to go? If you could go anywhere in the whole world?"

I didn't know where to begin in answering that question. It was so far from everything I was dealing with. What I really wanted was to understand my place in his life. I wanted to know what I meant to him.

I glanced up at the portrait, at which point . . . Was it possible? Was it possible I'd defeated her? Maybe she'd given up. Maybe she had been forced to accept that she was nothing now. To accept that she was dead.

My morning walk the next day began on the road around the lake, a regular walk I was growing used to. Afterward, I videoed portions of the gardens, narrating the landscape as I went. I was mildly encouraged by the success of my first post, and by Marguerite's submission. It was just a beginning, but maybe it was something to build on.

I brought a garden broom with me so I could gently knock the snow off tree and shrub branches from below. If I waited too long, the snow would turn to ice, and I wouldn't be able to remove it.

Bright sun poured into the kitchen through the French doors. Geoffrey was finishing a phone conversation with Taylor. I poured myself a cup of coffee. When I opened the refrigerator to get a carton of milk, I saw several individual containers of a fancy French yogurt, two six-packs of blackberry seltzer, and four bars of dark chocolate. In the pantry, I'd already noticed two boxes of organic granola bars from Trader Joe's. Gilda had purchased all of Taylor's favorite snacks because she was visiting soon. I was dreading her arrival.

Earlier, I'd seen Nina and Bess in Taylor's bedroom, stripping the beds and replacing the sheets, vacuuming, polishing, dusting, scrubbing. It struck me that the sheets were clean already. Everything was clean. No one had used that room since Taylor's last visit, but they were *recleaning* it, preparing for the arrival of a princess.

I sat down next to Geoffrey, who was now researching cars online. He told me he was buying a graduation present for Taylor. He said her car had broken down a few times recently. I didn't believe it. I thought he just wanted to buy her something to cheer her up. Geoffrey often behaved as though Taylor held something over him.

I found myself wondering why he didn't buy me a new car. But truthfully, I liked my truck. I had no desire for a new car. I couldn't picture when I would ever use it. Of all the things Geoffrey could buy me, a car might come last on the list. I didn't know what would come first on the list, if there even was a list.

His cell phone rang. Serge Kuhnert's name flashed. Geoffrey didn't pick up, but his whole body stiffened at the sight of Serge's name. Then he returned to his laptop.

Several minutes later, he groaned.

"What is it?"

"Marguerite's book. I said I'd have a draft complete with photos by April—that I just needed to sort a few things." He pinched the bridge of his nose with his thumb and index finger. "We need a boost from somewhere. Online sales are soft. Money's tight."

Geoffrey and Marguerite had always spent money like it was nothing. It was hard for me to understand what he was talking about. "You spend so much . . . on . . . all this." I gestured around me. I knew what it cost to keep up the grounds. I could only imagine the rest.

Geoffrey inhaled through his nose, like he was trying to control his temper. "The business is all about the image of Rosecliff. Image is everything." The muscles of his jaw tightened. He stood and paced the length of the room.

"You must have someone to help." It was better for me if he didn't have someone to help.

"Last year, we had to sack a couple of people on the content side. Wren and Amar don't know gardens. Neither does Basil."

"I can help you." I didn't have a lot of time. Geoffrey's requests for content were already taking time away from Brizzi's. But it didn't matter. Geoffrey and I needed to be partners. I could see a road to our unity. He needed to know that I'd share any burden. That I viewed his goals as my goals, his responsibilities as mine. I couldn't allow anything to divide me and Geoffrey.

He stopped and sat back down next to me, taking my hands in his. "Thank you." A moment later, he furrowed his brow.

"What is it?"

"It's . . . I don't want to saddle you with too much." He looked down at the floor. "It's not fair to you."

"Tell me."

"It's . . . her gardening show."

"What?"

"The producers want to create an AI voiceover identical to Marguerite's voice." I couldn't think of anything more disturbing than an AI version of Marguerite's voice.

Geoffrey looked up and met my gaze again. "We need an outline of the season. And Marguerite's words, too. A script."

"Hmm?"

"We need to give them . . . something." He tipped his head back to stare at the ceiling. "Marguerite pitched this show as 'gardening as a way of life.' That gardening can be incorporated into your day, even if you don't have a lot of resources. They want ideas for episodes."

"I can help you." I thought about filming in the garden of my New Milford house—a perfect example of success with no resources. But that was a terrible idea for so many reasons.

"Thank you, darling," he said.

I needed to become essential in Geoffrey's life—to the point that he couldn't operate without me. Not just a girlfriend. The gardening show, the social media, the book, all of it was a wall, a barrier—between me and Helen's house, between me and Rachel Hanna, Teddy, Frank, Taylor. Between me and the past.

"There's an event coming up in a couple of months," Geoffrey said. "Greenhaven is having a memorial in honor of Marguerite. Will you go with me?"

It was more than I had hoped for. To be seen publicly with him, at Marguerite's event. It was an acknowledgment of us.

"Really?"

"Yes, darling." He wanted me there. I could see it in his eyes.

But to go to Marguerite's memorial? Was that too much?

The next three days were filled back-to-back with client meetings. No matter what else was going on in my life, I was determined to maintain my position at Brizzi's. In many cases, I'd already made general plans with clients—to build patios or fences or plant trees. Early March was the time to lock down dates and collect deposits.

I was worn out on Saturday and would have liked to stay in bed. Instead, I shut myself into the rarely used TV room upstairs. I hadn't spent any time in this room since moving into the house. It was kind of hidden. No one could tell I was in there, unless they walked in themselves. A number of framed photographs hung on the walls, including one of Marguerite, Geoffrey, and Taylor as a little girl, taken in Venice. There was an older photo of an adolescent Marguerite in a frilly dress, with her parents on either side of her, in an expensive-looking apartment. And a school picture of a serious boy who resembled Geoffrey, maybe twelve years old, with a close-cropped haircut, wearing a military uniform.

I opened a drawer in one of the end tables and saw a small silver tray engraved with a poem.

Had I the heavens' embroidered cloths . . .
I would spread the cloths under your feet:
But I, being poor, have only my dreams;
I have spread my dreams under your feet;
Tread softly because you tread on my dreams.

—*William Butler Yeats*

And then the words:

For Geoffrey
From your loving wife, Marguerite

I read the line about "being poor" several times. The woman had no shame.

I put the tray back and closed the drawer, wishing that I hadn't seen it.

I watched five hours of one of Monty Don's famous gardening shows. He travels from one British home to another, and he talks about people's gardens in a soothing voice.

It was an escape from thinking about the investigation, Rachel Hanna, Taylor, Marguerite, Wren, Helen. Everything that was occupying my dreams. If only there were a portal into the world of Monty Don's gardening show and I could snap my fingers and enter and leave everything behind.

Monty Don tells viewers it's about the process. He says that if you don't work the soil yourself, "you don't understand it at a visceral level." Marguerite had never really worked the soil herself. She loved Rosecliff, but it wasn't in her bones the way it was in my bones. If Marguerite had engaged in the process, everything might have turned out differently.

If it were me, I never would have fallen from that cliff, no matter . . . I was too engaged in the process of stabilizing the cliff, too engaged in the question of exactly how unstable the cliff was. That was one of the things I spent my days thinking about. Everyone always talked about how well Marguerite knew her property. They said she knew every square inch. But she didn't know it as well as I did. No one knew it as well as I did.

Next, I watched *A Gardener's Delight, Gardening as Therapy, Gardening for a Long Life,* and *Paradise in Reach.* By Sunday evening, I had some ideas on what the *Marguerite by the Lake* show could look like. It made sense to focus on the "no resources" theme: What can you do with your garden if you have no time and no money?

Then I moved on to Marguerite's book. It was organized into different gardening topics, such as choosing plants, pruning, layering, fences, paths.

But the tens of thousands of digital photos on her computer were organized by plant type (folders on daffodils or hydrangeas) or by event (like last fall's book launch) or by date.

There was no folder on pruning or fences or any gardening topic. I had to scroll through hundreds of photos, one by one, to find images relevant to the pruning chapter. I allocated two hours each evening that week. It was tedious work. I hoped that Geoffrey appreciated all that I was doing to support him.

As I was working on the photos, I was skimming sections of the text, trying to insert the most relevant photos on each page. In one section, Marguerite had written: *First off, you've got to get rid of the water sprouts, basal shoots, and any diseased branches, which will drain the tree of energy.* I'd told her about the water sprouts. She inserted my advice into her book without mentioning it to me. Just like she did on social media.

I deserved recognition for my ideas and my work.

The notion of recognition was crystallizing in my mind. It was taking a clearer shape.

As I was finishing up for the day, I clicked to organize all photos by date. I looked at the most recent ones: the ten photos of the sunset over Lake Spiro that Marguerite had taken right before she died. And then I saw a picture that she didn't intend to take. It was a blurry photo of her sweater, just solid gray, nothing else. Except . . . on the edge, one very thin sliver of skin color that looked like the edge of Marguerite's finger. She was probably gripping the cell phone and covering a small sliver of the camera with her finger.

But actually . . . she wasn't.

It was my finger in the photo. My finger on her sweater. My skin was darker than Marguerite's. Not by a lot, but enough for me to tell. You could easily think, looking at the photo, that the finger was in shadow. And you'd interpret the color of the skin through that lens.

Maybe it *was* in dark shadow. Maybe it *was* Marguerite's skin.

But it wasn't. I knew it wasn't.

Rachel Hanna's team of CSIs would go back over these photos a thousand more times. They would eventually see what I saw. Wouldn't they?

If only I could delete the photo. But they already had it. They probably already had it.

I had a plummeting, hollowing sensation. I couldn't stop myself.

I returned to the pictures of the sunset. I went over them one by one. It was possibly the most spectacular sunset I'd ever seen. I hadn't been surprised that Marguerite was taking pictures. And then I remembered. That was why I'd walked back. I had started to take the same photo, but from farther away. Right before I saw Marguerite.

I opened up my phone. There it was. One photo of that remarkable sunset. I zoomed in.

No.

It was Marguerite in the distance, walking past the pylons. It was Marguerite.

I zoomed in on the background across the lake. Helen's house. Helen's lawn. No.

Someone standing on Helen's lawn, almost indistinguishable, but I knew who it was.

I was dropping through space. I was waiting to crash.

I needed the investigation to be over. I needed to shut it down.

On my own laptop, I pulled up my folder of photos and confirmed what I already knew. Nina was looking straight into the camera. Somehow, I'd known that Helen's house was a problem for me.

Did Nina see Marguerite fall? Did she see me?

Something Rachel said came back to me. She said Helen was confused and vague when they spoke. Did Nina tell Helen what she saw?

It was all I could do to carry on with my normal work routine. Taylor was arriving the following day. Taylor and Rachel Hanna had melded into a two-headed monster coming at me, fangs bared. Each of them, individually, terrified me. But together, they were overpowering. And now . . . those photos. Nina in that photo. I had to come up with a plan. I couldn't continue to react. I needed to develop a proactive plan.

For Taylor's first night, Geoffrey asked for a formal dinner in the dining room, prepared by Raoul. Gilda approached me in the morning, when I was on my way out the door.

"Which glasses and china would you like to use tonight, Miss Sullivan?"

I didn't have an answer. Geoffrey and I had been using the kitchen dishes. I had barely looked at the formal glasses and china, but even if I'd been studying them, there's no way I would have been able to describe any of them to her on the spot.

She must have realized I didn't have an answer. So she led me into the butler's pantry and pointed to some of the options.

I didn't want her to view me as indifferent. Though I *was* actually. Indifferent. I couldn't distinguish among any of the things in front of me.

I was scared of choosing a glass that was something special or sacred to Marguerite—and that Taylor would be offended. So I pointed to a shelf on the far right, with the simplest dishes and the simplest glasses I could find. "These," I said. "And these."

She smiled. "And for the wineglass?"

I pointed to another simple glass. "This one."

"For your *wineglass*?"

I pointed to the same one and repeated myself. "This one."

Gilda smiled at me. "Very well."

"I appreciate your help, Gilda. With everything."

Gilda clasped her hands together in front of her body.

"I know it was terrible for you." I was trying to connect with her. "Losing Mrs. Gray."

"Mrs. Gray and I were close." She held my gaze without blinking.

At five, the front door opened, and Taylor walked in—the spitting image of her deceased mother—the same blond hair, dark brown eyes, and ballerina neck, accentuated by a white turtle-neck. Geoffrey followed, rolling her bag.

"Taylor!" I said. "I'm so happy to see you." I'd been dreading this moment. I knew what Taylor saw when she looked at me. She saw a bounder who had pounced on her father in his moment of vulnerability. Or worse than that, she saw her father's mistress who tried to tear her parents' marriage apart.

"Nice to see you." Taylor tipped her head to one side.

I imagined her inner monologue: "I lived here for eighteen years with my mother and father. You were our gardener."

She twisted her hair back with one hand. "Dad told me great things about you."

Behind her eyes, I could see the words *gardener, gardener, gardener, gardener.*

Taylor looked through the grand foyer and into the living room. "Everything looks different."

"It's all the same, darling." Geoffrey smiled and the wrinkles around his blue eyes grew more pronounced. I was struck by how handsome he was. His perfect features still surprised me.

"It's not the same," she said under her breath.

Geoffrey put his arm around his daughter and squeezed her shoulder. Then he kissed her forehead. "I've missed you. I'm so happy you're here."

Gilda had set out cheese, crackers, and a bottle of Sancerre in the living room. When I realized that everyone was making a fuss over Taylor's arrival, I purchased a dress for this evening—

with Geoffrey's credit card. I wanted Taylor to know that I'd made an effort. When I saw that she was wearing jeans, I felt like I'd shown up at the wrong event.

Geoffrey and I sat on one of two red velvet sofas across from Taylor on the other one. I'd asked Geoffrey about the smell of roses, and where it was coming from. He suggested that the dormant rosebushes continued to give off a scent in winter that was making its way into the house. It was absurd. Dormant roses have no scent.

You couldn't enter the living room without looking up at Marguerite's portrait in its heavy gold frame. Even Taylor and Geoffrey, who were not new to it—their eyes automatically settled on Marguerite as if she were another person in the room participating in the conversation. I was surprised they didn't hear her. Or did they? She spoke softly, but clearly.

Leave, she was saying to me. *Go.*

A penetrating light pierced the canvas. Looking at her eyes was like looking into the center of the earth. The depth, the heat, the light that originated from some reserve deep inside her. I closed my eyes for ten seconds. When I opened them, the painting was . . . It was just a painting. It was paint on a canvas. Just paint on a canvas.

"Taylor, I wanted to tell you . . ." I tried to make eye contact with her, but she was looking down at her hands, at a broken fingernail. I continued: "I'm very sorry about your mother. If there's anything I can do."

"Thank you," she said, keeping her eyes on her broken fingernail.

Geoffrey placed several logs on the grate in the fireplace.

Taylor licked her lips, which were chapped. I didn't expect to feel sorry for her, but I did. She looked lost.

Geoffrey lit a piece of newspaper, then stuck the flaming newspaper up the flue.

"I've heard about how hard you've been working at law school," I said. "And on top of that, you have a job in New York."

Geoffrey stuffed the burning newspaper underneath the logs, and they went up in flames. The temperature of the room shot up in an instant.

"At the Whitney," Geoffrey said. "She'll be working under the General Counsel."

Taylor gestured to the painting over the fireplace. "Serge, my mother's friend, helped me get the job."

I thought I noticed Geoffrey stop what he was doing at the mention of Serge. But it could have been my imagination.

"Congratulations," I said.

Taylor looked in my general direction, but I couldn't quite make eye contact with her. It seemed she was looking just past me at her father.

A spark flew out and landed an inch away from the oriental rug.

Taylor stood and stomped it out with the toe of her trendy sneaker. She pointed to a hole in the rug. "I remember, on Christmas Eve, like five years ago, when Mom was making a fire and a spark burned that hole," she said. "She'd only just bought the rug on that trip to Morocco."

Taylor's gaze moved around the living room. "Every object in this house reminds me of her." Then her focus seemed to shift inward. It was like she'd forgotten that Geoffrey and I were in the room. Her shoulders rounded forward, her chest concave, and she became very still.

I suddenly wished I were someplace else. Anyplace else. I could feel how much she didn't want me there. I was causing her pain.

Geoffrey leaned forward and put his hand on his daughter's shoulder.

A moment later, Taylor crossed the room to sit down at the grand piano. She played for several minutes—something classical—her long slim fingers sliding confidently over the keyboard. Geoffrey joined me on the sofa. He clapped when Taylor finished playing. I followed his lead and clapped also.

"Wonderful, sweetheart," he said, then turned to me. "Taylor studied to be a classical pianist. But then she took a detour and ended up in law. The truth is, she's so disciplined, she could do anything she decides to do."

Past Taylor, I could see through the window to the outdoor patio, furnished with a dining table and chairs, all still covered for the winter. It was still too cold to eat dinner outside. But in another few weeks, it might be possible.

Taylor stopped abruptly. "Dad, the piano's out of tune."

I thought the piano sounded fine but I chose not to say anything.

"I, um . . ." Geoffrey frowned as if trying to remember.

"Armand tuned it in the summer," Taylor said. "But when the pressure in the house shifts, it goes out of tune quickly."

Geoffrey smiled. "Okay, darling."

Taylor pointed to a framed drawing of some kind of royal lady and her daughter at court. It was hanging near the piano.

"Dad, do you remember, Mom bought this for fifty pounds the summer we were in London, like fifteen years ago? She told me she chose it because of the love in the mother's eyes. She said she understood how that mother felt."

"Your mum loved you more than anything in the world."

Taylor was quiet for a moment.

"It's amazing," she said, "the drawing's worth half a million now."

"I'm not surprised," Geoffrey said.

"How do you know that?" I asked her. I genuinely wanted to know where you get this kind of information. These were things I needed to learn.

But maybe she took my question the wrong way. "My mother knew a lot about art," she said, as if she was explaining to a child. "I guess I . . . absorbed it."

"Tell me more about your mother," I said, trying my best to be sincere.

Taylor closed the keyboard cover. She walked back across the room and sat down in front of the fire, crossing her legs. She picked up a cracker from the silver tray and broke it in half. "It's easier for me to talk about my mom with . . . her friends." She put half of the cracker in her mouth, chewed, and swallowed.

I looked in Geoffrey's direction but couldn't catch his eye. "Maybe I asked you about her as a way of getting to know *you*," I said to her. "That was stupid."

Taylor nodded. She turned to her father. "Do you remember, in Madrid, when Mom and I bought ten drawings in one afternoon?" Taylor spread her arms wide on the back of the sofa. "She saw a piece of art and she knew immediately."

"Your mum had a good eye." Geoffrey stood to adjust the logs in the fireplace.

"She discovered Serge Kuhnert," Taylor said to me. "She knew before anyone else did."

I sensed a stiffening in Geoffrey's posture. His jaw muscles clenched.

She cocked her head to the side. "Where did you grow up, Phoenix?"

I felt like I'd lost control over the conversation, like I'd lost control over everything.

"Not far from here," I said. "I'm still holding on to my grandmother's house that I grew up in."

She nodded. "It's nice to have an extra house. Just in case." She laughed. "And you probably have so many memories attached, like I do with this house."

Taylor fingered one of her gold hoop earrings. "Where's the rest of your family?"

"My brother lives in New Mexico." I needed her questions to reach a dead end.

"You must miss him."

"Yes," I said.

"Blood is blood."

She was drawing a circle around herself and her father. She was telling me to keep out.

CHAPTER EIGHT

Raoul delivered on the dinner—beef tenderloin, potatoes au gratin, and asparagus vinaigrette, with silver candlesticks and bowls full of tulips as centerpieces.

A large Venetian glass chandelier lit the table and four crystal mirrors hung on silk-covered walls. Geoffrey was seated at the head of the velvet-draped ten-foot table, with Taylor and me on either side.

I was sincerely hoping that Nina was not serving us dinner. I couldn't keep it together if I had to manage Taylor and Nina in the same room.

"Why did Gilda set the table with two water glasses and no wineglass?" Taylor pointed to the glasses at her place setting.

I felt my face flush. "I like them. It doesn't matter. Does it?"

She smiled. "I guess it depends." She pointed to the shorter glass. "These glasses are meant for the staff. Same with the plates." She pointed to the plate in front of her.

I felt my stomach turn. "Yes," I said. "But they're still nice." I looked down at my plate, not wanting to see Taylor's expression.

I was careful about how much wine I drank. I made sure that I was drinking at the same pace as Geoffrey and Taylor.

During dinner, Taylor turned to her father. "Gabe and I broke up."

"Oh, sweetheart," Geoffrey said.

Tears welled up in Taylor's eyes. I could see her trying not to cry.

"I'm sorry," I said, though Taylor's torso and eyes were turned toward her father.

Geoffrey stood and walked to Taylor's chair. He bent over to kiss the top of her head. "Darling." Occasionally, I could see a resemblance between Geoffrey and Taylor. They had a similar slightly crooked smile and teeth. It was more subtle than the likeness between Marguerite and Taylor, but just as unnerving.

After a couple of minutes, Taylor seemed to recover. "I moved out of our apartment in New Haven. I wasn't expecting . . ." Her speech trailed off. She put her fingertips on her water glass, as if she was considering taking a sip, but she didn't.

"I'm sorry," Geoffrey said.

"I was thinking I would stay here for a couple weeks. I'm moving in with Caroline at the end of the month, when her roommate goes to Atlanta."

Geoffrey had told me Taylor was just visiting for one weekend. This news made me nauseous.

"Of course," Geoffrey said. I saw the way that he looked at Taylor. His eyes were filled with admiration. She was Marguerite twenty-five years earlier. She was the Marguerite from the painting.

Taylor's hand landed on a spoon she hadn't used that lay by her plate. She flipped it, and then she flipped it again. "I start my job in May," she said. "I've got to study for the bar."

Geoffrey nodded. "Absolutely."

"Absolutely," I said, though she didn't seem to be looking for my approval.

"By the way," she said to her father, "I'm meeting with Detective Hanna tomorrow morning." She turned to look at me. "I'm assuming you both talked to her already?"

We both nodded.

The subject of Detective Hanna sent my intestines into turmoil.

Those photos. Nina. Marguerite. My finger on the sweater. Bruises. Fertilizer. Russ Marks. Greenhaven.

I could barely look at the food on my plate.

After dinner, Taylor followed me down the hall, past the grand staircase, and toward the living room. She stopped and picked up a small porcelain lion from the hall console. It was lunging forward, mouth open in a roar. "My mother lives on through the items that she held and touched. That's what feeds my father, you know. He's in love with the memories."

"May I?" I reached out for the porcelain lion, and she handed it to me. I closed my fingers around it. I imagined the lion biting into my flesh and drawing blood. I quickly set it down on the console again.

Geoffrey was seated on the living room sofa in front of a blazing fire. Had Nina tended the fire while we were eating dinner? I hadn't noticed her walking in that direction. Geoffrey stared at the portrait. He didn't know that I was watching him. What was he thinking? Maybe Geoffrey hadn't grieved for Marguerite, because he'd never lost her. The painting was her presence—stronger than the real thing.

Again, I heard Marguerite's harsh whisper.

Leave. Go.

Could Geoffrey and Taylor hear it, too? Or was it only me she spoke to?

I gestured to the painting. "What an incredible tribute to your mother," I said to Taylor as we stood in the living room doorway. "I feel like she's here with us." Maybe it was a mistake to say that. Maybe I'd given Marguerite more strength by acknowledging her—that she was still holding sway over the house, and I was holding sway over nothing.

Taylor turned to me. "When did you and Dad become such good friends?" She touched her gold hoop earring again.

"Over time."

Her eyes locked on mine. "Really?"

I realized my mistake too late. I tried to swallow, but my mouth was too dry, like the saliva had been sucked out of it. "After your mother passed away. I talked to your dad about the garden. So, you know, we became friends in the last . . . couple of months."

She narrowed her eyes. "That's great, you've been there for him, during the hard times."

What kind of comment was that?

"He's heartbroken over your mother." I tried for a matter-of-fact tone.

"Dad is good at picking himself up and moving on." She tapped her mouth with her index finger. Marguerite used to do the same thing.

"He's been struggling," I said.

"Are you still our gardener?"

"What?"

"Dad said that you're still working for the landscape company, so I'm just wondering, like practically speaking, are you still our gardener?"

"I don't—"

"I hope so, because you always did such a great job," she said. "I'm not trying to be rude. I'm just curious."

Taylor's eyelashes were so light, they were practically invisible. Without mascara, she had the look of an albino.

Trying to ingratiate myself with Taylor had sucked every ounce of energy out of my body. The evening had wiped me out.

"Thank you for being lovely to Taylor," Geoffrey said to me as he climbed into bed. He kissed the tip of my nose, then brushed the hair out of my eyes. "She's the apple of my eye."

If he were confronted with a choice between me and Taylor, he would choose Taylor. "I can see that," I said. And then, because I couldn't bear to discuss Taylor, I said: "I've made some progress on the gardening series."

"Yes?"

I sat up in bed. "I think we should emphasize one hour a week. You can spend less than an hour a week on a one-hundred-square-foot garden and get excellent results."

Geoffrey's face lit up. "Yes." He laughed to himself. "Yes. I love it. It's fucking brilliant. *One Hour a Week for the Garden of Your Dreams.* It's fucking brilliant. Let's get together with Wren."

"Great idea. And one other thought." I paused. "So . . . the Instagram account is doing well. But the thing is, I've hit a plateau. I can't make much more progress with my limited access."

"Okay."

"I need Marguerite's login."

"Of course. I'll talk to Wren."

I couldn't tell if he meant it, but I chose not to push.

He turned out the light. I felt the warmth and weight of his body on mine. Geoffrey's presence made me better. Safer. Calmer.

Two hours later, I woke up with the image of Marguerite's bruised arm in my head. It wasn't just her arm that was bruised. There were bruises covering her whole body.

I tried to go back to sleep, but images of a bruised and

bloody Marguerite were hitting me in the face, like the wind on a fast boat. I needed someone to knock me out.

When I came down the stairs in the morning, Taylor had completely rearranged the living room furniture. She was using one of the console tables as her desk. She had moved a lamp onto the table and brought her desk chair from her room, along with all her books, notebooks, and laptop, which were now spread out on top.

Her back was to the door, and she was talking to someone on the phone. "Exactly. A little sus." She heard me and turned. "Okay, Maeve. Later."

"Good morning," I called from the doorway. "Did you have breakfast?"

"Yup. I've been awake for a couple of hours." She was wearing sweatpants and a T-shirt.

"Wouldn't you prefer to work in your bedroom," I said casually, "where you have some quiet?"

She shook her head and looked down at her laptop.

"It's a big house," I said. "There are a lot of rooms to choose from." Again, in a super casual tone.

"My mom's portrait is comforting to me." She gestured to the painting. "I feel like she's watching over me." She looked back to her laptop.

I didn't enjoy sitting in the living room, but I didn't want her there either. It seemed like a bad idea to let her take it over.

"It's a spectacular work of art." I paused. "I just . . . we should probably all discuss it, if you're going to spend your days working in here." I was hoping to address the question of where she worked as a logistical one, without weight or meaning.

"I mentioned it to Dad." She looked up at me. Her face was smooth, and her eyes were clear, like an innocent child's.

"I'm just suggesting," I said, "we should all consider each other's needs."

"I'm saving you from having to sit in here," she said. "Because my dad would sit in here all day long if he could. For him, it's a way to be close to my mother."

I coughed. I hadn't been aware of Geoffrey gravitating to the living room.

I heard the now familiar low whisper:

Leave. Go.

Did Taylor hear it, too?

"Anything you want is fine." I put my hand on the back of her head in an attempt at affection.

I could feel her flinch and pull away.

I clasped my hands together behind my back, to be sure they wouldn't make any more mistakes.

I was compelled to return to Helen's house. To stand exactly where Nina was standing that night and see exactly what she saw.

When I arrived, there were no cars in the driveway.

That photo was seared in my mind. I walked directly to the spot on the lawn where Nina had stood.

My eyesight was strong. I could see Rosecliff. I could see the position where Marguerite had stood taking photos of the sunset. I could see the place where I had stood taking the photo of the sunset. If Nina had my eyesight, she would have been able to see both. And even if she didn't, even without her glasses, she'd probably know, at the very least, that there was a second person. Wouldn't she?

I heard a car pulling into Helen's driveway. It was Helen's car. No.

Why was I standing here? Why was I here? Why hadn't I timed my visit to coincide with landscaping work?

I waved to Helen as she got out of her car. "Hi," I called out as I walked in her direction.

"Phoenix, I didn't expect you today." A strange look crossed her face.

"I was a little worried the last time I was here," I said. "Because it looked like you had some Japanese beetles. Before we spray the roses, I wanted to check and make sure. Rather not use the pesticide if I can help it." I sounded defensive, offering excuses.

"How are you?" She wanted to ask me something else.

"Great," I said. Helen and I had not discussed the fact that I was living with Geoffrey, but she knew.

"By the way," she said, "I've had a few conversations with that detective."

I nodded and maintained eye contact.

"She's been asking me what I saw the night that Marguerite died. The truth is that I didn't see anything. But . . ."

"Yes?"

"I'd like to help her if I can. Marguerite was one of my closest friends."

I nodded.

"You know that. Don't you? That Marguerite and I were very close?"

"Yes."

"And that I'd go to great lengths for my friend."

"Yes."

What was she trying to tell me? Was she threatening me?

I returned to Rosecliff at the end of the day. When I reached the top of the stairs, headed for our bedroom, I saw Taylor standing in the hall outside the door. Her body in an awkward turn, her hands clasped together in front of her chest. She smiled. "I've always loved this painting." She pointed to a watercolor on the wall—a picture of two small children, each one trying to pull a toy away from the other one. "I forgot about it."

Had she been in our bedroom when she heard my footsteps? I had packed up all of Marguerite's belongings. Finally, the room was almost mine. Not entirely, but almost. And Taylor's entry was a violation.

"The children are angry," I said.

"Hmm?"

"I mean, the children in the picture look angry. They both want the toy. Don't they?"

Why did I say that? I used to be good at saying something

that meant nothing. Just to keep a conversation going. But recently that skill had left me.

"Huh," she said.

Once Taylor went back downstairs, I opened my laptop, and the same tabs were still open.

What was she looking for? What could she have found that she would share with other people, with Rachel?

This had been her mother's bedroom. As a child, she had probably run in here to cuddle in bed with her parents when she was scared. She had probably helped herself to her mother's clothing if she needed to borrow something. She had felt free to wander in and out of the bedroom when her mother was alive. And now, there must be some sadness in knowing that it was off-limits. I wasn't married to her father, but she understood that the house wasn't entirely hers, the way it had once been.

I didn't want to make all of this worse for Taylor. But . . . she didn't think I had a legitimate place here. She dismissed my role. So I couldn't be as generous as I might have otherwise been.

I looked around Marguerite's bedroom. My bedroom. Was it mine? I'd removed what I thought were her personal items. But now I was realizing that there was a very blurry line between personal and impersonal, if any at all. Maybe the trouble was the furniture. The canopy bed, the two chests of drawers, the five paintings. Some of them were probably museum-quality antiques and works of art. How could I move those to storage? I could potentially move the rug to another room. The settee could be reupholstered. That might help. But if I was honest with myself, the rug and the settee were not the problem. It was larger than that.

I went through all the closet drawers to make sure there was nothing private that Taylor might have seen. It was only my underwear, shirts, hats, sunglasses. Maybe Taylor was looking for the J.Lo ring or the diamond bracelet.

As I passed Geoffrey's closet, I noticed that one of his drawers was partially open. I opened it all the way. Could Taylor have been looking in Geoffrey's closet? I could find nothing but socks. But now I wondered if there were other things here that I might have missed. I checked each of his drawers. Most were filled with clothing. I carefully looked underneath the clothing, just in case he was hiding something. It was only when I got to a drawer that contained scarves, scarves I'd never seen him wear, that I saw a flat wooden box in the back. I took it out and opened it. Inside were two dog-eared, wrinkled pictures of Serge. Serge? In one, Serge was lying on a picnic blanket, sunbathing in the park. In the other, he was painting a large canvas, completely focused on his work and unaware of the camera.

Why did Geoffrey have these photos of Serge?

I unfolded an old, yellowing handwritten letter, which read:

Geoffrey, As I told you, my friendship with Marguerite is paramount. I encourage you to look inside yourself and assess whether you are "husband material." Marguerite is in love with you. I don't want to see her hurt.

To be clear, whether or not you marry Margue-
rite, you and I have no future. "For of all sad words
of tongue or pen, The saddest are these: 'It might have
been!'"

I remain

Yours truly, Serge

I reread the letter three times.

Maybe I didn't understand.

It was . . . it was too . . .

And the dog-eared photos of Serge.

Why were these photos here?

Why was this letter here?

Did Geoffrey sleep with men?

Had he been in love with Serge?

The questions were going nonstop in my brain. A list of them that I ran through and repeated. Was Russ Marks a lover or a friend? Who were the other men? Who were the other women? Did Geoffrey care about me? Would he ever care about me?

From the living room doorway, I could see Taylor sitting on the sofa, the back of her shoulders shaking. She was looking at the portrait. At Marguerite, whose husband had been in love with her best friend. Was that true? How had Serge captured so many layers of pain in her eyes? Because he'd caused the pain himself? The Marguerite in the painting knew everything. I could see it. She'd held on to the betrayals. How many had there been? She'd managed to control Geoffrey and Serge in the end. To crush that relationship. Had she failed with Geoffrey and me? Or would she win in the end?

Curtis texted. Phoenix, call me.

Curtis still didn't know where I was living. I had to keep it that way for as long as possible.

An hour later, I walked past the living room and saw Geoffrey seated next to his daughter. She was resting her head on his shoulder. He was talking to her, comforting her. He didn't take his eyes off her.

I didn't know this man. Did I matter to him at all?

Geoffrey was absorbing his daughter's distress, as if he wanted to transfer some of that distress to himself. To suffer in her place.

Would he ever do the same for me—take on my distress as his own?

I felt a surge of panic, seeing them together like that. I knew Geoffrey loved his daughter. But now I wondered if he loved anyone else. And if so, who?

I went to bed. I waited for him. Lying in the dark, when I closed my eyes, Helen's house was the only thing I could see. I tried so hard to think of something else. I tried to focus on the gardens I was designing. Solving problems that my clients were having. Nothing worked. I could only see Helen's house, tiny in the distance, and then the barely visible figure of Nina standing in front.

My thoughts circled on Serge's letter. *Look inside yourself and assess whether you are husband material.*

It was hours later when Geoffrey came to bed. I told myself that was all in the past. That was thirty years ago.

I held him close to me. He was warm. I was grateful to feel him next to me.

Still, when I closed my eyes, I could only see Nina.

I lay there all night with my eyes wide open.

CHAPTER NINE

Marguerite was seated at the kitchen table when I entered the next morning. Blood rushed from my brain. My body went cold. I gripped the counter to steady myself.

And then . . . I saw. It was Taylor—wearing white pants and a nautical striped blouse. Her mother had worn an outfit identical to the one she had on.

I turned away from her and poured myself a cup of coffee while I recovered. My hands were trembling so much that I sloshed coffee on the counter and on the floor. I found a towel to wipe it up while trying to get my hands under control.

Then I sat down next to Taylor. I watched her slice a banana into her bowl of Special K. Each slice was perfectly identical to the others.

"What if you take a break today," I said, "and we go on a walk together in the afternoon?"

She gave me the smile that I was growing used to. The smile said: "I know you wouldn't understand the first thing about studying for the bar exam, so I won't try to explain it to you because it would be a waste of my precious time. And smiling is the easiest way to avoid talking to you, which I find practically unbearable."

Out loud, she said: "I'm meeting Maeve for coffee." I'd learned that Maeve was Taylor's best friend who lived a couple miles away. When I tried to picture Maeve, I imagined a woman who looked exactly like Taylor, but with dark hair. Snow White and Rose Red. I hoped I never had to meet her.

"Okay. Tell me if you need anything," I said. "I want to be there for you. This is huge . . . what you're doing. I'm blown away by all your accomplishments."

"I appreciate that."

I stumbled on my words. "I'm just . . . here to support you."

"Okay."

"I sometimes wish I'd gone to law school." I was trying to bond with her, but it also happened to be true. In sixth grade, I'd written an essay about how I wanted to be a trial lawyer when I grew up. That year, I spent a lot of nights with my best friend, Abby. Her mom was a criminal defense attorney, and I wanted to be one, too. But then . . . Abby and I grew apart. And common sense told me law school wasn't an option for me.

"You should have," Taylor said. "I mean, if you wanted to, you should have." She ate several bites of her cereal, then wiped her mouth with her napkin. Her blond hair fell straight down her back, like a Barbie doll's. "On the other hand, your career is what brought you and Dad together." Her eyes held on mine for a moment too long.

"Yes."

I met her gaze. And then it was as though a veil dropped from her face, and I was looking into Marguerite's large brown glassy eyes, staring into a churning vortex. The woman in front of me wasn't in the room. She was someplace else. Someplace I didn't want to go.

I looked down and bit the inside of my cheek.

Taylor asked: "What are you working on today?"

I made myself look up. "My clients have a tree that is struggling. I'm going there to help." That was true. My clients were deciding whether to take down a diseased ash tree. I understood the relationship between the tree and the other plants in my clients' garden. The removal of one tree can have a lasting impact on an entire ecosystem.

In the afternoon, I planned to work on Marguerite's book. But I didn't mention that.

Taylor's eyes drifted around the room and then back to her cereal.

I swallowed my coffee. "Plants and trees are like my children."

She took another precise bite of cereal. "They fill the void?"

"What void?"

She continued to eat her cereal. "Seems like there's always a void. No? For me, my mother left a void," she said. "What about your mother?"

I froze. How did she know anything about my mother? "My mother?"

She nodded.

"My mother's dead," I said.

"Then you know what it feels like."

"Do you want to have children, Taylor?"

"One day." She looked out the French doors and gestured to the lawn. "I can see retiring here in this house and watching my grandchildren run and play."

I held that image in my mind for several moments. Where would I be when she was watching her grandchildren run and play?

Taylor's gaze shifted away from my eyes to someone behind me. "Good morning, Nina."

No. I thought I'd timed my breakfast so that I'd be gone before Nina arrived.

"Good morning," Nina said.

"Nina, my sheets are so soft," Taylor said. "And they smell like the ocean."

"Miss Taylor," Nina said, "I try for to make the room nice."

I turned around and smiled at Nina.

I saw something in her face. An accusation. Was it an accusation? Her eyebrows lifted, her forehead wrinkled, and her mouth flattened into a half-smile.

She'd seen me on the cliff. She'd seen me. I could tell by the way she pursed her lips. By the way she interlaced her fingers in front of her. She knew. She knew. She knew. She knew.

In a matter of seconds, my shirt was drenched with sweat.

I couldn't bear to be in the same room as her for a moment more. I couldn't bear it.

I stood and quietly slipped out the back door.

Curtis texted: Call me.

I tried to think through the situation in a rational way. Nina would have said something to someone if she'd seen me there. She would have said something if she'd seen Marguerite fall. It was months ago. And I would already know. She wouldn't just go about her job without saying or doing anything.

Unless. Unless she *did* tell the police. Unless Rachel already knew that I was there. And she was just waiting to get all her information in order. To get corroborating stories. To get all her forensic evidence collected. All her witnesses lined up. So she could pounce on me.

No. That wasn't possible. Was it? Could Nina have seen Marguerite fall? I would know, wouldn't I?

That night, Geoffrey turned out the light on his bedside table. He kissed me and held me close to him. Then his hand slid over my breasts, down my waist. He whispered in my ear. I rolled away from him. What if he was still obsessed with Serge? I didn't have the courage to ask him. To acknowledge I'd looked through the secret box in the back of his scarf drawer.

I sat up and turned my bedside lamp on. I needed light.

If only I could make Nina tell me what she told Rachel Hanna. I was suffocating. I wanted them both to leave me alone. I wanted them to be gone.

Geoffrey squinted from the light in his eyes. "What's wrong?"

"Do you trust me?"

"Of course," he said.

"You treat me like I'm a low-level employee."

"What are you talking about?"

I needed control. "You're not paying me, Geoffrey, and I'm not asking you to. We're in this together. But the least you can do is trust me with your information. If you don't, then I'm not sure what this is. Our relationship. What am I to you?"

"Phoenix, darling, where does this come from?" he said. "Of course, I trust you. Of course, I do."

The next day, Geoffrey gave me Marguerite's login, so that I had full access to her account. Wren was trying to keep me out of the inner circle, but she'd failed.

I had a moment of triumph over her, but only a moment. Minutes later, I received a voicemail from Rachel Hanna, asking for a meeting. I ran through the options in my head. I just needed a few days to steady myself. Just to get a few hours of sleep. Because when I spoke to her, I had to know that my voice wouldn't shake, that my hands wouldn't tremble. I'd always been good at controlling what people saw and heard when they looked at me. But since I'd moved into Rosecliff, that control was slipping away from me. Sometimes the wrong words came out of my mouth. Sometimes I didn't know what words had come out of my mouth.

It was Taylor, here in the house, that had thrown me. She was supposed to leave at the end of the month. It was just a few more days. When she was gone, I could stabilize. I would stabilize.

I had far bigger concerns than Marguerite's Instagram weighing on me. But helping Geoffrey with the business was . . . something to strengthen my position. Possibly.

In the early mornings, before I left for work, I took pictures and videos of Rosecliff for Instagram. I was supposed to support Marguerite's vision but remain invisible. Wren and Geoffrey hadn't said that . . . exactly. But it was what they wanted. I was used to hiding. Even dead, Marguerite was so much more visible than I ever was.

These plants had a hard year, but they weren't defeated.

I narrated while I took a video.

The structure and formality of the traditional English garden, adjacent to the house, is so different from the wildflower meadow that flows down the hill.

Which one feels right to you? Which one belongs here at Rosecliff? Or do they both belong?

The post received eighteen hundred likes.

After work, I made a nice pitcher of fresh lemonade, with slices of lemon and lime. It wasn't exactly the right weather, but I was so thirsty. So very thirsty. I poured some into a tall glass, then set the pitcher and the glass on a side table on the verandah. I took several photos of the pitcher and glass together. Then I took a photo of the glass with my fingers wrapped around it. It was just a glimpse of me . . . of my presence. The last photo was the one I chose to post. It was an act of aggression. I was revealing myself, like an exhibitionist. I was saying, look at me, notice me.

The caption read: *Lemonade after a long day in the garden.*

I had a feeling of accomplishment. Maybe I could succeed in carrying this business forward, in the absence of Marguerite. If I could get past all the obstacles. Maybe.

My lemonade post got two thousand likes.

When I looked at the photo again, a glimpse of my fingers wrapped around the glass, I was reminded of the photo of Marguerite's gray sweater, with that sliver of my finger.

You fucking moron.

It was like I was going out of my way to call attention to my fingers—to my skin. Like I was saying to the police, *pay attention to the color of my fingers.*

I wanted to delete the photo. But it was too late.

It was obvious from the moment I saw Taylor. She wanted me out. It was my job to weave myself into the fabric of Geoffrey's life so completely that she couldn't eliminate me.

I was looking for ways to control my environment. I needed to be centered in order to address all the obstacles in my way. So when Taylor was out for the afternoon, I took the opportunity to meet with Gilda. We sat in the dining room.

"Geoffrey and I have talked about making some changes in the house," I said to Gilda. "He suggested that I should replace certain things." I knew I would not be able to get away from Marguerite if I was surrounded by her things. "But, of course, I don't want to replace anything with sentimental or monetary value. So, I'd like to understand some of the history." I gestured around in an all-encompassing way. "Here."

Gilda clasped her hands together in her lap. I could see both of our images reflected in three of the four crystal mirrors. I felt like I was in a fun house. "You'll find that the house and everything in it grows on you," she said. "Even if you aren't able to appreciate it yet."

What was she implying?

From a cabinet in the butler's pantry, Gilda took down four different-sized plates and a bowl. She said that this was the most formal set of china. Apparently, the Grays owned twenty of these place settings originally, but a couple of the dishes had been chipped. So they had only eighteen remaining. Each dish had a band of twenty-four karat gold around the outside. I ran my finger around the band of gold.

"These dishes were wedding presents," Gilda said. "Mrs. Gray used them for many dinner parties."

I wanted to ask her what the different plate sizes were for. But I imagined she would sneer at me with condescension, and I couldn't bear it.

"But these weren't actually her favorites." She opened a different cabinet and took down a more modern dinner plate.

"These were a gift from Mr. Kuhnert, the Ginori dishes, her favorites. For a special dinner, she'd always ask me to use the Ginori."

I had an irrational urge to throw the Ginori dishes against the wall, one by one.

Gilda left for a few minutes and returned with an old copy of a magazine. She opened the magazine to a page that was dog-eared and pointed to a large photo of Marguerite Gray, at her most glamorous. I could tell she was proud to show me this photo, as if she took some credit for Marguerite's beauty and fame. I skimmed the article on the opposite page and arrived at one section quoting Marguerite.

A dinner is a ceremony. Anything is important if you endow it with meaning. I can do that with crystal, silver, china, linens, flowers. These are layers of details, and they add up to something significant.

I couldn't help thinking that if I could really understand the distinctions between the different crystal glasses, I'd have access. I'd have power.

I skimmed the rest of the interview and landed on the final section quoting Marguerite:

My home is a reflection of me. I worked hard to put my stamp on this home. It's layers and layers deep. Any future mistress of this house will find it impossible to get rid of me.

I gasped and tried to cover with a cough.

Marguerite was talking to me.

I wanted to run screaming out of the house, but I tried to

rein in my emotions so that Gilda would not think I was fazed by what I had read. She had shown it to me on purpose.

She caught my eye. Could she tell I was choking?

"And these . . ." Gilda pointed to a china pattern with delicate green vines. "Mrs. Gray purchased these when she was traveling with Taylor in Hungary. She used them for informal luncheons."

I was able to recover enough to speak. "She liked to travel?"

"She loved to travel." Gilda smiled.

I continued on like nothing was wrong. "Did Mr. Gray join her on her trips to Europe?"

"He didn't share that interest." Gilda could have been telling me that Geoffrey liked chocolate ice cream and Marguerite liked vanilla, for all the animation in her face.

"What did they like to do together?"

"They worked together." She was holding to her talking points.

"I see."

She talked me through two dozen different silver trays, noting where and when Marguerite had acquired each one of them.

"How do you remember every single tray? So many of them look alike." I laughed lightly, hoping she found the tray situation as absurd as I did. But I could tell from her lack of response that she didn't. In fact, she seemed proud of Marguerite for having them.

"I've been here twenty-five years," she said.

"Geoffrey told me."

"These were the dishes that Mrs. Gray would use for a large catered event outdoors." She held up a plain white plate, the ones we'd eaten on several nights earlier, the ones I liked the best. "Or for the staff."

She went through all the crystal glasses, explaining that the finest crystal glasses were the thinnest ones. They would shatter most easily.

I felt it was important to catalogue everything in the formal rooms downstairs. The dining room, the living room, and the library. It was another way of claiming possession. If I just glided along the surface of this existence, Taylor would find it easy to slide me out of the way. It was important to dig in, so that moving me out of the way would not be easy.

In the living room, I photographed and measured each painting and each drawing on the walls. I ran my hand over each silk throw pillow. I noted which ones were torn and which were not. I memorized the fabric patterns on each sofa. As if I were in a witness protection program, or a spy, and I had to rehearse all of my answers, so it was believable that this was my house.

At one end of the living room, glass shelves sparkled with crystal and silver objects. I picked up each porcelain figure, each silver bowl, and each crystal vase, and I examined it as if I were at a store and going to purchase it, so I could actively choose to keep it. I planned to set aside an hour every day for this activity.

The objects in the house would continue to suffocate me unless I convinced myself that these things belonged to me. I needed to allow that sensation to seep into my bones.

The objects were connected to the kind of life that the Grays had led. Maybe that was the key. The key to understanding this life and connecting with Geoffrey might lie in a relationship with these objects. That could be the route to a lasting partnership with him.

The library felt the most like Marguerite's room. A shrine to her. I could feel her presence in an especially strong way. It was where she'd gone to be on her own—to be inspired. So far, I'd rarely used the room, but when I did, I felt like I was trespassing.

The backs of the bookshelves were lined with cream-colored silk. A whole row of Marguerite's trophies and awards stood on the top shelf.

On the wall, there was a photo of Marguerite and Geoffrey with President Obama and one with President George W. Bush, as well as half a dozen framed magazine covers—*Vanity Fair, Town & Country, Vogue*—all featuring Marguerite.

Most of the shelves were filled with books about gardens and landscapes—many by famous garden designers from around the world. I arrived at the far corner, and I could see that four shelves were dedicated to Marguerite's eight books. At least a dozen copies of each one. *Rows of Roses, The Gardens at Rosecliff, A Night at Rosecliff, All About Peonies, Decorating With Flowers, Bring-*

ing the Outdoors In, Sight Lines, Morning Has Broken. I pulled the books out one by one. I'd seen all of these in bookstores, but I'd never had enough money to buy them. I'd always read gardening magazines and blogs and newsletters. But having this library in . . . my home, it was so much better than that. I could surround myself. Immerse myself.

I opened *Morning Has Broken* to the title page. On the following page were the words to the song:

Praise for the sweetness of the wet garden, sprung in completeness where God's feet pass.

I flipped further forward to a section on daffodils. *Daffodils work well under high branching trees, so light gets filtered in. . . . The depth of the bulb should be two or three times its width. In colder weather, plant the bulbs even deeper. . . . Leave daffodils to wither in place.*

I'd told her all of that. I'd been flattered that she was interested in what I had to say. But now I realized I'd just given her everything. Seeing our conversation in a published book was even more offensive than seeing it in her rough draft.

I could picture Marguerite now, with her phone in her hand. She might even have been recording me. I couldn't learn anything new from her books because they were full of my own ideas.

I opened up *Sight Lines.* It was the same thing. She probably thought she had a right to my knowledge.

It was dark outside when I left the library and walked past the living room. I glanced up at the painting. I didn't mean to.

As I looked up, it happened right away. Cold fingers on my neck. The sound of breathing.

And then, just as quickly, it was a picture on the wall again, exactly like the image that appeared on so many mugs and T-shirts. Just a picture.

CHAPTER TEN

I spent the majority of the day at my clients' home in Kent. It was a large sprawling estate, an old horse farm that had been deserted for some time. The current owners wanted to restore the estate to its former glory. They were working with a landscape architect. Brizzi's was hired to execute the design. Had this been a year earlier, I would have wanted to design the landscape myself, but I was so overwhelmed by the investigation and Taylor and trying to help Geoffrey. I was relieved that this job didn't require creativity.

When I returned to Rosecliff in the early evening, I was greeted by the sight of Rachel Hanna's Dodge Charger in the driveway. I walked around the outside of the house, looking in the windows. In the kitchen, Rachel was talking to Nina. She was talking to Nina.

I checked my phone and saw another text from Curtis. Call me.

I slipped into the house through the front door.

Tell your own story, I told myself.

I walked straight into the kitchen.

"Hello, Rachel."

"Hello, Phoenix."

Nina hovered nearby, looking nervous.

It didn't matter what Nina had seen. What she thought she'd seen. What mattered was who was confident, who was unwavering. "Nina, would you please get us each a cup of tea?" I said. "Thanks so much."

I led Rachel to the living room. This was my performance. I turned on all the lights and motioned for her to have a seat.

Upon seeing the painting above the fireplace, she gasped. She was stunned into silence.

After several moments passed, she spoke. "I've never seen this before," she said. "I wasn't . . . in this room before."

I placed three logs on the grate in the fireplace. "Other than the *Mona Lisa*," I said, "there is no image that has been reproduced as many times as this one."

"Is that right?"

"It's the expression on her face that's so hard to put your finger on." I lit a piece of newspaper and warmed the flue with it. "It's this anger or frustration and something like 'You will not lie to me anymore.'" I placed the burning newspaper under the wood. The logs went up in flames.

"Thank you again for your help," Rachel said. "I was hoping to fill in . . . um . . . your background a bit."

"My background?" I adjusted the logs on the fire with the poker.

"Yes."

I laughed. "Rachel Hanna. We were in French together three years straight. You know my background!"

"Right. Well, let's see. Tell me a little about your grand-mother."

Why was she asking about my grandmother?

She looked down at her spiral notepad and flipped to a blank page.

I sat on the sofa across from her. "You probably met her at some school event. Didn't you?" My grandmother had never attended a school event, but Rachel didn't know that.

"No."

"She was an incredible woman," I said. "She sacrificed a lot for me and Curtis."

Nina entered with a teapot and two cups on a silver tray. She placed the tray on the coffee table without making eye contact.

"Thank you, Nina," I said.

She nodded with a nervous jerk and left the room.

I poured us each a cup of tea, trying to ignore the pain be-hind my eyes.

Rachel frowned and the vertical lines between her eyebrows deepened. "I remember when your dad died."

What did she remember?

"That was hard," I said. "But my grandmother did her best. She looked after me."

"Right. And I know about the car accident. I was very sorry to hear about that."

Why was she bringing up the car accident? Did she remember me in the rehabilitation facility? Over and over, she'd seen me in my lowest, darkest moments. And that wasn't enough. She was asking for more.

After she left, I took a very long shower, imagining that the rest of the world would go away. All this weight on me. Imagining that it would be gone by the time I stepped out of the shower.

On my way downstairs, I overheard voices in the living room. It was Geoffrey and Taylor.

"I think Mom might still be alive if it weren't for her," Taylor said.

I froze outside the living room, out of view. My body stopped working.

"Darling," Geoffrey said quietly, "every person who's looked at this incident has declared your mother's fall an accident."

"The witness saw a second person."

The witness. The witness. There was a witness.

Nina. Nina told Rachel. Fuck.

"Hanna's interviewing everyone who's come within fifty miles of this place." Geoffrey paused. "But . . . Christ, at some point, we have to . . . what on earth could Phoenix have done to hurt your mother? We've known this woman for years."

"I have such a bad feeling about her."

"Taylor . . ."

Taylor started to cry. "Gabe and I talked last night. He said I was too intense. I told him, I lost my mother. I don't want to lose him, too. He said he couldn't have fun with me anymore."

"Sweetheart."

Taylor kept talking and crying. "Phoenix's presence here has turned me into someone I don't want to be. I'm serious, Dad. I'm asking you, I'm begging you to end it."

"She's good to me, Taylor."

"You don't see what I see."

I could feel my body shutting down. And then I told myself panicking was a luxury I didn't have time for.

Curtis texted me for the fourth time in three days. We need to talk.

He still didn't know where I was living.

I'd lost ten pounds since I moved into Rosecliff. I couldn't sleep. My cheeks were dark hollows, and I had a rash on my neck. I was telling myself to speak loudly and take up space—to show strength and confidence. But I was disappearing.

At dinner that night, Taylor was wearing a long skirt and blouse. Her hair was parted on the side.

"I talked to Serge," Taylor said to her father. "He's trying to reach you. Maybe it's about Greenhaven? He's planning to attend."

I thought back on the calls from Serge that Geoffrey had ignored. That letter from Serge. *You and I have no future.* Was Geoffrey a scorned lover? Bitter and resentful?

"Oh, right. Forgot to call him back," Geoffrey said distract-edly. "Russ asked me to join him for an afternoon sail tomorrow. Anyone else?"

What was Geoffrey's relationship with Russ? And why did Rachel care about Russ?

"I'm busy, thanks," Taylor said. She was wearing a mauve-colored lipstick, similar to the shade her mother used to wear. Did she take it from Marguerite's purse after she died? Or did she go out and buy the exact same one?

"It's some serious male bonding shit," Taylor said to me. "Don't bother going."

"That's not true," Geoffrey said.

"Mom never went on your sailing trips."

"She didn't like sailing."

Taylor rolled her eyes.

I decided to take Taylor's advice. I didn't know how to sail. But even if I had known, I didn't have the nerve to push myself into Geoffrey's rendezvous. "I'm busy, too."

Taylor poured herself water from a silver pitcher. "So, I have an update from Detective Hanna."

I nodded, because I didn't feel confident about how my voice would sound.

"And?" Geoffrey said.

"There's a witness," she said, "who saw a second person." Taylor paused and her eyes rested on me.

"Really?" I said.

"Someone who's about the same height as my mother." Taylor's eyes stayed glued to mine. "She'll probably interview every-one again, in light of this development."

No one spoke for a minute. Taylor finished her water and refilled her glass.

"I saw your posts on my mom's Instagram," Taylor said to me.

I waited a beat hoping that Geoffrey would jump in, but he didn't. I tried to speak without emotion. "Wren had some really good ideas. We both agree, above all, we need to respect your mother and her brand. Because her followers are looking for continuity." I looked to Geoffrey, again hoping he'd jump in, but he didn't.

I had to keep all defensiveness out of my voice, or Taylor would spot weakness, like a wolf smelling blood.

She was cutting her steak into very tiny pieces. "We can't ignore the fact that my mom's gone." The muscles of her jaw were tight.

I swished my red wine in my glass. I'd taken to having two shots of vodka before dinner, especially if I knew that Taylor would be joining us. With the alcohol already in my blood-stream, it was easier for me to drink my wine at a slower pace. But on this night, the vodka wasn't enough. I wanted to down the rest of the wine in my glass. "All our followers know what happened."

"Do they?" She took a small bite of steak and chewed.

Flames from several candles in crystal candlesticks illumi-nated the table. For a moment, the bottom half of Taylor's face was well lit, but not the top half. Her mouth looked like a dis-embodied puppet. "Are you trying to copy my mom's voice?"

"My posts are factual. About the property." I picked at a loose thread in the tablecloth.

Taylor took another bite of steak. The Grays all liked red meat. On this particular night, the steak was bloody through the center. It turned my stomach to look at it. I imagined Tay-lor's canine teeth growing longer, so that she could pick up a piece of bloody steak and tear it apart.

"One of these days," she said, "you'll begin to appear in the photos." She put her fork down and rested her fingers on the edge of the table.

"What would be wrong with that?" I tasted my red wine. I was getting used to wine from the Grays' collection. I was learn-ing to appreciate it.

She was digging her nails into the table. "This business was built on my mother." She spoke with quiet intensity.

"Darling," Geoffrey said, "I don't know enough about gar-dening to do this on my own. Phoenix is helping me."

Taylor's voice broke out of its careful restraint, into a higher pitch. "Are you kidding me?"

"Otherwise," he said gently, "we're wasting all your mum's work in building her brand."

"This isn't okay for Phoenix to, like, *inhabit* my mother." She stood up. "It's disrespectful and it's disgusting."

She walked to the doorway, then turned back and looked at me. "You are not wanted in this house."

She left the room. Geoffrey followed her.

I sat alone at the dinner table. My hand was trembling so much that I had to hold my wine with two hands. I finished one glass, and then another.

I felt feverish and my pillow was wet from perspiration. Our room was too warm. Since Taylor had arrived, I couldn't sleep more than a couple of hours at a time. I sat up in bed because I heard something. I felt a familiar pull. It was like a magnet.

Geoffrey was sleeping restlessly next to me. The heat off his body was like a furnace.

I looked at the clock on my nightstand. It was 2 A.M. I got out of bed, put on my bathrobe, and walked to the top of the stairs. I felt the portrait beckoning to me. The grand staircase was lit by nine brass sconces. Each one was cast to look like a hand coming out of the wall, holding a torch. The hands were charming in the daytime, but I was scared of them at night.

Nevertheless, I descended and entered the living room. A rose smell of overripe citrus accosted me. I stood in front of Marguerite. I saw her eyes blazing. I saw her lips, rounded, barely open. Was it an impulse, a thought forming? Or maybe she wanted to swallow someone whole. I could feel her mouth enveloping me. I could feel my body breaking down, dissolving into her saliva.

She hadn't withdrawn at all. I'd thought that she would. She still hung high above the fireplace, relishing her position. She saw me as a crude replacement for her.

I'd come to believe that I understood her. If I studied her

carefully, I could figure out what she wanted. Her eyebrows arched higher. It was so subtle. Ever so subtle. Her chin shifted down. At night, we usually left one small lamp on in the living room, in the far corner on a chest of drawers. As a result, Marguerite's face was lit unevenly. I could see her right eye much more clearly than the left. It drilled into me.

She was angry. I was taking what belonged to her. She wanted to expel me.

The wind was whistling. I could still hear the faintest whisper from the painting: *You can go.*

Back in our bedroom, I took the diamond bracelet out of the secret drawer and put it in the pocket of my bathrobe. Then I walked down the hall to Taylor's room. I heard a sound coming from inside her bedroom. She was typing very loudly.

I walked closer to the door, leaned against it, and put my ear up to it.

The door opened, and I staggered forward into the room.

"Hi," I said.

"Do you need something?" Taylor stood by the open door, wearing an oversized Yale T-shirt. Her mouth was turned down. She was a little taller than me, and she literally looked down her nose at me.

"Your typing woke me up." I could hear how ridiculous that sounded. How could it even be true? She probably thought I'd been spying on her. I read that computers can decipher what someone is typing, just by listening to the sounds of their keyboard. Each key makes a slightly different sound.

I wasn't actually spying. I'd been considering giving her the bracelet that I found. Like a peace offering to Marguerite. But after seeing the expression on her face, I decided not to.

"I thought it was something else at first," I said. "Another kind of noise. And I wanted to check and see what was wrong." Every word out of my mouth sounded like a lie. I told myself to shut up.

"Nothing's wrong," she said.

I touched the cool metal of the bracelet in my pocket. "I wanted to check on you."

"Sure." She backed up and turned one shoulder toward me, in a signal that I should leave.

In our bedroom, I returned the bracelet to the drawer.

I wondered if there was something rotten about my relationship with Geoffrey. Rotten at its core. And the rot would eventually eat its way to the surface. All the ugliness would be exposed for what it was.

CHAPTER ELEVEN

"It will be easiest if you exit through this door here because it's the widest." Taylor was directing two twentysomething men who were carrying one of the living room sofas.

The men set the sofa down to take a break.

I entered the living room, having just returned from work. "Hi."

"This is Dimitri and Tom." Taylor smiled. "They work for our upholsterer."

"This is Phoenix." She pointed to me. "She's my dad's . . . um . . . girlfriend."

The men nodded in my direction.

"Don't worry," she said to me. "Freddie promised one week, and we'll have the sofas back."

"Sofas?" I was confused about why she was moving the furniture and couldn't find the words to respond to her.

Dimitri pulled out his iPhone. "Do you mind?" he said to Taylor, motioning to the Kuhnert painting. "For my wife?"

"Of course," she said enthusiastically. "I'll take it!"

Taylor took his iPhone and photographed him next to the painting.

Dimitri and Tom lifted the sofa and walked to the door that was propped open, with Taylor directing them. I followed the three of them down the walkway and to the driveway.

We arrived at the truck. Dimitri and Tom were focused on wrapping up the sofa in blankets.

"My mom loved that fabric," Taylor said to me, "but it's threadbare and she was planning to replace it. So I picked out something similar. It's red velvet but has a subtle pattern and texture. So it's the same, but it's different." She laughed lightly.

"This isn't about the fabric," I said.

Taylor put her hand on my shoulder. "If my mom had lived two more weeks, she would have replaced that fabric. She was about to. Actually. So I'm just following through on her wishes. And you can't deny, the woman knew what she was doing when it came to interior design."

"But your mom didn't live two more weeks," I said, and then quickly regretted it.

Who was I to object to a red velvet fabric with a slightly different texture? I'd been in the house for less than two months.

I wanted to laugh, it was that ridiculous. I knew nothing about velvets, or fabrics, or patterns, or sofas.

But I couldn't allow her to see weakness, or she would never stop.

Taylor lifted her chin and tilted her head to one side, just like Marguerite used to. She was wearing a turquoise bead necklace that looked similar to one I'd seen before. Was it Marguerite's?

"What I mean is, here we are now," I said. "And we have to look at the situation we face . . . now."

Taylor widened her eyes.

"I'm just hoping," I said, "we can respect each other."

She tilted her head in the opposite direction. "I hope so, too." She paused like she was searching for her thought. "I guess respect means different things to different people." She licked her lips, but somehow, she didn't disturb her mauve lipstick.

Her eyes met mine. "I grew up here," she said. And then her tone changed. "I promise you, my dad will be happy to know that I arranged to have the sofas reupholstered. These things matter to him. It's my mom's legacy."

Taylor waved goodbye to Dimitri and Tom. I felt cold and small.

I needed my life. I needed my life to be mine.

If Wren was angry that I'd gone over her head to get Marguerite's login, she didn't let on.

"I'm thinking that one episode is filmed each month," I said to her as we walked the property. "And that episode focuses on what a gardener should try to accomplish in that month.

"So right now," I continued, "for example, if we were filming the March episode, we'd talk about pruning rosebushes or Russian sage."

"Cool."

After a momentary silence, I said, "Taylor's having a hard time. I want to be supportive."

Taylor had just left for New York for a couple of days, to move some belongings into her friend's apartment. She would be gone for two nights. And then she would be moving out for good at the end of March. Four days left until the end of March.

I'd been looking at my phone, checking the date several times a day, as if the date might change from one hour to the next. There was a clock ticking in my stomach, like the crocodile's in *Peter Pan*. I wondered if Wren could hear it.

"She can't let go of her mother," Wren said.

"Prolonging this whole thing," I said, "she's the one who's suffering the most." I was trying to find common ground with Wren. Some way to bond with her.

I looked to her for a reaction—a hint of how she felt about Taylor, how she felt about me. But I got nothing.

While Taylor was away, Geoffrey and I had dinner out together. We watched a movie at night. Before bed, I showed

Geoffrey the chapters on pruning and fences that I'd finished putting together for Marguerite's book.

"Smashing." His eyes were shining with what seemed like pride.

"It wasn't hard."

I was telling myself that there was drama in Geoffrey's youth, and it was all over now. Russ was just a good friend, a sailing buddy.

"Who else could do this?"

It was an awkward question because obviously Marguerite could have done it. She had been doing it.

"I think this book is going to be better than Marguerite's last one," he said. Then he put his forehead up against mine and looked in my eyes. "Don't forget we have the Greenhaven event around the corner. Buy something lovely."

This was going to be my first black-tie event ever. Even that wedding years ago, the one that was hosted by the Grays, that wasn't a black-tie event. I spent a long time deliberating on the dress and shoes to wear. I'd ended up deciding on a dark rose ankle-length dress and a pair of low heels. Both arrived safely, and I'd already tried the dress on. It was prettier than anything I'd ever owned.

Geoffrey and I talked through a timeline and calculated how long it would take for me to finish the book.

Was it possible that we could overcome everything? His past and my past and Rachel and Nina and Taylor. Was there any chance?

"Soon, we'll have lots of nights like this one," I said. "In a few days, it'll be just the two of us again."

"Hmm?"

"When Taylor leaves at the end of the month."

"Right." He sighed loudly. "The thing is, I talked to her a few hours ago, and um . . . it looks like her flat fell through, poor girl. Caroline's roommate's not leaving. So . . . um . . . Taylor will be with us for a bit, until, you know, she finds something else. Probably a few weeks."

I felt like the room was spinning. I had no ability to orient or reorient myself.

"I knew you wouldn't mind." He squeezed my hand. "Right? This is a rough time for her."

"It's not okay." I needed Taylor to be gone.

Geoffrey wrinkled his brow. "She just lost her mother."

"She's rude to me," I said. "You've heard her."

"Us together"—he motioned between us—"it feels too quick to her."

"Either we're together, or we're not," I said. "And it can't be one way when she's here and different when she leaves. If you're not comfortable with our relationship, I should move out."

"I'm just asking you to cut her some slack."

"No." I couldn't live with Taylor. I couldn't tolerate her.

"Darling, please." He squeezed his eyes shut tightly.

"I need an end date," I said. "It can't go on like this."

I couldn't hold on to my center if Taylor was in the house. She would try to confuse me. She would climb inside my head, and I wouldn't have the ability to present myself to Rachel Hanna *like I needed to present myself.*

The entire time that Taylor was away, her room called to me.

She had left the door open. So each time I walked by her room, I had an opportunity to glance inside. To think about which drawers, which cabinets I would look inside, when I had the chance. There were certain things I could see from the hall-way, like the childhood photos that were taped to her mirror. I wished that I'd spent more time in her room before she'd arrived, back in February. I would have had much more leeway back then, when it was a semi-vacated room. Now, it would be more damning if Geoffrey or Gilda or Nina saw me. There was so much downside to searching her room.

But when everyone was out of the house at the same time, I couldn't control the impulse.

I debated whether to close her door behind me. Or to leave it open. A closed door would look more suspicious from down the hall. If anyone thought about it. Because Taylor had left it open. But if I left it open and someone walked by and saw me looking through things, that would potentially be worse.

I ended up deciding to close and lock the door. If I heard someone trying to get in, I would have a chance to put every-thing away. And then sneak out, either onto the balcony, which led to exterior stairs, or out the bedroom door.

Taylor hadn't lived in this house for eight years, but all her things—her high school yearbooks, her chemistry notes, her glitter lip gloss, her hair scrunchies, her stuffed panda bear—all her childhood belongings still cluttered the surfaces in her room, as well as the shelves and the closet. In addition, there was another layer on top—her more recent belongings, along with some of Marguerite's clothing, that she'd brought with her on this extended visit. I was like an archaeologist deducing the time period of various fossils.

In addition to the photos on her mirror, there were some pinned to a corkboard over her desk. Some of her as a baby in her mother's arms. Her younger mother looked so much like Taylor, it was disconcerting. And it wasn't just their features that were similar. It was their body language and their attitude. The haughtiness. The entitlement. I wondered what it would be like to have that entitlement deep in my bones. So much so that it would be obvious to everyone, even in a photograph. I thought about the luxury of walking around in life believing that you were better. Knowing that you were. I remembered the feeling of that J.Lo ring on my finger. I'd felt like I was playing Chutes and Ladders and I landed on a ladder. I could rise up. The ring was a shortcut—to belonging, power, safety, visibility.

There were at least a dozen pictures displayed of Taylor and Marguerite together. And probably thousands more on Taylor's phone. She didn't appreciate the twenty-six years she'd had with her mother. She felt sorry for herself because it wasn't enough.

I had only ever seen *one* photograph of me and my mother together. The one with her pushing me on the swing. But that one picture had buoyed me all these years. It was a treasure I kept in my heart. I knew what was true about my mother and me. No matter what my grandmother said. I'd been able to block out my grandmother's words for most of my life. There were only a couple of exceptions.

I saw some photos of Geoffrey and Marguerite together. Marguerite and Serge. Geoffrey and Serge. And all three of them together. A twentysomething Marguerite was standing between the two men, her arms around them. She was laughing. But Geoffrey looked ill at ease, like he did in all the old photos of him and Serge that I'd seen. Had he been in love with Serge?

There were also some pictures of Taylor's friends, several with the same group of five teenage girls on a campus in a rural setting. One of them was probably Maeve. Maybe boarding school. A different group of older girls in a college dorm. One was probably Caroline. And a boyfriend showed up in later photos, post-college, maybe Gabe.

I wanted to pack up her room—to take down the posters and the pictures and the decals. Rip it all out. And move the furniture out as well. Moving the furniture would be nothing to me. I could carry a five-year-old maple tree by myself.

I pulled out a plastic bin from underneath the bed. It was full of schoolwork and artwork from when she was a kid. I took everything out of the bin and finally got to the very bottom.

That was when I saw it. All the jewelry. More than twenty jewelry boxes. I opened them one by one. A sapphire bracelet, a pearl necklace, a pair of emerald earrings, diamonds, rubies.

I'd never seen this kind of jewelry, all in one place. It was like a jewelry store.

Taylor had taken *all this,* and she was still sneaking around, looking for the J.Lo ring.

Later that day, Marguerite came back. This time, it was her breathing. I could see her chest moving, just slightly; but the worst part was the sound. The light exhalation. It was constant. If you didn't listen carefully, you might not notice. But the sound of her breath followed me. It was faint, but my hearing had always been sharp. Geoffrey couldn't hear what I could hear.

Marguerite wanted to silence, suffocate, smother me.

I wanted to say: No. This is my life.

But once I was standing in front of her, I lost all my strength. I couldn't handle the pressure. I tried to overcome the portrait's control. But then, within seconds, I realized it was not a choice. I was under an influence. The portrait held me in place. I felt weight on all my limbs and my torso. Marguerite wasn't letting me go. I wanted to tell her, it was your *own fault. You* did this. I wanted to escape from her grasp, but I was a prisoner.

Marguerite called me to her, and I had to approach the painting. I had a desperate and perverse desire to communicate with her. I needed her. And then with equal intensity, she repulsed me. I was compelled to look at the painting. But then after I'd looked, I felt sick and frightened of it, frightened of my own weakness and the portrait's strength, so that I had to turn away and hide my eyes. There was a force stronger than me that was calling to me and I was in thrall to it.

I looked in her eyes and saw the expression in them that I'd seen when she was about to hit me. The rage. I could feel the heat of her skin radiating off the canvas. She was heating me from the inside out. She was entering me and imbuing my body with heat. A hot burning sensation shot from my fingertips and toes, through my limbs, into my internal organs. She might kill me.

And then the rage changing to something else. Surprise. Shock. Fear. Fear as she slid backward and tried to stop herself, but it was too late by then. She was over the edge.

In the morning, I noticed Taylor's new car in the driveway. She was back from New York. When Geoffrey told me he'd bought her a BMW i4, I wanted to remind him about his financial worries. But I couldn't object to a gift for Taylor. I couldn't object to . . . anything really. It wasn't my place.

I was on my way out the door, headed to work, when my eyes landed on an abstract drawing that included several overlapping spiral shapes. It was hanging in a prominent spot in the gallery— noticeable from the dining room and the living room. I stopped in front of the drawing to study it. I hadn't seen it before. The spirals were linked together, almost connected, but not entirely. Like they could have detached and separated at any moment.

At the far end of the living room, Taylor was working. Her hair was down in waves around her shoulders, and she was wearing her now customary mauve lipstick.

"Welcome back," I called out.

She barely looked up and nodded. "Thanks."

"That drawing." I approached her and pointed to the gallery. "The one facing the front door. I haven't seen it before."

"Do you like it?" she said.

I was surprised by her question. She'd never seemed to care whether I liked something. Was she just being polite, or was she truly interested in my opinion?

"It's beautiful."

She shrugged. "I just hung it this morning."

Had she moved it from one wall to another wall?

"I bought it in New York yesterday," she said. "Serge and I were walking through one of my favorite art galleries, just a hole in the wall. And that drawing . . . It was only three hundred dollars. And it came with the pretty wooden frame. We used to have a print there, but my mother gave it to Gilda a couple of years ago."

My face felt hot. "You can't . . ."

She turned back to face me. "What?"

I needed to control my environment. I needed to hold on to my center. "Hang a drawing without . . ." I paused, trying to find the right words.

I was trying to find my way through a maze in the dark. I kept circling. Did I have any right to choose the art on the walls? And if I did, if it were all up to me, how would I even begin to make the decisions?

But . . . instinctively, I knew that Taylor would marginalize me as much as I let her. So, I had to push back, no matter what. Otherwise, she'd grow bolder by the day.

"Hmm?" She furrowed her brow.

"We need to discuss it first." I was trying to sound open and collaborative.

She raised her eyebrows. "But you said it's beautiful."

I could feel beads of sweat breaking out on my nose. I was perspiring through my T-shirt. "That's not the point." It was an effort for me to stay on the ground. To feel the soles of my feet touching the floor.

"I just didn't see it as the kind of thing you'd be interested in doing." Her expression was serious, but there was a glimmer behind her eyes.

I worked hard to control my face. "You didn't?"

"Finding a drawing. Buying a drawing." She motioned to the drawings and paintings on the walls nearby. "I mean, have you ever done it before?"

No. I'd never done it. "Your father . . . we're building . . . a home together—"

She cut me off. "Really?" She pushed her hair out of her eyes, then whispered, "A home. With the shared history of the last two months. Or was it longer than that?"

I felt hollow inside.

I went for a walk in the dark at ten. A walk in the dark down our driveway, and then on the road alongside the lake. Because

I couldn't bear to go back in that house. I couldn't bear to be around Taylor for one more minute.

I turned around. Up ahead I saw someone. I couldn't make out who it was. I couldn't even tell if it was a man or a woman. The person was a considerable distance away. They got closer and closer. It was probably one of our neighbors. Who else could it be? It might be her. I was scared of her. Maybe I was scared of how I felt about her. When I was honest with myself, I had to acknowledge that I hated her. Hatred is dangerous. So is fear.

The figure was closer now. It's possible that it was a teenaged boy. Or a young woman. Now I was about fifty yards away. I could see her form. I still couldn't see her face. She approached closer. I thought it was Taylor. Now I was about twenty yards away. Panic surged through my body. I thought about running in the opposite direction. My heart raced. My face was hot. I had a sick feeling in my stomach. I couldn't bear to speak to her. I couldn't bear to interact with her. Now she was ten yards away. Her eyes were down. Now five yards. Now one. She lifted her face and the moon lit up one side of it. It was Marguerite. Taylor. Marguerite.

"Dad's looking for you." A puffy cloud of air escaped from her mouth.

"Okay."

Her arms were crossed in front of her body. "He asked me to help find you."

I nodded.

"Why are you out here?" She narrowed her eyes, just like Marguerite used to. "It's dark and cold. He thinks it's weird."

"I'll be home soon." I hadn't been aware of the cold until I saw Taylor. But I realized I could hardly feel my fingers in my gloves.

"Please come back now." She was standing so close to the edge of the slope. Really only one foot away. I wondered if she realized that. It was so dark out. She didn't remember this road perhaps. She didn't realize how precarious it was.

I pulled my hood over my head and put my hands in my pockets.

"I don't care what you do. But Dad is worried."

"Okay."

"So will you follow me?" She turned and walked back in the direction of the house.

No. I wasn't going to follow her. No.

When I returned, Geoffrey was sitting at the kitchen table reading a book about sailing. He looked up. "Bloody hell, Phoenix."

I could barely feel my hands or feet. My face was burning from the cold. "I needed some time on my own."

"You don't care that I'm worried about you?" There was disappointment and accusation in his voice.

I didn't tell Geoffrey that I was scared of his daughter. How could I?

He frowned. "You could just let me know what you're doing," he said. "Why are you out there at night?"

"I needed some air." I'd been trying to handle my relationship with Taylor on my own. Trying not to drag Geoffrey into it.

"What?"

"The stench inside this house, it was too much."

He startled, like I'd slapped him. "What's gotten into you?"

I didn't want to back down. "Your daughter's presence in the house is hard to take."

"What did she do?"

I tried to be rational. "She doesn't want me here."

He shook his head.

"We need to decide on some limits." I sat down at the table opposite Geoffrey, still wearing my coat, hat, and gloves and still freezing. "She can't stay indefinitely."

The words sounded absurd coming out of my mouth, but I tried not to falter.

He batted the air aside with his hand, like he was waving a gnat out of his face. "She doesn't even want to."

I took off my gloves. "I need to know what this is. Our relationship."

"What this is?"

I rubbed my palms against each other to warm them. "I want something solid. Something constant. I want to know I can depend on you."

"Of course, you can."

"Your daughter talks down to me." I took his hand in mine. "You and I have to be united."

"Phoenix . . ."

"If you can't manage your daughter, then I have to take some time away."

"I'll talk to her." He squeezed my hand.

"I refuse to live in a house that doesn't belong to me—a house your daughter considers more hers than mine." In that moment, I wavered. I didn't know whether I was bluffing. "And if you agree with her, then, I'm sorry, I have to go."

After only two months, by what right could I call this house mine?

But . . . I had to say it *was* mine. And say it loudly.

CHAPTER TWELVE

Geoffrey had refused to take anyone's side. He'd remained neutral, but that wasn't good enough.

It was a strange feeling, returning to my New Milford house. Like when I was twelve and went back to my kindergarten classroom, and I was surprised that it was all so small.

The brick pathway and patio that I had put in still looked good. That was one of many odd jobs I did for my grandmother as a kid, in exchange for room and board.

I was disturbed by how the kitchen looked. I'd never noticed that the floor tiles were bubbling up. The fifty-year-old laminate kitchen counters looked their age. The overhead light was harsh and practically green. It was so dirty compared to Rosecliff.

Now I understood, if there was a scale of how nice things

could be, my grandmother's house wouldn't even appear on the scale.

Curtis showed up in his typical costume of worn-out jeans and worn-out shoes. "So, what's up? You've been MIA."

Finally, I had to acknowledge to him where I'd been living.

He tilted his chin down and looked at me from the top of his eyes, a mannerism he'd had since I could remember. "You're kidding me, right?"

"I'm not kidding."

"You think it's a good idea to be hanging around there?"

"I'm not hiding from anything."

"But, actually, you are though."

I placed two mugs of strong coffee on the kitchen table, one with milk for me and one black for Curtis. I sat opposite him. I used to hear from friends that Curtis bragged about me when I wasn't around. He talked about how smart and successful I was. When friends told me that, my heart would hurt a little bit.

He circled his finger around the rim of his mug, and then circled it in the opposite direction. "So . . . um . . . Rachel Hanna's still out there talking to people."

Suddenly, I had a sour taste in my mouth. Like heartburn, but worse. "How do you know?"

"She called me again. I mean, I just picked up the phone, and she was like 'Hello-o-oh, this is the detective!' I couldn't hang up on her."

I felt lightheaded.

"She wanted to know all this shit going way back . . . about Mom and Dad. Were we close as a family?" He rolled his eyes. "She's really mining for stuff."

Blood was emptying from my brain.

"Same with Grandma. Every damn little thing about 'Did we love our grandmother?'" He added, "I said you adored her."

Why was Rachel asking about our grandmother again?

He bit his bottom lip. "Just thinking, maybe . . . keep your head down," he said, "for now. Right?"

I found out one guy on my crew was allergic to bee stings when he had an anaphylactic reaction. I felt like I was having an anaphylactic reaction to Curtis. It was the band of compression around my rib cage. And my tongue felt like it didn't belong in my mouth.

The afternoon my grandmother died, there'd been nothing unusual about that car ride. Grandma was talking, and I was listening. "Your mother couldn't stand to hold you," she said. "She couldn't stand it."

I didn't see the truck. The sun was in my eyes, and I couldn't see.

I was trapped in a hospital bed, with eighteen broken bones, for nine months.

Every doctor said the same thing. A miracle I survived.

Curtis shifted in his seat. "Listen, Maya has some friends visiting next week. So, can I crash here for a few nights?" I could hear a note of entitlement in his voice. Or was that my imagination?

I took a sip of coffee and burned my tongue. "Sure."

"Thanks, Fee-Fee. And one more thing. Can you spot me a hundred?"

I looked down at my lap. "I wish I could help you out, but . . ."

"You're living in a fucking castle." He smiled.

I looked him in the eye. "It's not my money." A fly was buzzing around the kitchen. It landed on the windowsill. I stood up to look for my flyswatter. But then changed my mind and sat back down, so that I could get this conversation over with.

Curtis frowned. "You need more cash in your own account."

I noticed a small chip in my coffee mug. "I'm fine."

"How is . . . what's his name?"

"Geoffrey?"

"Nice guy. I met him once, the summer I worked for Frank."

"His daughter is visiting," I said. "There's a little tension between us."

"His daughter?"

"Yes."

"How old is she?"

"Twentysomething," I said. "She's a lawyer."

"You don't want to fuck with a lawyer."

I felt a motor going in my stomach.

He finished the rest of the coffee, then stood and turned to go.

"Don't worry about Taylor," he said on his way out. "You can handle her."

It was a few minutes after he left that I realized I hadn't said her name.

For the next few days, I threw myself into work to avoid thinking about Geoffrey and Taylor and Marguerite. It was late March and Brizzi's was in overdrive. We had to remove and compost dead annuals, cut back the ornamental grasses and shrubs, spray fruit trees, replenish mulch, not to mention follow through on all newly initiated projects.

On my third day staying at my New Milford house, I received another voicemail from Rachel Hanna in the late afternoon. After one vodka tonic, I forced myself to call her back. I left a message. I said I was pulled onto a project in Massachusetts and would be working there through the week. I would meet with her when I returned. Brizzi's had one project in Massachusetts, and I'd already made a point of telling Frank that I'd be the one liaising with the client.

Rachel wouldn't be happy. But it was something.

I collected two large bags of my old clothing, along with some old sheets and blankets, to give to the Salvation Army, and I put the blue sweatshirt and the jeans in one of those bags. First, I spilled some mustard on the sweatshirt and jeans, then tried to wash it off, so it would look like I had a real reason for giving it away, if someone were really going to dig deep. I'd given clothing to Salvation Army on several occasions, after my father died, after my grandmother died, and a few other times, too.

I was on my second drink when I saw, through the kitchen window, Geoffrey's Audi pull into my grandmother's driveway. I hadn't visualized him here at my house. I felt naked. Exposed. He knew I didn't have much money. But knowing and seeing are two different things. My eyes landed on the grout stains and the peeling laminate of the counters. The inside of my house was not presentable. I stepped outside and surveyed the garden, seeing it through his eyes. It wasn't as stunning as Rosecliff, but it was charming. I'd taken a lot of care with each corner of it. I didn't mind him seeing the garden.

He got out of the car. He was wearing khakis and a polo shirt. It was a warm night.

I walked toward him.

He opened his arms slightly, as if he was waiting to see if I'd embrace him.

I kept my arms by my side. "Hi."

He lightly touched my shoulder. "Aren't you going to invite me in?"

"Uhhhhh, nope."

I saw his eyes land on the weeping willow, which was already leafing out quite nicely. And then the Adirondack chairs underneath. A client had thrown the chairs in the garbage eight years earlier, and I'd salvaged them. But seeing them through his eyes, I kicked myself for holding on to them all these years. It wouldn't have killed me to buy some new chairs.

"Phoenix." He laughed. "You're kidding me. I want to see your house." He gestured toward it.

The siding on my house was probably fifty years old, but I'd never noticed how bad it looked until now. "No, it's . . . I had some plumbing issues."

Geoffrey walked toward the back door.

"No." I held his arm firmly. "No."

He stopped and turned to me. "Then come back with me." He cupped my face in his hands.

"I've got a lot going on here." I gestured in the direction of the house.

"Well . . ." Geoffrey continued toward the back door. "If you don't come back with me, I'm going to have to move in *here*."

I tried to laugh. "You'd hate it here."

"Not if I'm with you." He stopped again, put his hand on the back of my head, and kissed my forehead. "I miss you."

"I need to know when Taylor's leaving."

He looked anxious to please. He wrapped his arms around me. "I'll take care of it."

"I need to know."

"I have something for you." He unzipped his jacket pocket and reached his hand inside. "I want you to know what you mean to me."

He pulled out a small blue velvet box and handed it to me. I recognized that box. I had opened it often. I knew exactly what was inside.

The J.Lo ring.

I had a huge rush of hopefulness.

He placed it on my ring finger. I'd gone for a manicure the

prior week, for the first time in ten years. How had I known? Still, the pads of my fingers and my palms were as hard and rough as sandpaper.

"Do you like it?" Geoffrey said.

"Is this an engagement ring?"

His hand wrapped around my waist. "It's whatever you want it to be."

What did the ring mean?

I tried to block out thoughts of Serge and Russ and the red-headed woman and the brunette. Was he still in love with any of them? Was he still in love with Marguerite?

Did Geoffrey care about me?

I could choose to believe that he did.

With this ring, maybe I could manage Rachel Hanna. Maybe the ring would make me safe.

I could see myself wearing it. Standing under Titania's bower, in a gauzy full-length pink dress, gold sandals, and the J.Lo ring. I could see myself. Oxlips, violets, and musk roses surrounding me, with woodbine overhead. Hundreds of guests lined up to tour the gardens.

I could see myself. The lady of the manor.

"I don't want to be a guest at Rosecliff," I said. "I need to feel like I belong there."

Taylor saw me wearing the ring at dinner the following night, but she didn't say anything. She pretended she didn't notice it, but I knew she did.

"I spoke to Serge," she said. "He's planning to stay over here the night before Greenhaven."

Geoffrey smiled. "Great."

"Why aren't you returning his calls, Dad?"

"Just busy, that's all."

"It's just weird. I mean . . . like you're avoiding him?"

"No, sweetheart. It's not personal. I'll ring him tomorrow."

"Okay. I'm going to arrange to have the leak in the gallery patched up," she said to her father. "It's been like that for the last nine months." She ate a small potato off her fork in one bite.

"Thanks, sweetheart."

It was happening again. This wasn't acceptable. Sidelining me like I was no one. "I'll take care of that." I wiped my mouth with the inside of my napkin, and then returned it to my lap folded over, as I'd seen in one of the YouTube videos I'd watched on table manners.

Her eyes landed on my diamond ring again.

She carefully cut a piece of chicken, the exact same size as the one she cut before. "You don't know the contractor."

"I'll figure it out."

"No, I'll do it." She took a bite and chewed.

"Geoffrey," I said. "Please tell her."

"Tell her what?" He was pretending that he hadn't been paying attention to the conversation, but I knew that he heard everything.

"Our conversation." I tried to catch his eye. "That this is my . . . my house."

A silence fell over the table. I didn't even believe it myself. But the pull of the undercurrent took me there, and I was glad it did. Even if the consequences . . . no matter the consequences.

"Who cares who calls the fucking contractor?" Geoffrey said.

"Geoffrey, tell her," I said. "Tell her."

"Phoenix will make the calls," he said finally.

"Dad . . ."

Geoffrey leaned back in his chair. He pushed his hair straight back with his fingers.

Taylor gripped her wineglass with such ferocity. For a moment, I thought she might crush it with her bare hand. "Mom's memory lives here."

"Look, sweetheart . . ." Geoffrey reached his hand out to take Taylor's, but she pulled back from him. "We can talk this through. We can get to the other side."

"This isn't right." Taylor took a large sip of wine. "Phoenix just coming in here. This house and the business—these things are Mom's domain." She pushed her chair back away from the table. "And in case you forgot, Marguerite by the Lake is a business revolving around *Marguerite*."

"Taylor." I tried to keep my voice even. "The platforms need gardening content."

Taylor stood up. She had two bright spots of pink in her cheeks. "This is about so much more than a fucking tulip. My mother had a vision. *Marguerite by the Lake.* Yes, she liked flowers. But she liked a lot of things. Millions of people admired her. It wasn't all about gardening tips. Do you think Phoenix can inspire millions?"

"I know this is a hard situation," Geoffrey said.

She froze and a mask hardened over her face. "You can hire any gardener off the street to come up with gardening tips. But you can't replace my mother. I won't allow you to replace my mother."

I tried to swallow, but I felt like I was choking. The ignorance, the disrespect. People could spend several lifetimes learning about botany and horticulture. But in one sentence, she'd grouped me with the least-skilled gardeners.

I'd thought she would cower when she saw the ring on my hand. I'd thought everyone would cower. But it wasn't working like I thought it would. The ring wasn't working.

"Taylor, sweetheart," Geoffrey said. "We're trying to attend to her legacy. And . . . I . . . we'd love your help and your participation with that, too."

Taylor sat back down, her eyes glazed over. Geoffrey stood and walked behind her chair. He wrapped his arms around her shoulders from behind.

"Taylor has a lot going on," I said in a matter-of-fact tone. "The bar exam. A new job. Geoffrey, I don't think we should burden her with the business right now."

"Her participation can be . . . modest," he said.

"Geoffrey," I said. "Tell her what we discussed."

"Let's save that for—"

"Your father and I are engaged," I said. "We're engaged to be married."

I placed my left hand across my chest, close to my neck, so that she would have a full view of the ring. No shrinking. No hiding.

Taylor turned her head to look at Geoffrey for confirmation.

He shrugged. "Well . . . it's something that could happen at some point."

"Geoffrey," I said, "you promised me." I couldn't allow him to betray me.

"Are you engaged?" Taylor asked.

"Yes," I said.

"It's nothing definite," Geoffrey said at the same time.

"This is what I feared." She closed her eyes and put her palms on her forehead. "Let me point out to you, Dad, that in a matter of months, Phoenix has taken over everything that was Mom's. Why the fuck is she wearing Mom's ring? You don't see any of it. You're just clueless. I'd like to know . . ." She turned to look at me. "I'd like to know, for example, what time you left the house the night that Mom died. I'd like to talk with your alibi. I'd like a background check."

"Honey," Geoffrey said. "Please."

I tried to retain composure. Treat her like a child. Like a willful teenager. Dismiss her. Dismiss. But it was more and more difficult to dismiss her.

The ring wasn't the effective tool I needed it to be. The ring wasn't working the way I thought it would.

My tongue was too big in my mouth. I thought I might choke.

"I want information," Taylor said. "If I can't get it from Hanna, I'll hire a private investigator. Trust me when I tell you, I'm not going to stop."

None of our roses had bloomed yet. But the following morning when I woke up, I felt nauseous from the smell of decaying roses, like I had all winter long, only now it was growing stronger, more intense. It was impossible to ignore.

In the living room, I looked at the piano music that Taylor had been playing. I'd always wanted to play the piano. I thought about Taylor's childhood compared to mine. She had no idea of all her advantages. It's too late to learn an instrument when you're an adult. It's too late for a lot of things.

"She's distraught over Marguerite's death," Geoffrey had said the night before, when we were alone in our bedroom. "I'm asking for compassion." He repeated, "Compassion," as if I didn't have any.

I looked out the window. We'd uncovered the patio furniture so that we could have dinner outdoors sometimes.

And then. I looked at the painting.

The colors changed. Marguerite's dress, her face, her hair, her shoes, her tense hand clasping the shears, every part of Marguerite, the colors became darker, stronger, so that her figure was distinct from the rest of the painting and the background of the lake and surrounding hills faded to white. And all I could see was her figure becoming darker and darker. And then, Marguerite, she wouldn't stay inside the painting. She was pressing out of it. Her lips, teeth, and tongue forming words that escaped from her mouth and reverberated through the room.

I know a bank where the wild thyme blows . . .

Her face pushed up against the canvas, stretching forward beyond its frame, so that the painting transformed into a frieze. It seemed like the canvas would crack.

Where oxlips and the nodding violet grows . . .

I choked.

I turned and ran. I ran so fast and ran straight into Gilda. "Hello, Miss Sullivan."

I turned toward the powder room, pulled Gilda in behind me, and locked the door behind us.

"Miss Sullivan . . ."

"Please be quiet." I put my finger to my lips and whispered from inside the bathroom. There was a pounding on the door. "That's her."

"What's her?"

"She's trying to break in." I whispered more loudly, because she didn't seem to understand.

"Miss Sullivan," Gilda said. "There's no one." She unlocked the door and opened it.

"Noooooo!" I screamed.

A strong blast of air pushed me back.

But then I opened my eyes, and I saw no one was there.

CHAPTER THIRTEEN

"It was Nana's ring," Geoffrey said calmly. "Your mum didn't care for it. She never wore it."

"Mom assumed you'd give it to me."

I was on the patio off the kitchen, pruning the large viburnums, all of which had bloomed early because of the heat spell. Temperatures were expected to get up in the eighties. The French doors were open, so I could hear Geoffrey and Taylor in the kitchen through the screen doors, but my view of them was blocked.

I closed my eyes, allowing a butterfly to circle my face. When I opened my eyes, I realized it was actually a wasp.

"You have loads of her jewelry," he said. "And you never wear any of it."

"It's a betrayal." Taylor's words came out with an uncontrolled duck-like sound.

"I'll make sure it goes to you eventually."

"Dad . . ."

"I'll tell Phoenix that's the way it has to be," Geoffrey continued speaking gently.

"I want that in writing." Taylor's speech was strident. "The ring goes to me. It stays in the family."

I didn't hear what Geoffrey said in response.

If it was my ring, it was my ring.

I took a bath in Marguerite's bathtub. Would I ever think of it as my tub? Probably not. But it was better than her shower. Lately, when I was showering, I felt cold fingers on my neck.

I left my phone in the bedroom on purpose. The sight of it filled me with apprehension. A part of me wanted to throw it in the lake. My phone brought me problems, but I needed to know what the problems were, so that I could find my way out of the abyss of this investigation.

I got out of the bath and applied expensive lotion to my body, like Marguerite probably would have. When I looked in the mirror, my ribs, elbows, and hips were sharp bones sticking out from my body. I stepped on the bathroom scale. I'd lost twenty-three pounds in two months. These days, I was careful to wear loose clothing that disguised my body.

I had dark circles underneath my eyes, worse than Frank's. In the last two weeks, I'd started to wear undereye concealer, though I'd never worn makeup before. If I didn't, I looked like a ghoul. I ran a brush through my hair twice, but I stopped because too much hair came out in the hairbrush.

When I walked into the bedroom, Geoffrey was holding my phone in his hand. He started when I entered and put it down on the dresser. "Just checking the weather."

Why was he looking at my phone? What did he see?

Once dressed, I sat on the small patio on the front side of the house, the side that didn't face the lake. A direct view of the lake tended to contribute to my anxiety.

On Instagram, there was a selfie of Taylor, in jeans and a sweater, standing where the new patio was to be built. She was holding a large mug.

Looking forward to my morning cappuccino here, once we build our patio. A wide semicircle with lake views. A cozy room outdoors.

No one told me that Taylor was going to start posting—that she was going to steal my ideas and present them as her own, exactly like her mother did.

If I'd kept a lower profile, maybe she wouldn't have come after me. She wouldn't have tried to push into my territory.

Only now . . . What could I do to stop her?

I needed some information that would help me in this battle.

I had a feeling that Marguerite's email login would be the same as her social media login.

I was wrong. It wasn't the same. I tried eight variations and none of them worked.

It wasn't clear to me what I would look for if I did get into her email. What did I want to find out?

I was about to give up, when on my ninth try, I succeeded.

I saw a lot of back-and-forth with Wren, Amar, and Basil. To and from Taylor. Emails related to Marguerite's gardening show and recent book. A number of notes to and from Serge. There was one from Serge, dated mid-October of last year.

> *Marguerite, Thinking of you. I'll do anything you need me to do. Anything.*

I reread the email several times. I felt nauseous. *I'll do anything you need me to do.* What did that mean?

I found another note from Serge, dated August of last year, with the subject line *Greenhaven.*

> *Maybe they're accounting errors. Regardless, you can't blame yourself. Geoffrey placed his trust in a con artist. I think you have to cut your losses.*

Accounting errors? Who was the con artist? Was it Russ?

I heard the sound of a car and looked up to see Curtis's 2008 Hyundai coming up the driveway. I hadn't given him the Rosecliff address.

I walked briskly through the bluestone courtyard, down the granite walkway leading out to the motor court.

Curtis opened the car door and stepped out. He looked slightly better than usual, like he'd had a shower and shave.

"Phoenix!" He opened his arms wide to give me a hug.

"What are you doing here?" I whispered.

"Just stopping by to see the best sister in the world." He smiled. "Is there anything wrong with that?"

"Please leave."

"Come on, Phoenix," he said. "I drove all the way over here."

From the pathway into the woods, I saw Taylor returning from a walk. She was wearing white jeans and a fleece jacket, an outfit I was sure I'd seen her mother wear.

She stopped in front of Curtis and her mouth dropped open. "Curtis!" Her face lit up with a smile.

I felt like someone was playing a trick on me.

And then she put her arms around him like he was an old friend.

What was going on? Curtis and Taylor were . . . what . . . what were they to each other?

"Oh my God. Taylor!" Curtis laughed.

"Do you know each other?" I asked.

"Yeah," Taylor said, beaming. "Wow. It's been a while."

I couldn't take it in. The trickle of information that was making its way into my brain was frightening me more than anything else had—more than Rachel Hanna. More than Nina.

And I was simultaneously so enraged. I wanted to scratch and claw at Curtis. How dare he keep this from me? After all I'd done for him. And then to show up here. To show up here with this mixed loyalty. This subtle implication that he might be on Taylor's side. I wanted to scratch his eyes out.

Curtis turned to me. "The summer I worked for Frank," he said, "I spent a lot of time here."

"You never mentioned Taylor."

"I didn't?" He turned to Taylor. "Phoenix is my sister." He held his hand out, as if he was presenting me.

"Your sister?" She widened her eyes. She was confused. "Oh. Wow."

"I'm very sorry about the death of your mom." Curtis put his hand on Taylor's shoulder. "I heard about it from Phoenix."

There was some kind of affection between them. Or some kind of intimacy.

"You did?" I saw a flicker of what I thought was curiosity in her expression.

"She told me . . ." He paused.

"Yes?" Taylor had become slightly more alert and focused. "Do you want to come inside? For a glass of . . . something."

My attention was heightened to a sharp point, waiting for the response.

"Sure," he said.

"Great," Taylor said. "I'll just get cleaned up."

Taylor walked ahead and Curtis hung back with me, until she was far enough ahead that she could no longer hear us.

"You look like you saw a ghost." Curtis smiled.

"You know Taylor? What the fuck are you doing?" I spoke

softly, aiming my words at the ground so the sound wouldn't carry.

"Not that well," he said. "She was having a hard time and . . . It was a confidential situation."

"Confidential, my ass."

"She needed someone, and I was there," he said. "I can help neutralize your relationship. She likes me."

We were close to the house. Once he was inside, it would be impossible to get rid of him. I turned and looked him in the eyes. "Get out of here."

He smiled. "If you want my help," he said as he was leaving, "I've got your back."

I ran inside and barely made it to the toilet before I vomited.

I felt as though Taylor could see my insides. As if every horrible thing that had ever happened to me, every horrible thing I'd ever done, she had access to all of it. She had access to Curtis's brain. That meant she had access to me. To my past, my thoughts, my actions, my desires. All the ugliness that existed inside me. All the ugliness that I wanted to put behind me. Taylor could get to that information now. Because she was friends with Curtis. She'd been friends with Curtis. Maybe they'd been lovers? Was that possible?

"I talked to Curtis," Frank said at our weekly meeting.

The sound of Curtis's name was like nails on a chalkboard.

"He wanted some advice on his restaurant."

"Yes?"

"He stopped by. He asked me, you know, permits, all this, I know this stuff. I said I'd introduce him to the right people. I know all of them."

"Don't put yourself out."

"For you and your brother, I'll do anything."

"But . . ." I wanted to say, don't trust him. But I held the words in my mouth.

Frank served me a plate of lasagna. He was old-school and lunch was a cooked meal, same as dinner.

"You're too skinny," he said. "You've gotta eat something."

We sat in his kitchen. The smell of lasagna was making me sick. I pushed the food around on my plate to make it look like I was eating.

"So, the other thing is," Frank continued, "he's like me. Doesn't believe the stories."

"Hmm?"

"Mrs. Gray. You know. He said he's friends with the girl. He's worried about the girl."

The passage in my throat was getting narrower, too constricted.

"Curtis and me, we both talked to the lady detective again. So did Teddy and the rest of the guys. So did Mrs. Spielman."

I had an image of the blood in my arteries slowing down, like it didn't have the stamina to make it all the way to my heart.

"Mrs. Spielman?"

"She had some new information for the detective."

I held my face still. Like stone. Lips drawn together, like I was drinking from a straw.

Frank continued: "I asked Curtis what he knew. He said, 'Phoenix is the one who knows about that night.'" Frank's words expanded to fill the room. "'Ask Phoenix. She was there.'"

I backed up. Into a corner. Hoping that I could melt away, vanish, if I backed into a corner that was dark enough. I pressed my back against the wall.

He crossed the room and put his hands on my shoulders. "You going to pass out?"

I took two steps forward into the light.

"You're sick." He pointed to a chair. "Sit down right there."

"What did you say?"

"I said, put your bum in the seat. Right there."

"What did you . . ."

He walked to his bar and poured us each a glass of brandy. "Here, kid," he said. "Drink."

I'd been moving through a fog for two weeks, trying to avoid Rachel's questioning and Marguerite's attacks. Now, the connection between Curtis and Taylor had pushed me to the point that I was barely functioning.

I sat by myself on the porch at Rosecliff. The pink sky cast a pink glow over the white stone of Helen's house across the lake. The more I stared at the house, the more saturated the color appeared to me—deep pink, almost magenta. After a few minutes, I couldn't bear to look at it anymore. Helen's house was growing in its toxicity. Helen had information for the detective. Nina told her what she saw. Helen talked to the detective.

The Marguerite Gray shrub roses were now blooming. It was only March. I'd never seen any roses bloom in March. Maybe because Marguerite had been so particular about where and how we planted these roses, with the optimum sunlight and best drainage. Or maybe because we'd had a whole week with temperatures in the eighties, like an apocalypse on its way.

Marguerite had been using the scent of her roses to poison me. She was channeling her fragrance into the house through air ducts. The roses had been making me sick, the same way that the painting had been making me sick. My tremor was practically constant. Marguerite was causing me pain. I wanted her to suffer as much as I was. I wanted to destroy the roses.

But roses, flowers, plants, they were my children. I worked so hard to nourish them and give them the very best chance. I understood them. I cared deeply for them. And the Marguerite roses were my pride and glory.

They were deep velvety crimson, with loose shell-like petals, and a strong Old Rose scent with notes of lemon and wine. Their fragrance was growing stronger every day. At this point, I could smell them from across the lawn. They dominated and displaced the scent of every other flower. I had smelled them through every season of the year, even in the house, in the winter, when they were supposedly dormant.

There are things one can do to kill a plant. The most effective is glyphosate solution. I put some in a nondescript plastic misting sprayer, and I applied it to the roses. I felt I had no choice. With each spray of the solution, I visualized snuffing out this spirit that was torturing me. Three days in a row, I applied the solution. On the third day, I did not see a noticeable change. In fact, it seemed as if they were stronger and healthier than before. I questioned whether I had mistakenly put fertilizer in the spray bottle, instead of the solution. So I repeated the entire process. This time, I triple-checked that it was the glyphosate solution. This time, I didn't dilute it. It was twice as strong as the time before. Again, three days in a row, I sprayed the solution. And at the end of the three days, I saw no difference in the roses.

Late at night, I woke up and went outside. I circled the rose bed, like a dog. I ripped one of the blooms off.

Stop it, I told myself. What are you doing?

I ripped another bloom off, involuntarily. My hand moved out from my body toward the red bloom. It was like a bloody tumor. And another and another. After each one I removed, I planned to stop. I held my hands behind my back, linking my fingers together. And then I looked at those blooms, each one a hideous growth, and I couldn't contain myself. Each one needed to be blasted away. I held one of my wrists with the other. Trying to restrain my hands. I told myself to leave, to go back to bed.

But I couldn't. And then it was like a current passed through my body. And I plunged my arms into those bushes, ignoring the thorns, with no gloves and no protection, and I ripped and clawed and savaged the flowers with my bare hands. I had to exterminate them.

Hours later, I lay on the grass. The sun was beginning to come up. I didn't have much time until someone saw me.

I pulled the winterizing blankets from the garden shed. I draped the blankets over the beds. No one at the house would know the difference. But Brizzi's crew would be showing up in two days. My arms were raw and covered in cuts, from my fingers to my shoulders. I could get by with wearing long sleeves. Maybe. But when Rachel Hanna came to talk to me, she would see the scratches on my wrists and hands. She might guess what had happened.

The next morning, Taylor smiled at me. "What did you do to the Marguerite roses?"

I froze. I couldn't read her. What did she know? What did she guess?

"I looked underneath one of those blankets this morning," she said. "Wow."

I nodded again, not sure what else I could do.

Her eyes landed on my ring. I never took it off anymore. I was scared that she might come in my bedroom and take it.

Did Taylor talk to Curtis again? Did they have plans to meet?

Curtis was the black sheep. Why did Taylor like him more than me?

When she went back upstairs, I went outside and lifted the blankets to inspect the roses. The blooms had doubled in number and each one had doubled in size. They had pushed out beyond the borders of their bed, too, into the other flower beds nearby.

I wanted to say to Geoffrey, don't you see that this is Marguerite, wreaking havoc? She wants to kill me. She will take all the oxygen, all the air, and the only air left will be the putrid, rotting air filled with the smell of old, dank fruit and death.

Would I shrivel up and turn into a worm who would make its way through the earth here and fertilize all the roses for Marguerite's glory? Her energy could not be suppressed. How would I kill these flowers who refused to be killed?

I pulled all the blankets off the roses. And even as I did so, I felt it was possible that the roses were growing fatter, wider, fuller and multiplying. Before my eyes. The roses each with their delicate, soft petals, but each petal was almost the size of my hand now. And each bloom was almost the size of a cantaloupe. And I felt the roses talking to me and they were saying: *We will not be stopped. We are here. We know you.*

When Rachel Hanna looked at the Marguerite shrub roses, she might make the connection. She might realize that the roses were unspooling and releasing to tell the world.

I wished that I could go back in time and reverse everything. I wished that Marguerite was still alive. I could pack up my belongings and go. I'd return the J.Lo ring. I'd return to buying what was on sale at the grocery store, to margaritas with Curtis, to my pink bedroom. It all sounded so much better than where I'd landed.

But there was no way to go, except straight ahead. Straight ahead to . . . what?

In the living room, I walked around without turning on the lights, familiar enough with the room now that I could circle it blindfolded, avoiding each chair and table. I ran my hand over the grand piano and noticed a very fine layer of dust. I sat in each chair. Like Goldilocks. I sat down at the console table where Taylor's notes were spread out: Constitutional Law, Trusts, Wills, Estates.

My eyes landed on Marguerite. I was looking for movement. Her expression changed each day, just slightly. Tiny changes, and then the portrait would return to its original state. On this day, her eyes had narrowed slightly. Her chin's position had shifted. The flush in her face was exaggerated. Normally pink, her cheeks today were red.

I was aware of the molecules of the painting vibrating in place and then sliding past one another, circling one another, as if the painting was liquefying. Then Marguerite's image darkened, and the rest of the painting faded to white, so that I could only see Marguerite's image in the foreground, like before, except this time the shears had doubled in size. It was as if Marguerite was a small child holding an instrument that was far too big for her to manage. Her three-dimensional form broke through the canvas and into the room, so that she was suspended in front of the frame.

I was completely exposed. There was no wall between me and Marguerite—no wall, no moat, no fence, no channel. She had found a way inside me, in my blood. The painting was her vehicle. It was like the head of the snake was still alive in that painting. She was the control center. Managing her emissaries—Rachel, Nina, Gilda, Helen. Maybe Frank, Teddy, Curtis. They might all be her agents.

And then . . . a flash of a blade in front of me. Cold fingers on my throat. I screamed.

I turned and ran. I ran so fast. Screaming. I ran like I was flying. I could feel Marguerite's ability to crush me. My legs moved, propelling me down the long hallway, through the dining room. I felt her behind me, the blade on my back, on my hair, as I crossed the kitchen, out the back door and across the bluestone courtyard and down the granite walkway. Flying. My lungs were burning. I accelerated. My heart was pounding.

I looked over my shoulder. I kept running and turning to see if she was behind me. Was she gaining on me? The distance between us was closing. I veered off the walkway and ran across the wide lawn. She circled and appeared in front of me, then a blast of air caused me to fall backward. I landed hard on my back. One of her hands, with cold fingers, enclosing my throat.

I screamed as loudly as I could. "Help me! Help me!" I felt like I might be swallowed whole.

Taylor's face appeared, looking down on me, just as Marguerite's face vanished into the distance.

"Are you sick?" Taylor looked confused and repulsed.

My lungs were burning. The damp grass had soaked through my shirt. I couldn't speak.

"What are you doing?" she said.

I paused, trying to recover. "I . . . thought . . ."

"Why are you on the ground?" She held her hands out in front of her. "What's wrong with you?"

"It was . . ." I searched for an answer. "A bear."

"A bear?"

"Yes."

She narrowed her eyes. "If there was a bear, it's gone. You can calm down."

I stayed out on the lawn for a long time. I couldn't stand to go back inside. With Marguerite. With Taylor. Until finally, the air grew too cool. I stood and walked slowly toward the house.

CHAPTER FOURTEEN

"You remember that Serge is arriving tomorrow?" Geoffrey said, before he switched off the light on his bedside table.

"Mm-hm."

"We'll have a lovely time."

I couldn't see his face, but his voice sounded taut.

Was it possible to have a lovely time with Serge? His visit would add to Taylor's strength. Maybe he would support her absurd ideas. Maybe he would speak with Rachel Hanna and give her some kind of damning evidence against me. Marguerite had told him that I was having an affair with Geoffrey. She could have told him any kind of outrageous lie.

Curtis texted me in the morning. We need to talk.

The sight of Curtis's name on my phone frightened me. As much as Serge's arrival frightened me.

What had he shared with Taylor? The realization that Curtis could be communicating with Taylor. Yesterday. Today. Tomorrow. The possibilities made me dizzy. Curtis had never been reliable, but up until now, I hadn't worried about him choosing someone else over me. Because I thought he didn't have strong feelings for anyone. But . . . maybe I was wrong about that. My conversation with Frank came back to me. *He's friends with the girl. He's worried about the girl.*

Serge was scheduled to arrive at six. In the afternoon, I hurried to get ready. I looked in the mirror and was dismayed by what I saw: blotchy skin, white lips, limp hair, a hollow face with dark circles under my eyes. I tried three different kinds of concealer, two different kinds of foundation, but nothing seemed to help. I looked like I'd aged fifteen years.

My pulse quickened at the sight of a Jaguar pulling into the driveway, an hour earlier than expected. I followed Geoffrey downstairs.

Gilda and Raoul were already on the steps outside the front door, greeting Serge, like little children who were too excited to wait. "Mr. Kuhnert! Hello!"

"Gilda!" Serge called out. "Raoul!"

Once inside, Serge embraced Gilda and shook hands with Raoul. "My dear friends," he said. "The sight of you two warms my heart."

"The man of the hour!" Geoffrey said.

"Hello." Serge smiled, lips closed, no teeth.

Then Geoffrey introduced me to Serge.

"A pleasure, Miss Phoenix."

Serge wore glasses, a cashmere sweater, and leather loafers, like a polished college professor. He didn't look untidy the way I thought a painter would look. I'd only ever seen him at Marguerite's funeral, wearing a suit, but I'd imagined that all of his other clothes were covered in splotches of paint.

Geoffrey and I sat across from him in the living room, in front of the fire, while we waited for Taylor.

Geoffrey made three whiskeys with large spherical ice cubes and handed them out to each of us. "Cheers," he said, nodding to Serge and to me.

I'd already had a couple shots of vodka, recognizing that I would need to show Serge a calm demeanor. I'd pulled my hair back in a clip, but the clip kept falling out. On this particular evening, the feeling of hair on my face was intolerable. It felt like a spider.

Serge's eyes wandered over the room. His gaze settled on his painting of Marguerite. He contemplated it while he drank, then looked up at Geoffrey. "Nice whiskey."

"Thanks, mate," Geoffrey said.

"You must be proud of our girl," Serge said.

"Definitely," Geoffrey said. "She should be here any minute."

Geoffrey asked Serge several questions about his work. He was lounging back on the sofa, trying to come across as relaxed. But he wasn't. Neither was I. I drank my whiskey faster than I intended to.

Nina appeared with a tray of hors d'oeuvres. The sight of her paralyzed me.

"What a lovely tray," Serge said. "Many thanks."

Nina nodded. "A pleasure, Mr. Kuhnert."

Everyone stopped talking while she rearranged the coffee table to make room for the hors d'oeuvres. She started to leave, but then stopped in the middle of the room. She turned back and looked directly at me.

My heart was so loud in my rib cage. I shrank from Nina's gaze, my eyes on the floor. "Miss Sullivan." I couldn't make eye contact with her. She raised her voice. "Miss Sullivan." Why was she repeating my name? She raised her voice even louder. *"Miss Sullivan!"*

I looked up. "What do you want?"

"Would you like another drink?"

"No! No!"

"Phoenix, darling," Geoffrey whispered. "You don't look well."

"Just a . . . headache."

"Maybe a glass of water, Nina," Geoffrey said.

"Of course," she said, then left the room.

Geoffrey took a few almonds from a silver bowl of mixed nuts that was resting on the coffee table.

Serge cleared his throat. "So, Geoffrey, I left you several messages."

"Ay, ay, ay." Geoffrey threw his hands up in a gesture of surrender. "Just trying to do too many things." He leaned over the bowl of nuts, looking for more almonds. He found one and popped it in his mouth.

"The subject is our financial arrangement," Serge said.

"Hmm?" Geoffrey's face looked blank, as if he hadn't listened to any of Serge's messages.

Serge set his drink on the coffee table. "We need a fair structure." He adjusted the cuffs of his sweater on each side.

"A fair structure?"

"I need a percent of revenue."

Geoffrey laughed lightly. He stood to tend the fire.

"Marguerite offered me a percentage when you first started using my work," Serge said. "I declined."

Geoffrey adjusted the logs in the fireplace with the poker, like the fire was the important thing that required his attention. Like Serge's demand was so ridiculous, it didn't deserve a response.

"It was a gentleman's agreement with Marguerite," Serge continued, "and we both understood there was flexibility built in. So, it's time now . . . for a fair arrangement."

Geoffrey turned to grin at Serge. "Nice try, man." Then he returned his focus to the position of the logs. "We'd have chosen a different image if you were going to charge us."

Serge sipped his whiskey.

I perused the cheese tray, then picked up a piece of Brie and a green olive, just to have something to concentrate on. The olive didn't make it all the way to my mouth. I dropped it on the rug under the coffee table. I leaned down to retrieve it. When I was coming back up, I bumped my head on the coffee table.

"You all right, love?" Geoffrey said.

"Yes." I smiled. "Fine."

Geoffrey sat next to me on the sofa. "You can't introduce this idea after fifteen years," he said to Serge.

Serge shifted in his seat. He wiped his mouth with a cocktail napkin. "I was hoping the two of us could come to something simple and reasonable."

Geoffrey clenched his jaw. "With Marguerite gone, the business is vulnerable. Money is tight."

Serge picked up his whiskey and studied it before taking a sip. "Marguerite did mention something about a drained bank account."

Geoffrey's jaw clenched.

Serge's gaze drifted to the fire. Then to *Marguerite by the Lake.* "Let's remember, you don't own the painting. You're the custodian."

"Cheers to adverse possession," Geoffrey said, raising his glass and drinking.

"Our lawyers can sort this," Serge said. "If you'd prefer?"

"Come off it, man."

The conversation stopped when Nina entered, carrying my glass of ice water on a small silver tray. She presented the glass to me. I took it without looking at her.

"By the way," Serge said to Geoffrey, "thanks for offering me a ride tomorrow. But I've got to get back to New York."

Nina cleared some napkins from the coffee table before leaving the room.

Serge turned to me. "What are your plans for tomorrow night, Miss Phoenix?"

"Hmm?" I drank the full glass of water and started to feel slightly better.

"While Geoffrey's at the Greenhaven deal," Serge said. "Do you have a good show?"

"I'm going with him," I said. "We're going together."

Silence fell over the room.

"You can't be serious," Serge said, turning to Geoffrey.

Serge and Geoffrey locked eyes.

I had a sensation of falling. I had nothing below me. Nothing to catch me.

"Look, Serge," Geoffrey said, "this is none of your affair."

"It *is*, actually. I'm not sitting at a table with your latest paramour and answering questions about who's living with whom. I'm not going to smile and nod like I think the whole damn thing is fine. Because I'm not so sure it is."

Heat was rising to my face. A whirring sound behind my eyes and my nose, filling my head. I turned to Geoffrey, but he wouldn't look at me. Would I have to stand up for myself? How could I win against Serge?

"I wasn't going to raise this," Serge said, "while sitting here by the fire with our whiskeys on ice, because I don't want to embarrass the lovely Miss Phoenix." He turned to me. "Perfect name by the way. You *do* rise from the ashes, don't you?" He turned back to Geoffrey. "If you think I'll consider publicly desecrating the memory of my dearest friend in the world by attending her memorial with the woman who has replaced her in your heart and in your home, when your wife is not even *cold in her grave*, you are sorely mistaken, dear boy."

I expected Geoffrey to fight back. I expected him to defend me. But he said nothing. Nothing.

It took every ounce of courage I had, but I stood and spoke to Serge. "If you don't feel comfortable going," I said, "we understand. Geoffrey and I will attend without you." I tried to say the words with confidence, but my voice was trembling the whole time.

Geoffrey remained silent.

Serge stood and walked to the door. "Allow me to refresh my drink."

When Serge had left the room, Geoffrey mumbled, "I think I've made a bit of a muddle of this." He pushed his hair straight back.

"What?"

"I want you with me. Of course." He took both my hands in his. "But this is an event to remember Marguerite and her contribution to Greenhaven. And maybe it is a bit awkward for me to have another woman with me."

I felt like he'd punched me in the face.

"You invited me. You're not allowed to disinvite me."

"But . . . people have this incredible loyalty to Marguerite," he said. "And . . . it's complicated. Isn't it?"

"No." It wasn't complicated.

"There's public perception to consider." Geoffrey frowned.

"And I'm not sure why you'd want to go anyway. What does it have to do with you?"

"I'm ... what ... why I'd want to ..." The thoughts were coming too fast, and my lips and my tongue couldn't keep up with the thoughts. "Everything ... I'm doing everything for ... you. ... the book, gardens, for the series, the garden tour ..." I wanted to tighten my hands around his throat so that he couldn't breathe. I wanted to make him feel as irrelevant as he was making me feel. "Everything ... I'm doing all of this for you. And you don't ..."

"Sweetheart, please," he said. "It goes without saying that I want you by my side." He extended his arms as if to hug me. I moved away from him. "But for these first months following Marguerite's death, maybe I should tread lightly. Maybe it wasn't wise for me to invite you to the event. I wasn't thinking straight. Because I was just so grateful to you. And you make me so very happy."

It was a deep humiliation. Everyone would know. Taylor. Serge. Gilda. Everyone would know I was disinvited. And I couldn't complain. I was that insignificant. He could just keep me around as his mistress. As unpaid labor to keep the business afloat.

I thought the J.Lo ring meant something. I thought it was a symbol of my value.

"I apologize, Phoenix," he said. "Can you forgive me?"

No, I couldn't forgive him.

I couldn't.

No.

Serge returned to the living room with a fresh drink. "So, Phoenix," he said upon entering, "did anyone tell you that Marguerite, Geoffrey, and I were roommates in our youth."

Geoffrey stiffened.

Serge sat back down next to the fire, across from me and Geoffrey. "I lived in their spare room for almost two years," he continued, "and during that time . . . let's just say that Geoffrey . . ."

Geoffrey cut him off mid-sentence. "Don't listen to him."

"Pursued me," Serge said. "Though he was in a relationship with Marguerite."

I wasn't taking in what Serge was saying. I could only think about this colossal humiliation. About the dress and shoes I foolishly purchased. About Gilda's expression of triumph. My stomach churned. Taylor would love to see me in the role of concubine, to witness the last strand of my self-respect being stamped out.

It was easy for Geoffrey to marginalize me. It didn't pain him at all. He smiled and took another handful of nuts. "I don't know what the prat's going on about."

"You told me if I slept with you—"

"It's a load of crap," Geoffrey said as he chewed.

My focus finally shifted to the conversation in the room. Processing the conversation in the room.

"If I slept with you," Serge said, "you'd allow me to stay."

What? Could this be true? It couldn't, could it?

Geoffrey laughed. "Are you high?"

"Marguerite didn't want to believe me," Serge said. "So, I moved out."

It was like I was listening to people I didn't know. And after a few moments, it dawned on me, these *were* people I didn't know. Including Geoffrey. Especially Geoffrey.

"He didn't like my friendship with Marguerite," Serge said to me. "He tried to play us off each other."

"Shut up, man," Geoffrey said.

"At one point, I was dating a young poet and had him over to our apartment for a drink. The poet wanted me to read his work. He spread out a few of his poems on the coffee table.

"Geoffrey walked in and picked up one of the poems. He read it out loud in a mocking voice. He laughed. He repeated one of the lines. And laughed. Then he crumpled the paper into a ball and threw it into the fire."

"I have no memory of this," Geoffrey said. "But if there was a poet moping around the place, I'm sure he was a pretentious bore and deserved what he got."

"Geoffrey couldn't stand for me to be close to anyone," Serge said. "Not the poet. Not Marguerite. He was obsessed with me."

He was obsessed with me.

"But I refused him, and he couldn't take the rejection."

"Come off it," Geoffrey said. "You imagined the whole damn thing."

No. Serge hadn't imagined it. Geoffrey had been in love with Serge.

"You were a frightened fool, dead broke, and sponging off

us," Geoffrey said. "You moved out when we got engaged. End of story."

Serge sipped his whiskey. "Quite a nice whiskey, this."

Geoffrey's face and neck were red. His mouth twisted. But Serge remained calm. He continued to speak in a matter-of-fact manner. "Marguerite was worried about her marriage," Serge said. "From the beginning to the end."

Geoffrey stood up. "Fuck off."

"She told me about you and Phoenix," he said to Geoffrey.

This was confirming what I feared, what I knew.

Geoffrey paced the room. "If our marriage had any trouble, it was your fault," he said. "For thirty years, you were whispering in her ear. I couldn't so much as look at a woman without you reporting to her that I was having sex with someone." He stopped two feet away from Serge and looked him in the eye. "Just because you never had any lasting relationship of your own, you had to screw that up for Marguerite."

Serge smiled. "Marguerite was like my sister," he said. "Once you were married, I said nothing. But she was sharp. You didn't hide your sex life as well as you thought you did."

The more I listened, the more I realized that my relationship with Geoffrey was an empty well of ignorance. I didn't know him. Not at all.

"I saw the letters," Geoffrey said, pacing again. "You tore me down, so you could make yourself look good. You told her not to bring me into the business. You told her I didn't add value. You told her I was a cheater, that I married her for the money, that I was a no-talent loser. Don't think I don't know this for a fact."

"I only told her the truth."

We heard a car in the driveway. Everyone stopped talking.

Geoffrey froze. "That would be Taylor."

Gilda and Nina passed around coq au vin, braised carrots, and fried potatoes.

"Look at this girl." Serge beamed at Taylor, who was sitting across from him. Her long blond hair framed her face. "This accomplished *woman*. This Yale lawyer. The rest of us are going to be coming to you for advice from now on. I hope you're ready."

Taylor rolled her eyes, like she was being modest.

What did Taylor know about her father's love life? What had Marguerite told her?

"Gilda, darling, the carrots are divine." Serge winked at Gilda as she refilled his wineglass, and she smiled back.

The dinner conversation centered on Taylor's new job and Taylor's new apartment. No one mentioned the event I was disinvited to. No one mentioned that Geoffrey liked to fuck men. No one mentioned Marguerite. Or the investigation. It seemed like they'd all decided to avoid that subject, like they'd been discussing it ahead of time and decided not to bring it up. The room became warmer and warmer. I stood to open a window.

"Your mother was going around telling anyone who'd listen that you were editor of *The Yale Law Journal*. Oh my God," Serge laughed. "She couldn't stop!"

I wanted to bolt out of the room and run outside.

"Taylor this . . . Taylor that . . . All she wanted was to marvel at you."

I couldn't bear to hear another word and was relieved when Taylor excused herself from the table.

Serge turned to Geoffrey. "I forgot to ask you," he said quietly, "is Russ Marks attending the memorial?"

A silence fell over the table.

"I have no idea," Geoffrey said.

"Seems like he might be there, in his capacity as CFO. No?"

"Maybe." Geoffrey leaned back in his chair, trying to appear relaxed. But I didn't think he was.

"I'm planning to go early and attend the major donors' cocktail party," Serge said. "It's an opportunity for some due diligence. Truthfully, I'm concerned. I have to make sure my dollars are going to the right place."

Geoffrey's face looked pale. Why was he upset? Was he scared of something?

Maybe Russ had been stealing from Greenhaven. Maybe Geoffrey had found out his friend was stealing behind his back, and that was why he looked so ill now. Maybe.

But the voice in my head told me it could just as easily have been Geoffrey stealing.

Taylor returned to the room and sat down.

"Did you tell your father and Phoenix about our plan?" Serge asked her.

She smiled. "No."

I had a bad feeling about this. What plan?

"So, the other day, when Taylor visited me in New York," Serge said, "I was sitting outside at a café, and walking toward me, I saw Marguerite. Now, this is not an exaggeration. I thought that Marguerite had come back from the dead to visit me. I was certain it was her. But it wasn't. It was Taylor.

"I can't tell you how happy it made me, even once I realized it was Taylor," he said. "It wasn't just a physical likeness. It was the way she carried herself. It was so comforting to see her. My dear friend."

I sipped my water, breathing slowly through my nose so I wouldn't gag.

"And I thought to myself," Serge continued, "Marguerite had millions of admirers who are grieving over her. And wouldn't it be a comfort to them to have the same experience that I had?"

"What's your plan?" Geoffrey asked.

"It's a surprise," Taylor said. "A terrific surprise."

Whatever the surprise was, I knew I wouldn't like it.

Lying in bed that night, hours passed, and my eyes wouldn't rest. They were locked open, unless I pressed them closed. I went downstairs, with just the hand sconces lighting my way. The painting was glowing. Drawing me all the way across the living room, until I was standing two feet away, looking up at Marguerite. Her dark brown eyes, her dark brown eyes were coal-black eyes. It was a mirror ahead of me. I could see the rage. Pain. Seething. All the way into the dark, empty center of my soul. I am Phoenix. I am nothing. I make things happen. I'm a magic killer.

I was looking to find something human, but the very best I could see was an animal moving through life. Claiming. Holding. Clawing. Reaching. Securing. There was no poetry or religion. There was a pool of absorption and reflection. There was an animal—bent on survival.

In the morning, when I woke up, I didn't remember anything at first. And then it all came back. I couldn't recognize my life anymore. I felt pressure against every inch of my body, growing heavier all the time, like the weight of gravity was multiplying.

I checked my iPhone and saw a new post. It was a photo of Taylor standing in profile, chin up, her perfect nose in the air, next to the vegetable garden's new location, with one hand gesturing toward it. She was wearing all white, like Marguerite often had. *Moving and expanding the vegetable garden so it will have full sun! #betterthanever #margueritebythelake.* Eleven thousand likes.

That was more than five times the number of likes on my posts. She was stealing from me. Like Marguerite.

In his dark wood-paneled office, like a British men's club, Geoffrey's desk faced out toward the lake, a blue sky, and white clouds.

I leaned over his shoulder to show him Taylor's post on my phone.

He sighed. "Taylor wants to feel like she's a part of her mother's legacy."

"If this is important to Taylor," I said quietly, "then I can step aside."

"No! I just . . ." Geoffrey took off his reading glasses. He pressed his thumb and index finger where the glasses had made an indentation on either side of his nose, as if he had a tension headache. "I think it's good for business for Taylor to be involved."

"Okay." I nodded. "And what about the gardening content?"

"You won't . . . ?" He raised his eyebrows in a look of surprise.

It was unspoken, but understood, that I'd committed to supporting the business.

He wrinkled his brow, then leaned back in his chair and looked at the ceiling. Flames from the corner fireplace made the room glow.

"Can you just be patient?" he said.

What did that really mean? "I have another meeting with Detective Hanna." It was looming over me. In three days.

"It's a pain in the ass," he said. "I know." He wiped the lenses of his glasses with a microfiber cloth, then put them back on and turned his attention to his laptop. He was pretending to read something so that he didn't have to look me in the eye.

The fire made the room too warm. "I moved in with you right after Marguerite died," I said. "And I think that seems strange to Hanna." It would seem strange to anyone.

He waved his hand dismissively. "There's nothing to worry about."

I sat down in the dark green leather club chair across from him. "Please look at me." Finally, he looked up.

"I'd like your help with . . . you know . . . the meeting," I said.

The crackling of the fire filled the silence.

He frowned. "Do you have anything to hide?"

Dry land was just out of my reach. "I don't have the reputation that you have." I was trying my best to keep the panic out of my voice. "I'm vulnerable."

His face darkened. "I'm fully as vulnerable as you."

"I'm scared," I said. But I could see in his eyes that wasn't the right thing to say.

He spoke with a sharp edge. "Scared isn't an option."

Curtis texted: I need to see you. It's urgent.

I could feel my heart pounding in my chest. I could feel perspiration seeping through my T-shirt. What did Curtis want with me? What did he tell Taylor?

On Instagram, I saw that Taylor had posted a childhood photo of herself covered in dirt, holding a child-size shovel and watering can; Marguerite was standing behind her, arms draped around her daughter.

Mom and I planting tomatoes together when I was five #tomatogirl. Two hundred thousand likes.

Tears sprang to my eyes. I would not allow them to fall.

I blinked them back, widening my eyes. I blinked them back, behind my eyeballs. No tears. None.

I saw my situation clearly now. Two hundred thousand likes. I understood how small I was. I understood Taylor's outsized power.

I returned to the selfie of Taylor standing next to the vegetable garden's new location. She had no idea which vegetables would thrive here. She was a pretender. In all the years that I'd been working at Rosecliff, I'd never seen Taylor so much as touch one of the flowers, much less water or weed or mulch.

Two hours passed, and Taylor posted on Instagram again. It was . . . a photo of *Marguerite by the Lake,* the painting . . . then I looked more closely and saw it was a photo of a real person. It was Taylor . . . in a long billowing skirt, and she was standing in the exact same spot, with Lake Spiro in the background. The text read:

Re-creating something special. RIP Marguerite Gray.

She already had 324,000 likes.

The room was so warm. The room was hot. I wanted to jump out of my skin.

Taylor and Serge were forcing me to replay one of the lowest, darkest moments of my life. To endure this clone of Marguerite. To look at it and react to it. Taylor was weaving together all these threads of misery. Taylor, Marguerite, the painting, the cliff. They were woven so tightly around each other; I could hardly distinguish one from another. And those threads were tightening around me, too. Along with new threads, new hideous threads,

Rachel Hanna, Nina, Helen, Serge, all tightening around me like a strangling corset.

Later, when I saw Serge and Taylor through my bedroom window, Taylor was still wearing the same long billowing skirt. Serge was in black tie, ready for the event. They stood side by side near the cliff. She pointed to the place where the spruce tree used to stand. Then she pointed back to the cliff. They turned and walked down the new driveway. My crew had already started digging holes for the three dozen trees to be planted alongside it the next day. Taylor looked around, as if she was making sure no one was in earshot. She leaned in to him and appeared to whisper. She was telling him something about me.

Even though I was far away from them, and inside the house, I could hear her whispers. I could hear what she was saying. She was saying, "It's over."

And then her whispers merged with the whispers from the painting. Now the whispers from the painting were the same as Taylor's: *It's over. It's all over.*

The whispers from the painting didn't stop. They grew so loud I could hear them from any room in the house. I went outside to try to get away from them. But no matter where I was, I could hear Marguerite saying, *It's over.*

Taylor posted another re-creation of *Marguerite by the Lake.* This time there was an image of the Kuhnert painting next to the photo, so followers could compare the two. It was uncanny.

We love you, Marguerite. One and a half million likes.

I couldn't press the tears back behind my eyeballs, as hard as I tried. The tears came against my will. Water pouring down my face, like rain. My value, what I could offer, it was actually nothing. Nothing compared to Taylor, and what she was, and what she would always be. I was nothing. I was nothing. I was nothing.

I saw Taylor say goodbye to Serge. His car pulled out of the driveway. Was he on his way to interrogate Russ Marks?

Taylor had changed out of her skirt and was wearing jeans. She turned and walked in the direction of the woods.

I signed into Marguerite's email account on my phone. I was still looking for more information—information I could use to defend myself, if attacked. Something about Taylor or Geoffrey or Marguerite. Something to help me understand who I was dealing with. I was coming to recognize how little I knew. I was at a severe disadvantage.

There was an email from Geoffrey I hadn't read before. It caught my eye because of the date. It was the day before Marguerite died.

Marguerite, I'm on my way back tomorrow. Will arrive early afternoon. I'll see you for dinner.

A nauseous feeling traveled through my body.

Geoffrey wasn't home that day. Everyone knew Geoffrey wasn't home.

If he was home, why wasn't Marguerite reported missing?

I found Geoffrey in his office, working on his laptop. He was also in black tie, dressed and ready for the Greenhaven event.

Was it possible I'd grown to hate him in the last twenty-four hours?

"Geoffrey . . ." I showed him the email I'd read. "I don't understand this."

He pressed his lips together tightly, but he didn't respond.

"Geoffrey." I repeated myself. "I don't understand this email. You weren't here."

He turned to me, and the glow of the fire lit up his face. He removed his glasses and rubbed his eyes. "The night that Marguerite died," he said, "I actually came home earlier that afternoon."

What was he saying? What?

He smiled. "Russ dropped me by the lake, and I walked the rest of the way."

No. How could that . . . how . . .

"I took a nap on that sofa." He pointed to the sofa behind me. "When I woke up, I looked out the window to admire the spectacular orange sky."

No.

"I noticed two people near the edge of the cliff. You and Marguerite."

It was the same sensation of a fist in my stomach. It had only happened once. And again now.

Geoffrey leaned his elbows on his desk and rested his forehead in his hands. "It was soul crushing to be a disappointment," he said quietly. "I could see it in her eyes every day."

My intestines lurched.

I was exposed. He saw me. He saw everything.

No. *He* was exposed. He was . . . He knew *everything* and . . . He'd been . . . He knew.

He leaned back in his chair and looked at the ceiling. "In the moment, I felt relief," he said. "And that relief was so . . . loud. I couldn't bring myself to . . ."

I felt faint, dizzy. I didn't know if the room was moving, or I was moving.

Did he ever love her? Did he ever . . .

"Marguerite didn't believe in me." His eyes locked on mine. "I felt small when I was with her. But any relief I got from her death. It was short-lived. Because now"—he smiled—"I know something ugly about myself. And I can never unknow it."

I could see in Geoffrey's eyes he knew what I was thinking. He knew I saw his spirit. And what I saw was . . . dark. When I walked into his office, I hated him. But so quickly, it had changed to something else. This was a different man than the one from three minutes earlier. It was a different man now.

This person in front of me, he didn't call the police. He didn't . . .

He was here. He saw her fall. He didn't run to her. He left her. He left her to die.

He left his wife to die.

He gazed at the lake, through his window. "I was in love with her. I'm still in love with her," he said. "But I couldn't make her see me the way I wanted her to. When I saw that expression of pity in her eyes . . ." His voice grew louder and more strained. "When she pretended that she was impressed by something I did . . . I wished . . . I wished her dead. Sometimes."

A feeling of terror squeezing my heart. Tighter and tighter. I had no words. In that moment, Geoffrey frightened me more than Rachel Hanna. More than Nina, Taylor, Curtis. More than anyone. I backed up, one step at a time. As I neared the door, it flew open.

I turned to see Taylor standing in the doorframe. She was no longer a graceful, well-groomed lawyer. Her fever-red face was caving in. Tears and mucus were covering her nose, cheeks, and chin. Her body was caving in, too.

She was a cat, landing on top of Geoffrey's chair, on top of his body, her claws in his face, drawing blood.

"*Who are you?*" she said.

How did I find myself here? It was a free fall. A drop. Down. Endless now. How could I find a hold—a way to climb out of this deep, bottomless . . .

"*You . . .*"

Geoffrey wrested himself away from Taylor. He pushed his daughter off himself, and she landed on the wood floor.

"It's not what you think."

She was up on her feet again. "*I heard what you said.*"

He saw me there. He knew. The layers and layers of lying.

"You are *evil*." She was lacerating his chest, his face.

Geoffrey pushed her away from him again. He ran out the door of his study, down the stairs.

Taylor followed Geoffrey, screaming at the top of her voice. *"You're a killer!"*

"I'll explain when you calm yourself," he said. "I'll explain when you're calm."

He didn't want the investigation. Of course. He'd never wanted it. It was all just . . . He was there. He saw me there.

Taylor was on his heels as he reached the foot of the stairs. "I'm calling the detective," she said.

Geoffrey grabbed her wrists. He held them together in one hand. His pale blue eyes flashed.

"Get your hands off me," she hissed, "or I'll file an assault charge."

"You don't know anything," he said. "You're not calling anyone."

Taylor had turned into a snake, spitting her words at her father like venom. "What are you going to do to me, *Dad*? You think you have any control over me? You don't. You don't."

Geoffrey looked terrified of Taylor. I was scared of her, too. She'd transformed into someone I didn't recognize. He released her wrists.

"I'm ashamed I have an ounce of your blood," she hissed at her father.

He ran out the door, heading to the driveway. Taylor followed him out of the house, spitting and hissing, "You are evil. Evil!"

Geoffrey's Audi pulled out of the driveway.

"*Evil!*" Taylor screamed after him.

I had to get out of the house. I had to get away. I had to run.

I longed to feel cold wind on my face. I ran down the winding driveway and then continued around the lake. Some nights, like tonight, I carried a large flashlight, it was that dark.

Curtis called me, and I picked up.

I could barely hear him over the wind. "Taylor's talking to the detective tomorrow."

Was that a threat? Or was it a warning?

"I didn't tell her anything," he said. "I didn't say anything."

If he was trying to support me, he was too late.

Taylor knows.

Geoffrey knows. Geoffrey always knew.

Conversations flew through my brain, like a child's flip book. Like fast-forwarding a movie. About the investigation, Rachel Hanna, Marguerite, that night. "I'm fully as vulnerable as you," he said.

I couldn't operate from a place of fear.

I walked for an hour. Maybe two. Maybe three.

Geoffrey knows. He always knew.

Who is this man? What does he want from me?

I heard someone behind me. I stopped and turned to look. I couldn't see who it was, but I could recognize the rhythm of her steps. As she came closer, I could recognize her gait and her posture, the angle of her chin, and the movement of her long arms.

Taylor stopped about five feet away from me. She was spinning. Her hair looked like straw. I could see the bulging veins in her temples and in her forehead. She was falling into pieces.

"Do you need something?" I raised my voice over the sound of the wind.

She was wearing a black down coat and a black scarf around her neck.

She had something hidden in her coat. I couldn't tell. Was it a weapon? It was . . . I thought she was going to do something to me.

"You got your grandmother's house," she said, "in the end."

Marguerite stood in front of me at that moment. In the body of Taylor, it was actually Marguerite. "Didn't you?" The motion of her lips and the sound of the words were not completely aligned, like a movie that's out of sync. "You took what you needed, and you dumped the remains.

"It's interesting how you pulled that off. Your grandma's house. Maybe you think you can do it again. Find a crack. Pry it open. And force your way into our home.

"That's not going to happen," she said. "Sorry."

Geoffrey knew. The entire time.

"I know who you are." It was Taylor. Marguerite. Taylor. She raised her voice over the roaring wind. "I know what you did. I know everything."

I'd been walking on this road every day since I moved into Rosecliff. I knew which spots weren't safe. I knew the exposed sections of the road. I knew when and where I was at risk.

I thought to myself, Taylor could push me if she wanted to. Off the edge of the road. And who would be nearby to witness what happened?

I turned my flashlight on and shined it on the road in front of me, holding it like a weapon. If she attacked me, I could shine it in her eyes.

Branches of the trees around us were battered by the wind. Leaves and debris flew through the air, into my face, momentarily blinding me.

"Did you kill my mother?" The wind was so loud, I could hardly hear what she was saying, but with the flashlight, I could read her lips. She took steps in a slow plodding circle. Her eyes were pinned on mine. "She trusted you." Her words were so similar to what her eyes had been saying all along. "Did you push her?" Her upper lip lifted, exposing her foamy teeth and gums in a feverish grimace.

I turned my back to Taylor and started to walk toward the house. I wouldn't dignify her with a response.

I felt something fly over my head, in front of me and around my waist. It was her scarf. She pulled me backward, toward her with a strong jerking motion. "What are you doing?" I tore it from my waist and threw it to the ground. "You have to get control over yourself."

She narrowed her eyes. Her eyes were identical to Marguerite's. "You're a monster," she said. Her mouth opened so wide when she said the word "monster." The rest of her face disappeared. I could only see her mouth, with white foam across her teeth and gums, all over her tongue, and down her throat.

She picked her scarf up and held it high overhead.

Then she lunged away from me, sprinting down the middle of the road, head thrown back, screaming into the dark night air. She disappeared from view where the road turned, but I could still hear her voice. Moments later, she emerged again from around the curve, running full speed, her arms stretched in front of her, straight at me.

Behind her, a car appeared on the road from around the bend. It was driving fast, directly toward her. Was it possible this was happening again? Like with Marguerite? Even if it were an accident, no one would believe it.

The wind drowned out the sound of the car. Taylor's long black coat blended into the night.

I shined my flashlight into the driver's eyes.

I was trying to light the road for Taylor. That was my intention.

The road was so dark, pitch-black.

Of course, my intention was to light the road for Taylor.

But then the scene in front of me exploded. And I heard an awful cry.

CHAPTER FIFTEEN

Her body lay in the middle of the road. Taylor. Marguerite. Taylor.

The driver veered into the rock mass on the side of the road.

He staggered out of his wrecked car, blood across his face. He stumbled toward the body of Taylor.

I ran to her, screaming at the top of my voice. *"Help!"* I didn't stop screaming the whole time. In the driver's face.

The driver looked to be in his eighties. He was confused, in shock. "She wasn't there. I didn't see her. I couldn't see her. I didn't know. The light in my eyes. I couldn't see." On he went, until I told him to call 911.

When the police arrived, the driver was still incoherent. "I couldn't see. That light. When I turned the corner . . . I didn't even know. A deer, a dog. I didn't even know. And I swerved the car into the side. But I didn't know . . ."

He wasn't looking for a way out. He blamed himself. He took all of the blame.

The police had to reach the next of kin. Geoffrey was . . . I didn't know where. Would he go to the Greenhaven dinner?

This is Geoffrey Gray. Please leave a message, and I'll ring you back.

I left a voicemail. *Geoffrey, please call me.*

I tried him five times in a row.

I texted him. Geoffrey, it's an emergency.

The weight of what had happened was sinking into my body. I had to tell Geoffrey before anyone else did.

In the prior two days, everything I thought I knew about him . . . everything . . . I didn't know anything. I had no idea what he would do to me. Because now I thought he was capable of . . . anything really.

Geoffrey, it's an emergency.

While these thoughts were cycling through my awareness, I began to feel something. To hear something. It was a humming sound at first. And then a buzzing. I could feel it throughout my body, vibrations in my feet and in my legs, growing stronger and louder, then my arms, my throat, behind my eyes. It was Marguerite's fury. Unspooling, unraveling, unleashing. On the road. In the car. In the police station. In the police car. An officer drove me to Rosecliff. I could feel the buzzing—the vibrations of her rage. And I knew this time, I would not survive her wrath. She would end me. Getting closer and closer. I knew she would end me.

As I approached, the buzzing amplified. Once we pulled into the driveway, the sound was so loud, and the vibrations so strong, like intense voltage coursing through me. I would have covered my ears, but the sound was coming through every square inch of my skin into my body.

Walking from the driveway to the house, I considered turning around and running back to the police car. With every step I took toward the house, the vibrating grew stronger, louder, more intense and more painful. And then, the moment I entered the house . . .

Like a switch, it all stopped.

And was replaced by Marguerite's whispers.

Have you forgotten whose house this is?

I walked straight to the living room.

Marguerite by the Lake.

The molecules of the painting were circling, melting, liquefying. Marguerite's face and body darkening, grotesque now, bulging out of the painting. Her hair flying away from her face, around her head in every direction, like the thick, glossy mane of a lion. And she was roaring with her whole body. Her body, breaking out of the painting, straight at me. A deafening roar. In a guttural thunderous voice, she was roaring: *TAY-LOR.*

The lion was coming for me. Its intense yellow eyes glowing in the dark. Its mouth was wide open. Bellowing with large teeth, white foamy saliva, red slippery gums, and a purple tongue. The roar: *MY TAY-LOR.*

I ran to the kitchen, to the new set of knives and took the largest one from the block.

I returned to the living room. To the gaping, cavernous mouth, three feet in diameter, suspended in the air. Ready to tear me to bits with its razor-sharp teeth.

How could I fight the lion. How could I win.

It was a howl. It was a roar: *TAY-LOR.*

The lion was bearing down on me, its mouth opening wide, its pointed white teeth glistening, its yellow eyes fixed on mine. It would tear me apart, limb from limb.

It raised its claws in the air to roar its anger, eyes to the ceiling, and at that moment, I ran, with the knife out in front of me.

I ran with all my might.

Toward the painting.

I reached up as high as I could, and I stabbed the painting right in the center. I stabbed Marguerite in the heart.

Another booming roar: *TAY-LOR.*

I stabbed again.

A resounding roar: *MY TAY-LOR.*

I twisted the knife in the canvas.

TAY-LOR.

I pulled the knife out and stabbed one final time. With all my strength.

The roaring stopped.

My brain was quiet.

I turned around. The lion was gone.

Silence.

The relief I experienced was . . . In that instant, I didn't care if I went to jail. Because I had quiet. I had one moment of peace.

I was alone with the painting. The dead painting.

But I had to make sure. I couldn't risk any small chance.

The painting was hung in a brass frame. I lifted it off its hook. I carried it into the kitchen and placed it on the kitchen table.

I took my knife, and I stabbed again in the exact same spot, but this time I dragged the knife across the entire width of the canvas. Then I dragged the knife across the canvas vertically, so that now I could see a cross, like a crucifix, on the painting and a drop of blood on the canvas from a small cut on my hand.

It was what I'd been longing to do since I walked into this house. I'd been aching for this moment of ending Marguerite.

I took a pair of scissors from the kitchen drawer and cut across the entire canvas.

With patience and accuracy.

Horizontally thirty times. Thin strips. Then vertically. Thin strips.

So that the canvas was approximately nine hundred little pieces. It was like a poison had been infecting me and finally the toxin had a way out of my bloodstream.

I held one of those pieces of canvas between my fingers.

For the first time in my life, I had the upper hand over Marguerite. I'd finally conquered her.

When I finished cutting the canvas, I was overcome with

thirst. I filled one of the Marguerite by the Lake mugs with water, drank, and then filled it again and again. I sat at the kitchen table to appreciate this moment I had earned with blood, sweat, and tears.

The house was quiet. I had stillness.

I looked in several kitchen drawers that were filled with miscellaneous odds and ends, like rubber bands and tape, but I had no luck. Next, I checked the utility closet. On the back of one of the shelves, I found a tool kit, which I brought with me to the kitchen. I used a screwdriver to disassemble the frame.

I remembered seeing suitcases in the linen closet, but those were all roller bags and none of them would serve my purpose. I returned to the utility closet again but saw nothing there either. Eventually, I recalled what I'd seen in the coat closet. A stack of Marguerite by the Lake duffel bags. I took two of them.

I put the canvas pieces and the frame pieces in one. I carried that first duffel bag, along with the empty one, and headed to the gardening shed, which wasn't far from the house. The path was not well lit, but I had my flashlight with me. Inside the gardening shed, I found what I was looking for on the first shelf. A twenty-pound bag of soil. I placed it in the second duffel bag.

Then, with my flashlight leading the way, I started at the top of the driveway at the first of three dozen holes that had been dug for the new trees. The trees were scheduled to be planted the following morning.

I buried a few pieces of the painting and the frame at the

bottom of that first hole and covered them with a thin layer of soil.

I repeated that routine for each of the remaining holes.

The next day, the trees would be planted. It would be impossible to find anything.

FIVE WEEKS LATER

I'm standing in the rain outside the screen door. It's hardly stopped raining for all of May. I hear them in the kitchen— Gilda, Raoul, Nina. They repeat certain names and certain words. The investigation into Marguerite's death has traction. Rachel Hanna's team is making progress. They are getting close.

Geoffrey sleeps in the coral guest room now. When he eats at Rosecliff, it's very early or very late. He catches sight of me and quickly turns away. Is he scared of me? Of what I might say, what I might do? His face is gaunt and sallow. Maybe grief has made him sick.

I see him in Taylor's room, studying the photos taped to her mirror. He lies down on her bed with her stuffed panda in his arms. He rubs his nose against the panda's nose.

No one else goes in Taylor's room.

No one goes in the living room either. The deep gouges in the empty wall over the fireplace where the heavy painting used to hang are reminders of all the house has lost.

I move through the house like a ghost. Sometimes I'm not sure I even exist.

Serge arrives. I listen at the door of Geoffrey's office. I think Serge is trying to convince Geoffrey of something—to get his support. I hear him say something about *Marguerite by the Lake*. I hear Taylor's name. I hear my name. Is he blaming me . . . for everything?

Is it possible that Geoffrey will back him? Doesn't he realize, if I go down, he goes down with me?

Serge leaves, and the house is silent again.

I do my laundry in the basement in the middle of the night, when no one's around.

I lie down on the sofa in the TV room with all the lights on.

I can't bear to be inside my own head. Not for one minute.

I watch travel shows about Brazil, Andorra, Australia. I was told I'm not allowed to leave the state. But my overnight bag is packed anyway. I know how to move quickly. No one has asked me for the J.Lo ring. It is hidden in the side pocket of my bag. The ring is too big for me now. It falls off every finger.

In the early morning, the rain finally subsides, but the wind is still strong. The sun hasn't risen yet. I dress in a clean pair of jeans and a clean sweatshirt. I look out the bedroom window.

The Japanese maples are growing tall because of all the rain. They have leafed out and their brilliant colors are on display. I chose them for their red leaves and their scale. They're even more beautiful than I'd imagined.

I move silently down the stairs and out the front door, closing it behind me as gently as possible. The house is empty, except for Geoffrey. He is probably asleep. Outside, the sun is beginning to rise in the pink sky. I stand at the top of the approach to take in the rows of crimson foliage—three dozen glories lining the drive on either side, then descending and disappearing around the bend.

When they were planted, the root ball of each tree was four feet wide and four feet deep. Even now, those roots are stretching out, finding their way. I feel the connections forming between the two rows, underneath the drive. I belong to them. They belong to me. It's the trees that have kept me here. I've poured my heart into them.

I approach the sweetest, smallest maple. It's delicate and fragile, but I sense its ambition. It might be the one I'll come to love the most. Once it's sturdy, once its roots are deep and wide, I'll climb to the very top branch, where I'll have a view of all the gardens. I'll sleep in its boughs, where the branches come together to form a cradle.

The trees are keeping me safe. They know what I would do for them. They'd do the same for me.

I continue slowly down the drive. But halfway down, I have an uneasy feeling.

I stop to examine each individual maple on one side of the drive, and then the other.

I study one of the taller trees more closely. It has more muted colors. The branches, the leaves, even in the short time I've been outside, I think I see a subtle change in the tree's stance. A few moments earlier, this same tree was embracing me. Including me in its life.

But now, no. The leaves and branches seem to be twisting away.

Is something shifting?

I turn to consider the tree with orange and yellow leaves, unlike the others, just behind me. Is it shutting me out, too?

Could it be all of them? Could it be that they're all turning on me?

A terrifying realization is penetrating the edges of my brain.

Could this be her?

Is it possible Marguerite found her way inside all the trees? That she is inhabiting them, channeling her power into the trees, through the trees?

Yes. I can feel what she's trying to do.

And they're . . . giving in to her. But it's not their fault. She's too strong.

I think the trees . . .

They want me dead.

Will they choke the life out of me?

Try to strangle me with their branches and their roots?

Yes. They will. I know they will.

I have to kill them. I have no choice. Now is the time to do it, when no one will see.

In the gardening shed, I find what I'm looking for, in the very back, on the second shelf.

I stand at the top of the drive, holding the torch high in the air.

Ribbons of fire wrap themselves around the smallest maple. It is the one I love the most.

The drive glows bright with flames dancing on either side.

The wind is blowing in my favor.

I close my eyes and feel the heat surrounding me.

I am the source. The fire is me.

ACKNOWLEDGMENTS

I am overwhelmingly grateful to my brilliant agent, Stephanie Kip Rostan, for her magical ability to see the possibility of a book in a three-page scene and guide me toward that book. I wouldn't be on this path were it not for her. Thank you to Stephanie's colleagues at Levine Greenberg Rostan Literary Agency, including Jim Levine, Daniel Greenberg, Miek Coccia, and special thanks to Courtney Paganelli.

Heartfelt thanks to my outstanding editor, Catherine Richards, for her direction and her razor-sharp notes, which elevated and expanded this book into a grander and more propulsive story. Thank you, Catherine. I'm unusually fortunate to have had the chance to collaborate with three editors on this project and this book is so much better because of it. Thank you to Kelly Stone for her terrific insight and support. Endless gratitude to Kelley

Ragland, who was with me for the last edit, which was invaluable. I had the benefit of her astoundingly perceptive notes, and it was implementing them that allowed the story to take off.

To the incomparable Sarah Melnyk for her work on *Marguerite* and *The Photographer*, going above and beyond every step of the way, even going so far as to provide ideas and research on invasive vines and rhododendrons! To Sara Beth Haring, I'm excited for the opportunity to work with someone as talented as you.

To the gifted David Baldeosingh Rotstein for designing a truly inspiring and inspired cover.

Thank you to Andrew Martin for his belief in this book. To Paul Hochman, Gail Friedman, Alisa Trager, Kiffin Steurer, Shawna Hampton, Kenneth Diamond, Julie Gutin, Omar Chapa, Rowen Davis, Maria Snelling, Elishia Merricks, Drew Kilman, Kayla Janas, Hector DeJean, and McKenna Jordan. And to the entire exceptional team at Minotaur Books and St. Martin's Publishing Group and their extraordinary publisher, Jennifer Enderlin. I thank my lucky stars that I ended up working with you all.

Many thanks to Jo Dickinson, my phenomenal UK editor, and all her colleagues at Hodder & Stoughton.

To Michelle Kroes for seeing the potential in this story.

To Helen Schulman, Luis Jaramillo, and the Creative Writing Program at The New School.

If this book has dimension, it is in large part thanks to the tremendous wisdom of Anika Streitfeld, whose notes were intuitive, incisive, and spot on.

And to early readers Dina Lee and Nicole Starczak, for your thoughtful comments and your consistent generosity.

Thank you to Manfred Flynn Kuhnert for inspiring the character of Serge Kuhnert and giving me a lifelong window into Serge's world.

To my amazing family—all the Carters, as well as the Holbrooks, Heaths, Wiesenthals, Cohens, Schonwalds, Carter-Weidenfelds, Wellers. In particular, Jon Carter, Pamela Carter, Whendy Carter, Ellen Carter, Ali Marsh, Fred Weller, Eve Holbrook, Claus Sørensen. And especially Ginna Carter.

To my parents for their love and support: Arthur Carter and Linda Carter. In remembrance of Dixie Carter and Hal Holbrook.

And my other parents, Nancy and Don Kempf. As well as the Kempf and Bâby families, including Donald Kempf; and Susan and Charlie Bâby, who lent me their beautiful home in which to write.

I'm grateful to Daryl Beyers for advising me on plants, gardens, and landscapes. And to Harrison Carter for advising me on the art world. In both cases, any errors are my own. To Jay Haddad for a fabulous story about a house that was moved across a lake. All my gratitude to Susie Stangland, as well as Beowulf Sheehan, Ilsa Brink, and Michael Carlisle.

Thank you to the generous authors who have gone out of their way to support my books: Lisa Lutz, Jennifer Hillier, John Burnham Schwartz, Anna Downes, Katherine St. John, Sally Hepworth, Rachel Hawkins, Laura Zigman, Gregg Hurwitz,

Mo Rocca, Faith Salie, Deborah Goodrich Royce, Zibby Owens, and so many more. To the booksellers and independent bookstores who have done the same, especially Community Bookstore in Brooklyn, The Mysterious Bookshop in NYC, and The Hickory Stick Bookshop in Washington Depot, CT.

To my dear loyal friends for supporting me and my writing.

Above all, thank you to my husband, Steve Kempf—to whom this book is dedicated—who brings me immeasurable joy every single day. And to my children, Eleanor and Henry. You are each an infinite source of happiness and wonder.

ABOUT THE AUTHOR

Beowulf Sheehan

Mary Dixie Carter is the author of the critically acclaimed novel *The Photographer*. Her writing has appeared in *Time, The Economist,* the *San Francisco Chronicle,* the *Chicago Tribune, The Philadelphia Inquirer, The New York Sun, The New York Observer,* and other print and online publications. She worked at the *Observer* for five years, where she served as the publishing director. In addition to writing, she also has a background as a professional actor. Mary Dixie graduated from Harvard with an honors degree in English literature and holds an MFA in creative writing from The New School. She lives in Brooklyn with her husband and two children.